Emma Wolf

A Prodigal in Love

a novel

Emma Wolf

A Prodigal in Love
a novel

ISBN/EAN: 9783337001698

Printed in Europe, USA, Canada, Australia, Japan

Cover: Foto ©Andreas Hilbeck / pixelio.de

More available books at **www.hansebooks.com**

A PRODIGAL IN LOVE

A Novel

BY

EMMA WOLF

AUTHOR OF "OTHER THINGS BEING EQUAL"

—" As wind along the waste,
I know not whither, willy-nilly blowing "

NEW YORK

HARPER & BROTHERS PUBLISHERS

1894

A PRODIGAL IN LOVE

CHAPTER I

" You will grant," said Brunton, as they paused before Rembrandt's " Head of a Boy," "that these trans-
parencies of the flesh are marvellously acquired and natural. The color upon the cheeks seems almost to waver
with life. You—"

He stopped abruptly, conscious that his companion's
attention was directed in another quarter. Following
his gaze, he saw that it rested upon a trio moving
toward the great Millet at the farther end of the room.
Brunton leaned lightly upon the hand-rail with a look of
expectant pleasure in his quiet eyes.

The two girls hanging upon either arm of the young
woman seemed, despite their animation, to be deferring
their opinions to hers. She was undeniably noticeable,
though her attire was dark and extremely simple. She
was tall, and with a round, mature figure which she carried with unconscious stateliness. A black straw hat
rested upon her mass of gold braids and shaded the pale
ivory hue of her face. Her expression was deep and
thoughtful; the air of youthful deference which the girls
evinced appeared in natural keeping with the strong per-

1

sonality which marked her. As she turned to speak to a distinguished-looking old gentleman who had accosted them, the girls dropped their hold, and, wending their way through the crowd, made a hurried dash toward the picture before which Brunton and his companion still stood.

"Oh, Geoffrey!" they exclaimed, standing still at sight of the former.

"We wanted to get another look at this lovely boy before we leave," continued the younger, a tall school-girl, with a warm, animated face and voice, " so we left Constance for a minute while she talks to Mr. Glynn. We're in love with him, aren't we, Grace?"

"With whom, Edith, the boy or Mr. Glynn?" asked Brunton, looking with friendly amusement from her bright face to the gentler one of her sister.

"With the boy," answered Grace, a shy smile dimpling her mouth. "His cheeks and lips are as soft and flushed as if he had just had a nap. He looks so—kiss-able."

"That expresses it better—eh, Kenyon? This is Miss Grace, and this Miss Edith Herriott—Mr. Kenyon, girls."

They looked up with rosy cheeks to acknowledge the salutation of the tall stranger.

"Am I possibly speaking to the cousins of Severn Scott?" he asked in a full, deep voice, his dark, glowing face holding them fascinated.

"Why, yes!" Edith bubbled forth, delightedly. "And are you—can you be Hall Kenyon?"

"Oh, Edith," expostulated the quieter girl, flushing over her sister's irrepressibility. The stranger smiled, showing his handsome white teeth.

"You have guessed it," he said, courteously. "Mr. Brunton wished to confute some of my Eastern estimates of the Far West, so he brought me in to see your loan exhibition. I'm moving slowly in the direction of your residence as per promise to Scott."

"We shall be glad," returned Grace, with shy pleasure; and, as Edith plucked her by the sleeve, she nodded swiftly and darted toward the entrance, where they joined their former companion and passed on out.

"That was an unexpected flash," remarked Kenyon, moving slowly on with Brunton. "I intended calling on Miss Herriott to-night. Have you ever noticed how a contemplated action will evolve something associated with it just before the consummation? Oh, by the way, can you tell me who was that young woman with them?"

"That was their sister, Miss Herriott."

"Ah!" After an indistinct pause he rejoined, "An unusually beaut—handsome woman. Do you know her?"

"Yes; I am their legal adviser."

They walked from picture to picture, and finally came out of the warm rooms into the crisp spring atmosphere, and turned briskly up Montgomery Street.

"I've heard a great deal of these Herriotts from Scott," pursued Kenyon, suiting his long, nervous stride to Brunton's leisurely gait. "Their history is quite unique, I think. The father killed himself, did he not?"

"Exactly; and without reason. He was a strangely excitable man, and lost his head at a sign of disaster. Once imbued with an idea, he was not to be stopped in his course. His individuality might be described as the Chinaman expressed the locomotion of a cable-car: 'No

pushee, no pullee, go like hellee.' He had made an un-
wise speculation in grain—not, however, at all ruinous—
and, through overlooking two significant ciphers, he sent
a bullet through his head."

"I've heard it all before—a somewhat selfish perform-
ance for the father of a large family."

"There was no egoism in the act. The egoist is, at
worst, thoughtful. He had lost his balance entirely ; he
was practically insane."

"His daughter does not impress one as having inherited the tendency."

"You refer to Constance—Miss Herriott. She is quite
different, by virtue of her position — the guardian, you
know, of the family. But Herriott certainly perpetuated
himself in one or two of the younger children. Where
are you going?"

They had reached the corner of Pine Street, and Kenyon came to an abrupt stand-still.

"I promised to meet Joscelyn up here at his club at
four o'clock. I'll be at your office without fail to-morrow to see about that title, if no other inclination inter-
venes." He laughed lightly as he moved off. "Well, so
long."

With a nod the two men separated.

Kenyon would have more thoroughly appreciated
Brunton's characterization had he been a witness to the
little scene enacted in Eleanor Herriott's bedroom at
about half-past eight that evening. She had been dressing for her first ball, and the children sat waiting in eager
expectation.

As she moved into view there was a long sigh of admiration. The Herriotts' admiration for one another was

quite undisguised; they expressed it with an utter disregard as to what others might think of their family fanaticism. They were, however, equally frank with their disapproval, being heedlessly imprudent in pronouncing words which rushed to their lips on the impulse of an impression. Honest praise, however, seldom hurts; like a pleasant cordial, it sends a grateful tingle through the coldest blood.

Edith, perched on the foot of the bed, clapped her hands in applause.

"Oh, doesn't she look lovely! Oh, Eleanor, I wish I were grown up!"

"Look at her hair; it's a heap of fire-flies there with the light on it, her cheeks match, and her eyes are torches; the men will light their wits at them. She looks as though she would burst into flame. She'll surely be the belle."

"Keep still, you silly girls. Constance, put a pin in that rose in my hair, or I'll dance it out. There! Now while I put on my gloves you can give me praise galore; I like it."

She stood, a young, graceful figure in white satin, under the chandelier. The deep red rose in her bronze hair, the glow upon her cheek and lip, the restless, flashing gray eyes charmed as does a flash-light in a dark night. In the pause which followed her words, she turned to Constance in demure, laughing expectancy.

" Well, Constance?"

"Beautiful, dear," came the ready answer, in the low, tender voice. "I feel very proud of you to-night."

The younger girl threw her a kiss and swept her a deep

courtesy. Then she turned to the quiet little figure standing with her arm around Constance's waist.

"Want to see me, Nan?"

"Yes; just stoop a little." The tall, flower-like head
bent within the child's reach, and Nan's fairy-light fingers moved from the rose in the hair, over the exquisite
face, touched the slim young shoulders, and passed over
the simple fashioning of the gown. This was Nan's
sight. "You must look like a tiger-lily," she said, as she
finished her inspection.

"Take care, she'll spring at you," cried Edith, from
her perch. "She does look sort of tigerish, doesn't she,
Constance?"

"I'm not a bit fierce, Edith, to-night."

"No, but you're wild."

"That's not fair," put in Grace, critically regarding
her sister askance. "You are only too bright-looking.
You should go veiled; you hurt people's eyes, like the
sun. Catch a little of Constance's moonlight beauty."

"Moonlight fiddlestick," returned Constance with a
laugh, as she straightened a loop of ribbon on Eleanor's
shoulder. "Don't dance yourself to a bundle of rags,
Eleanor. You do so exhaust yourself with enjoyment.
Live to repeat the tale."

"Of my gown? It will get soiled at the first round.
Is that the carriage? Mr. Vassault said they would be
here before nine, as he is one of the Reception Committee.
Look and tell me, Edith."

"Bring us your favors," they cried, while Constance
hooked the soft white wrap about her, "and be sure
to be the belle. Good-night! I hear Mr. Vassault's
voice in the hall. Have a good time!"

"Hush, girls," remonstrated Constance; "you're making an unconscionable noise." And she hurried down after the white-robed figure.

"No, I won't come in, thank you, Miss Herriott," said Vassault, with a good-humored laugh at her invitation. "My wife says she will never forgive you if you keep me talking, and I don't want you to incur her august displeasure. Ready, Miss Eleanor? And looking as lovely as ever. I'll see that she accepts none but eligible favors, Miss Herriott, and that she bestows her own in official corners. We'll see you at Mrs. Glynn's reception next week, I hope."

"Perhaps. Mrs. Glynn takes a refusal as a personal affront. Good-night. Thank you for taking care of Eleanor. Enjoy yourself, dear."

She closed the door softly behind them, lowered the gas, which was flaring at full height, and ran quickly upstairs.

"Let us clear up this litter," she said, entering the large, untidy room where the children were still congregated. "Grace, hang this gown away, will you? Edith, put those things straight in the bureau drawers, and close them while—"

"Call Betty," advised Edith, with a yawn.

"Betty is tired, I suppose. Here, Nan, roll up this ribbon, dearie, while I pick up that mess of curl-papers and rose leaves from the dressing-table. Hush! is that Marjorie calling?" She stood still and listened. "Yes; I'll be back in a minute, girls."

She moved swiftly into the dimly-lighted next room. The child sitting up in bed looked cross and tired.

"What is wrong, little one?" she asked, sitting down

on the bed with a scarcely perceptible movement of weariness.

"Everybody makes such a noise," whined the child, "and Ede came in and pulled my hair, and I can't sleep."

"Lie down, darling, and I'll lie beside you."

The child snuggled down in her arms, put up her hand to stroke her face, and so dropped off to slumber.

In the next room the talk and laughter were unabated.

"Eleanor has all the fun," grumbled Edith, in a moment of reaction. "She goes off like a princess, and leaves us to clear up after her as though we were her servants." She gave a footstool an impatient kick. "Leave those things alone, Grace. Betty will pick them up in the morning."

"You mean Constance," said Nan, from the lounge. "Constance won't go to bed knowing the room is in disorder. She always says something might happen in the night, and if strangers chanced to come in and found a frowsy room she would feel her left ear burning."

Grace moved slowly about, picking up the scattered articles. There was a gentle, somnolent ease in her large though girlish figure, a dreamy thoughtfulness in her eyes.

"Constance *won't* rest," put in Edith, conclusively. "She divides her days into pigeon-holes, and is busy keeping them filled. I know what I'd do if I were in her place."

"What?"

"Let things run themselves; I've learned something about momentum. But Constance thinks she has to steer a rolling ball, and gets tired running after it."

"Dear Constance!" murmured Nan, with a resentful flush in her delicate cheek.

"Poor Constance!" sighed Grace, gathering up a handful of fallen rose leaves from the table. "I wonder if she feels as old as a mother of five girls does."

"Or a father," supplemented Edith. "It's a good thing, girls, that Constance is a big woman; otherwise she'd have been a lean, sour old maid long ago. How old is Constance, Grace? Thirty?"

"Why, no. She's only twenty-six."

"Only five years older than Eleanor! You'd never think Eleanor was only twenty-one yesterday—the lucky thing! I wish I were in her place, and going down to see Geoffrey to-morrow about my share of mamma's legacy. There goes the bell! Who can it be at this hour of the night?"

With abrupt curiosity she tiptoed into the hall, and, catching sight of the maid with a card in her hand, she followed her into Constance's room.

They both hurried over to the bed, and looked down for a second at Constance asleep, with the sleeping child in her arms. There was something so peaceful in her attitude that the maid drew back. But Edith had no such qualms.

"Wake up, Constance," she whispered, shaking her ruthlessly. The girl released her arms from the child, and sprang softly to her feet, awake on the instant.

"What is it?" she asked, in a hushed undertone, moving toward the door. "Something has happened to Nan—"

"No, no," laughed Edith; "it's only a visitor. Give her the card, Betty." She peered over her sister's shoulder in the dim light. "'Hall Kenyon,'" she read, slowly. "Severn's friend, Constance; we saw him this afternoon, you know. Hurry down."

Constance swiftly smoothed her hair and shook out her gown. She paused a moment to collect her rudely-awakened senses, and went down-stairs.

The stranger stood with his back turned toward the door. It was a broad, straight, young back, the brown, columnar neck supporting a powerful, somewhat massive, head.

"Mr. Kenyon," she said, softly.

He turned with a start. Her first impression was of a flash of white teeth and the glow of a dark young face as she held out her hand.

"This is an unpardonably late hour," he said, swiftly; "I was unexpectedly detained. But as I had determined to come to-night, I came, nevertheless. Scott said my name would not be entirely unfamiliar to you." He seated himself opposite to her, his hazel eyes resting upon her with startling brilliancy.

"His letters have always been full of your name," she replied, "and now they quite overflow with your fame. Severn is such an unselfish fellow; he always wishes the world to have a share of his good-fortune. I feel as though I had been a sort of spiritual companion with you on many of your summer jaunts and yachting tours. Is Severn well?"

"Quite well," he answered, an intense pleasure speaking in his voice. He had wished, at her first words, that the tender, peaceful voice would fail to pause that he might grow accustomed to its grave music as to the uncommon personality of the woman herself.

She was built in the large, easy lines of the great goddess
—round, full bust, and curves of quiet strength. A
wealth of pale, lustreless, golden braids crowned her, the
matte complexion of her colorless, dispassionate face
being in unusual combination with her hair. Her broad
gray eyes looked across at him with the easy directness
of truth. In her quiet, experienced pose, in the repose
of her firm mouth, there was not a suggestion of emotiveness. And Kenyon felt himself speaking less exu-
berantly than was his wont.

"He is quite well," he repeated. "Scott seems to
keep well through sheer bravado. He pays tribute to
no power outside himself, and one can always count upon
his bobbing up serenely in club, wood, or office, in spite
of the indisposition of weather or business. He is a man
who lives for the day, you know."

"Yes," smiled Constance, "he is a cheery pessi-
mist. Do you think he has ever thought of settling
down to a home and fireplace of his own?"

"I think so," replied Kenyon, with unexpected warmth,
meeting her eyes with a flash of sudden insight. Constance felt the stain of color rising to her temples. The
fingers of her white hand closed tightly over the arms of
her chair. She had given little heed to his words; the
man himself disturbed her oddly. His luminous hazel
eyes, under straight, fine brows, struck her as discon-
certingly intuitive; his nose was finely chiselled; his
mouth, unshaded by a mustache, left an impression of
wilful sensuousness, in striking contradiction to the
broad, firm chin. The lack of beard upon his face lent
to it an air of boyishness which the impulsive color in
his olive cheek strongly augmented. The glowing wine

of summer emanated from every inch of his wholesome physique.

"Why do you think so?" she asked, quietly.

"Oh, well," he laughed, throwing back his head as a child sometimes tosses back a refractory curl from his forehead, "ever since his return from his Western trip he has seemed to simmer."

"Simmer?" she repeated, questioningly.

"Exactly. As a pot, set back after boiling, browses over its recent exploit. It is a sort of retrospective calm which bodes—something."

"He was tired, I suppose. Did he describe all the wonders of the coast?"

"No; he recommended me to a guide-book for that. He was not very discursive, except on one point."

Constance regarded him expectantly. She knew from the animation in his face that the point in question would be divulged.

"The Herriotts," he answered, at once. "Fact is, Miss Herriott, I know you all from A to Z, in every mood, tense, number, and person."

"That was not fair of Severn."

"It was his unselfish friendliness again—the desire to share, you know. He had you all labelled, and when he called you by name I immediately knew the character of whom he spoke."

"What were the labels? May you repeat them?"

"Certainly. They were Con — Eleanor, the beautiful witch; Grace, the dreamer; Edith (pardon me), the little devil; Nan, the dove; and Marjorie, the lamb. Have I them straight?"

"Quite — according to Severn's cousinly reckoning. Are you going to make a long stay, Mr. Kenyon?"

"That depends on my lawyers and inclination. You know I came out to settle up an inheritance of my late uncle, Seth Cope."

"I did not know. Do you speak of Seth Cope, who used to live in that pretty cottage over at Sausalito?"

"Yes; that cottage is part of the legacy of which I am trying to dispose, meanwhile growing attached to it by living over there in its rose wilderness. Do you know Sausalito, Miss Herriott?"

"From base to summit. We lived over there one whole summer and autumn. It is just opposite the Rev. Dr. Granniss's place, is it not?"

"Yes; he and his wife have proven very companionable and neighborly. Do you know them?"

"They were very dear friends of my mother. I know them well. But I should think you would find the quiet distracting after the friction of New York."

"I should if I were unoccupied. But it seems to have tumbled upon my mood most opportunely."

"Does Pegasus like the herbage?" she questioned, spontaneously.

He was startled at the divination, and flashed one of his bright, restless looks over her again. "He seems to thrive," he returned, with an almost shy flush. "I am breaking him into a new gait."

"I liked the old one."

He made a military salute with his hand, and rejoined, hurriedly, "He cut too many capers. Got tired of them. I have struck into a long narrow lane, and he must walk sedately."

"I think that will be impossible," she said, with a kindly shake of her head. "The grass springs under his feet too ardently. His movement must be swift and to the fray."

"I hope not. My ambition lies in another direction. I am writing a novel."

"Are you? It will be good, I am sure."

"You are kind to be so prejudiced. I hope your prognostications will be fulfilled. But its success has met with an unexpected barrier."

"How?"

"In my windfall. The muse, you know, flies from affluence as from the pest. She is more at home in a garret or—"

"Or," she supplemented as he paused, "in the throes of a great sorrow or struggle. Then you must become unhappy to become happy. Even your heaven knows its purgatory. I advise you to stay out of heaven in consideration of your preface."

"No," he said, a sudden stubborn intolerance steeling mouth and eyes, "no."

They sat in silence for a few seconds, and then Kenyon arose with a start. "I have stayed too late," he said, standing tall and powerful before her. "But I wish to come again—to see the children."

"Do," she responded, rising; and putting her hand into his. "Will you come Friday night? That is the night on which they put on all sorts of fresh resolutions and good manners—their weekly moral cleaning."

"I have heard of some of your institutions," he said, still holding her hand, and letting his eyes travel over the passionless peace of her face and figure. "Also about the singing."

"And your violin?" she asked, quickly. "Have you brought that with you?"

"What do you know of my violin?" he demanded, with curious brusqueness.

"Nothing—as yet," she faltered, in surprise. "Except through Severn."

"I'll. introduce you Friday night," he said, with inconsistent lightness. "Will the children be up?"

"You must come to dine—at seven. Can you?"

"Thank you, I can. Good-night."

She lingered a moment in the moonlight after he had run down the steps, and then returned aimlessly to the drawing-room. She stood with her hand on a table without moving. Presently she raised her head with a long sigh. "He is a very handsome m—boy," she thought, strangely. Then, as if by analogy, she walked over and looked into the great mirror. "I am old," she murmured, gazing at herself drearily—"I am an old woman." She stood for a space, seeing only the loss, none of the wonderful womanly charm. "And yet," she reflected, "he—that Hall Kenyon—must be years older than I. Severn is over thirty—they are nearly of an age. Bah! what a fool I am! I suppose it is his bright exuberance which makes me regret mine to-night." She moved with an impatient gesture, and turned off the light.

She mounted the steps slowly, and entered the large room where Marjorie slept. The taper had burned out, and the room was steeped in moonlight. She moved noiselessly over to the bed, and looked down at the sweet, flushed face of the sleeping child. Unconsciously she brushed back the clustering curls from the brow, and drew the coverlet more closely about the little figure. Then she turned slowly, and walked over to the window.

She sat down and looked out at the night. The moon advanced with slow, regal steps along the path of turquoise, in all the grandeur of loneliness. The spire of the church seemed to bar its way—a sentinel arresting a spirit. It appeared wan to Constance, despite its radiance. The face looked like a woman's. She had seen, that afternoon, a picture—something like it—called "Penelope," by Cabanel. The woman, with great wan eyes, stands looking over the water—it is significant that she looks over the water; in that fact, thought Constance, Cabanel painted Penelope's hope. Some poet once said that the sea-gods quit their sunken palaces by night and seat themselves on promontories to gaze out over the waves. Mortals do otherwise; night holds the future— in dreams—upon its bosom. Without a past, the present is a child; without a future, it is an adult grown blind. Constance's present was not a child; neither had it grown quite blind. She often rose from her depths and looked beyond; but oftener her gaze was backward. In retrospect lay her strength.

Six years before she had been a gay, laughing girl. One day Robert Herriott, as has been said, in a frenzy of despondency, sent a pistol-shot through his brain, and blotted out the brightness of those nearest him who were old enough to realize its import. It subdued Constance as a thunder-bolt hushes the moment which follows; it sent into life a frail blossom before the world was ready for it, and snapped asunder the erstwhile powerful heart which had been mated to his.

The mother's battle for life was a desperate one, but she lost. And, dying, she called her daughter to her.

"Constance," she said, in a weak, supplicating voice, "I must die, and I cannot."

The girl gazed at the despairing face dumbly.

"Constance," whispered the mother, pleadingly, "there are all those children."

"I am here," answered the girl, pityingly.

"But, darling, there is Nan—and the baby."

"Yes, mother."

The woman's eyes gazed at the pale-faced girl with a wordless message. As long as she lived Constance Herriott could never forget that look.

"I am here, mother," she said again, in hushed solemnity. Upon the face of the dying mother there flashed an eager light; she was waiting. Finally the answer came:

"I shall never leave them, mother." And over the face of the dying mother there dawned a peace that passeth understanding, but which stretched from the dead to the living in a tie everlasting. And as long as she lived Constance Herriott would never forget that look.

So, when the grave man had asked her for the gift of her young womanhood, it had been easy to answer, "I have only my friendship left to give you, Geoffrey; the rest is given to these children."

And that was all. The young, inexperienced girl slowly developed into the motherly woman. The children turned to her as the flowers to the sun, and she was always there to supply the need. Her arms grew stronger—they had much to support; her heart grew braver—it had much to contend with; her brain grew manly—it had much to adjust; heart and form of woman, will and execution of man—one of necessity's curious combinations. Robert Herriott's miscalculation had unnecessarily warped many lives. There was enough left to keep the bodies in comfort—the one saving clause in the burden upon the young shoulders.

There had never been a day when the shoulders had fretted. But to-night, as she looked back at the face of her vanished youth, she shuddered violently, and laid her head against the cold window-pane as if for comfort.

She suddenly noticed that it had grown strangely still in the street below. The cable had ceased to whirr. Her hands were cold and numb. They grew slowly warm as she lay awake beside the sleeping child.

CHAPTER II

ELEANOR HERRIOTT waited in a corner of Brunton's outer office with a feeling of intolerant impatience. The quick passage of men in and out of the private rooms, the apparent absorption in business which hurried them to and fro, the rapid interchange of greeting, and careless, almost unnoticed exits, all excited her through their atmosphere of serious purpose. She was too much of a coquette to be unmindful of the swift glances in her direction, but too conservative a woman to be entirely pleased to pay the popular tax which beauty levies upon its possessors.

She was finally admitted into Brunton's presence, and entered with a sigh of relief.

"Ah, Eleanor," he said, putting out a hand across his desk by way of acknowledgment, but continuing to write for a few seconds, his fine, strong face bent closely over the document. There was a suspicion of elegance about Geoffrey Brunton which stood out markedly in his uncompromising law - office. Eleanor could not decide to-day whether the impression was supplied by the sweep of his brown mustache or by the bit of cape-jasmine in his button-hole.

"Sit down," he said, presently, removing his hand from hers, and carefully placing a blotter over his work. "We have a little business to settle, have we not?" He raised a pair of penetrating blue eyes with the strained scrutiny of the near-sighted. This same near-sightedness was a remarkable softener to an otherwise somewhat severe visage.

"Let me see," he said, musingly, "when did you come into your legal majority?"

"The day before yesterday."

"Good." He leaned across to a box, and extracted a packet of papers. He quickly ran them over, and selecting one, handed it to her. While she was putting up her veil, in order to read more clearly, he continued:

"You will understand the provisions from the words of the will, I think. Read it, and let me know whether you get a thorough comprehension of its details."

After reading it slowly and carefully, she met his eyes with a slight flush of delight.

"I gather from it," she announced with precision, as though curbing her tongue, "that as each of my mother's daughters attains her twenty-first birthday, she is to have the interest of seven thousand dollars paid to her monthly, which she can use as she sees fit; or, should she marry before, or whenever she does marry, the principal shall be handed to her intact. Is that correct?"

"Quite. But during these six years of your minority the principal has accumulated to something like ten thousand. This will give you a tidy little income for notions and nonsense, as the family fund will continue to provide for your necessities, as heretofore. So I suppose you will want your pile of bank-bills every month."

"I do not know," responded the girl, coloring deeply. She looked down at her slender gloved hands for a moment without speaking. Then, with a little self-conscious laugh, she looked up into the face of her friend.

"Geoffrey," she ventured, "could that clause about handing over the principal intact be broken?"

He suddenly remembered an amusing incident connected with Eleanor Herriott's inherited deplorable rashness. She was a child at the time of its happening, walking down-town with her mother, whose well-filled purse she carried in her little hand. As they entered a large dry-goods establishment Mrs. Herriott asked the child for the purse.

"I haven't it, mamma," she 'declared, excitedly; "I gave it to a poor little boy who had no coat on, and only rags for shoes. He looked so sick. I saw him while you were looking in a show-window. Wasn't it lucky!"

Brunton regarded her at this moment with some concern.

"How do you mean?" he asked. "Come, we are not at home, and cannot chat. What extravagance are you contemplating?"

"Well," she returned, tapping the floor nervously with her foot, "the Vassaults are going to Europe next month, and—"

"And you wish to go with them?"

"Oh, Geoffrey, it is such a chance!"

"But, my child, have you the means?"

"Can't it be taken—outright—from my capital?"

"It could—with the consent of your guardian. What does *she* say?"

"I—I have not spoken of it to Constance."

"Then there is no need in discussing it with me. Why don't you ask Constance?"

"You know how stubborn she is. Let her once take a stand, and—"

Her complaining voice died into a wavering, indistinct murmur. Brunton was regarding her coolly, critically, with an intentness which she comprehended with annoyance.

"Well," she insisted, "you must admit that no amount of reasoning or alteration of conditions will make Constance change front. A thing once true and just with her is always true and just. You know that as well as I."

His slightly sallow skin showed a trace of pallor at the girl's insinuating temerity.

"Nevertheless," he returned, coolly but carefully, "her guidance has not led you astray as yet. Even though you are of age, you will, I hope, trust to her maturer judgment in all serious undertakings."

"Why, Geoffrey!"—she flashed a look of anger toward him, her voice vibrating uncontrollably as she spoke —"you know that Constance is our only one, father as well as mother. Have I ever appeared refractory? Don't we all depend upon her approval in every action? Do you think I consider myself sufficient just because I have acquired a nominal independence!"

"That sounds sensible, Eleanor! I only hope you will stick to such colors. Then — about this European plan —you are ready to rely on her decision?"

She scratched at a spot of ink on the desk without looking up.

"I want to go," said she, in a low voice; after a few seconds she raised her eyes defiantly—"and I shall. You can advance me the money, can't you?"

"I can; but without Constance's approval, I shall do nothing of the sort. Still, why argue about it? Since you are so anxious to go, why should Constance object?"

"Because she does not like Mrs. Vassault."

"Ah!"

She regarded him expectantly, but he vouchsafed no further remark. He arose, put the mother's will back into its compartment, and turned his tall, slightly stooped figure toward her, waiting deferentially for her to move. She arose perfunctorily, her teeth set tightly together.

"I suppose you will agree with Constance," she said. "You generally do agree with her. But the money is mine now, and I shall do with it what I wish, or somebody will be sorry for interfering."

Brunton suddenly understood the meaning of the purple shadows which so often encircled Constance Herriott's eyes.

"I am not your guardian," he said sternly—"only your lawyer, whom your sister has honored by intrusting with other friendly matters. If you will stop to consider your words, you will acknowledge that they sound not only unlovely but childishly wicked toward your sister, to whom you owe more than you can ever appreciate. Despite your twenty-one years, you are like the child who says, 'Give me what I wish and I'll be good, but not otherwise.' You—"

"I am not a child, and that is where all the misconception lies. Credit me with a little judgment on my own account. Constance is not infallible. Besides, a chance like this does not offer itself every day to a girl in my position, and since I desire to go so strongly, I shall not allow a little personal prejudice on her part to deter me."

She moved across the room toward the door, with her head held high in defiance. Brunton, taking in the grace-

ful figure more minutely than interest had hitherto im-
pelled him, recognized that it would take even more
strenuous arguments to move her than would be necessary with her sister. Constance Herriott would have to
be convinced through her reason, Eleanor through the
sudden suasion of an overpowering moral impetus. When
the latter was in this condition she was, figuratively, deaf
and blind to any but her own perturbed sensations.

"Good-afternoon, Eleanor," said Brunton, holding out
his hand, which she did not notice, "I trust things will
shift themselves according to your pleasure."

"But you will not help me, I suppose."

"I shall talk the matter over with Constance Friday
night, when you can come to a better understanding of
the disposition of your resources. Don't fight with your
own shadow. Go home and be good, and probably you
will be happy."

He ended with a laugh.

"And have a dreary, flat old time. Thanks, I'm not
seeking such negative happiness. Good-bye."

His hand closed over hers on the knob.

"Take care, Eleanor," he admonished.

"Others can take care; I'll take something gayer."

She turned the knob sharply, and left him standing
looking after her quickly retreating figure with a feeling
of impotent anger. He was too intimately allied with
the Herriotts to be indifferent to such a revelation of
character. "Little termagant!" he apostrophized, the
vision of a quiet, womanly form rising beside its fever-
ishness like a piece of marble endurance.

Eleanor turned out of the office with a hot face and
knitted brows. Her pulses were hammering with wild

displeasure. To be thwarted was a laceration at which,
in first moments, she tore rabidly. Contentment or submission were surgeons at whose methods she jeered. At
the risk of being called unamiable or unreasonable, she
gave her leanings full headway. The perpetually amiable
are fools, was her defensive corollary—a sentiment born
more of vanity than of philosophy.

As she reached the corner of the passageway before
emerging into the hall proper, she paused to brush some
dust from the edge of her gown. At the same moment
a man, turning the L shortly, brushed sharply against
her bent figure, almost knocking her down. Eleanor staggered against the wall, and looked up indignantly.

"I beg your pardon," exclaimed a full, contrite voice,
as the man stood bare-headed before her. "I trust I have
not hurt you."

Eleanor looked up with a feeling of bewilderment.
"No," she answered, oddly; "it is nothing, I believe."
She turned to go, but a wrench of pain in her ankle de-
layed her.

"I am exceedingly sorry," he said, moving closer.
"Will you let me assist you down the stairs? I am sure
you are in pain."

"It will pass," she returned, with a nod of dismissal, as
she moved on more slowly. "What a face!" she thought,
with a swift revulsion of feeling. "What a surprisingly
vivid face!"

By the time she reached the car the pain in her foot
had subsided. On entering a street-car she generally assumed a preoccupied air, which her chance fellow-pas-
sengers would have described as haughty. It was her
own way of showing that exclusiveness is not always an

outward fact; that in a crowded public conveyance
Eleanor Herriott's spirit proper rode alone in its own
private carriage. Two Chinamen entered, and seated
themselves with ease beside her; Eleanor's face gave no
evidence of her inward shudder of repugnance. A bux-
om, bejewelled dame was reiterating, at full pitch, her indignation over her friend's having paid her fare. A man
with a package of sausages was seated opposite her;
Eleanor hated the odor of the very word sausage. Two
women were retailing, for the benefit of all hearers, stories of their household grievances and economics; a
school-girl was giggling over the unsolicited information.
A man on the back platform was chewing tobacco. When
Eleanor got off at her corner her nerves were in the ruf-
fled state of the fretful porcupine.

There are days when, from the hour of rising to retir-
ing, every detail seems to rise in malicious anarchy to
desire and comfort. This was such a day for Eleanor.
When she reached the house, she found Edith leaning on
the gate.

"Let me pass," she commanded, crossly.

"Don't be in such a hurry," advised Edith, suavely.
"There is that in the drawing-room which truth forbids
me to call charming, but which is awaiting you impa-
tiently."

"Who is in there?"

"The Plague."

"Mrs. Ferris? Is Gertrude with her?"

"She is."

"Pshaw! I suppose I shall have to go in. Edith,
will you move aside? I am not in a mood to tolerate
your nonsense."

" Your words are unnecessary evidence," admitted her sister, allowing her to open the gate and pass in.

The Ferrises were just rising to go as she entered, but sank back to chat a moment. Mrs. Ferris, an eagle-nosed, ferret-eyed woman, with a lorgnon and an " air," passed inspection over the new-comer's toilet, and allowed her to move on to her daughter, a sweet-faced girl, while she resumed her monologue. To entertain Mrs. Ferris was to listen.

" Yes, as I was saying when Eleanor entered, Miss Herriott, a mother has·more duties than she herself can enumerate. The secret of my children's well-being lies in the fact that I even sleep, as it were, with my hand on them. Unconsciously I direct their very dreams, and—"

" Do they ever have the nightmare ?" interrupted Eleanor, softly.

" Figuratively speaking, never. I have often thought of you, Miss Herriott, with your five girls, and wished I could be of some real benefit to you. Now, for instance, if you ever need a chaperon, say at a dinner, or a tea, or any of the pretty little functions which you may undertake for yourself or sisters, you can count on me at any time."

" Thank you, Mrs. Ferris, but I have grown accustomed to considering myself sedate enough to be the children's chaperon, and they are certainly sufficiently numerous to be mine."

" But, my dear girl, you know what prodding-forks and microscopes are used on an unmarried woman's actions. Now, for example—merely for example, you know—how could you explain your very intimate relations with Mr. Brunton to a suspicious stranger ?"

"I never vouchsafe explanations to strangers. To my friends my actions need no justification."

"Indeed, that is true. But Mr. Brunton, otherwise so very hard to draw into polite society, is continually—"

"Oh, mamma!" murmured Gertrude Ferris, with a shamed face.

"My dear Gertrude, Miss Herriott understands that my intentions are purely motherly."

"For whom?" asked Eleanor, innocently. "Constance, or—"

"Really," broke in Constance, with an uneasy laugh, "I have never supposed that I was such a cynosure, so I have never posed. Everybody knows that Mr. Brunton is our lawyer and a sort of friendly guardian of the children, besides being a family friend ever since he came to the city, more than twenty years ago. He was a boy going to the university when I was a little toddler of four or five. His father and mine had been old college-mates."

"Indeed? How very interesting! Those old friendships grow quite romantic sometimes. It must make you feel as though you had an elder brother."

Constance smiled her acquiescence.

"And now we must go," exclaimed Mrs. Ferris, bustling up. "Come, Gertrude. Oh, by the way, Miss Herriott, did I understand my Helen aright when she said that you contemplated giving Grace a graduating tea?"

"We spoke only of a sociable little afternoon for some of her intimate school-mates—something quite informal and friendly."

"I suppose you will have tête-à-tête tables and music?"

"Oh no. We like our own round-table for general hilarity and fun."

"Don't think of it, Miss Herriott—not for a moment. I speak from experience, and know that, notwithstanding the size of your room, there is less trouble with small tables. Take my advice"—she was on the door-step by this time—"and profit by my experience. I shall be in to assist you. Good-bye. No thanks necessary. I am not a woman who believes in confining my whole interest to my own. Good-bye."

Constance closed the door after them, and returned to the drawing-room and Eleanor with a merry laugh.

"Well," remarked Eleanor, taking off her hat and leaning back with an air of relief, "I should like to choke that woman."

"You came very near being rude to her."

"Can't help it; she makes me savage. Her only virtue is that she is the mother of her daughter, and Gertrude's most deplorable failing is that she is the daughter of her mother. Poor thing! if she had been born without a mother, it would have been better for her. The man who can face, without flinching, the prospect of Mrs. Ferris as a mother-in-law is yet unborn; a man likes to be his own manager. And now she has Geoffrey in her eye, the wary angler!"

"You have just come from him, have you not?"

"Yes." She sat filliping the rose in her hat.

"Did you read mother's will?" continued Constance, softly, surprised at Eleanor's sudden silence.

"Yes."

"Of course we always knew that she had devised her property to us in this way, but it seems more real after reading it."

She scanned her sister's face anxiously, conscious that some untoward event had robbed it of its bright charm.

"Is anything wrong, Eleanor?"

"No, only— Constance, you know the Vassaults are going to Europe next month."

"So you told me last night."

"Well, they wish me to go with them, and I wish to go, too. May I?"

"It is not a trip down-town, dear. It requires a nice little sum to get ready, go, stay, and return."

"I know; but I have it now, and I wish you would let me take some of it for this. Oh, Constance, I am just wild to go. I have never been, and I have longed for it so often."

"You know, Eleanor," said Constance, gravely, "that I dearly wish you to go, too—but not with Mrs. Vassault."

"Why not?"

"She is too young—and careless."

"She is as proper as you," burst forth the girl, violently. "She goes with the best people, and you have often let me go out with her."

"But this is quite a different affair. Certainly, Mrs. Vassault knows and keeps the proprieties—she does that by instinct; but she also does some very foolish things."

"Am I not to be trusted?"

"I do not know."

"Try me. Constance, darling, just this first trial! You always want to give us what pleasure you can. Say yes, Constance."

She was kneeling at her feet, her arms about her waist, her lovely face raised pleadingly to the troubled beauty of her sister's eyes.

"Dear, honestly, I cannot."

The girl made a passionate movement with her hands, sprang to her feet, and threw herself on the divan in a fit of sobbing.

"It is easy enough for you to sit there and refuse me so calmly!" she cried. "You have had your pleasure. You were twice across; and because we grew up after the trouble, you think it is an easy thing to have to renounce everything out of the ordinary rut. A mother would not act so. A mother gives in once in a while. Oh, mamma, mamma, I wish you were alive!"

Constance had witnessed such an outburst before. Nevertheless, her face showed, in its pallor, the heavy contraction of her heart caused by the bitter words.

"Poor Eleanor!" she said, rising, and laying her hand on the silky hair; "poor girl! I am sorry, too, that you have no mother. I am only doing my best, sister; I am sorry it is so bad."

The girl sobbed on, her face smothered in the cushion.

"You never stop to consider that we are younger than you; that we have no father, or brother, or relatives to take us about, but have to rely on the kindness of friends. You are unjust and hard. But I won't stand it!"—she arose suddenly, and confronted her sister with a distorted face—"I swear I won't!"

She had frightened Constance before into acquiescence, and now the latter drew her hand over her brow with a weary, uncertain gesture.

"Hush, Eleanor!" she said, hoarsely. "Let me think it over, will you?"

Eleanor drew in her breath hard. Her strong young arms went about her sister and strained her close. "I am a devil," she whispered, fiercely; "but I can't help it. And I — I do love you, Constance." She rushed from the room in a flash.

Five minutes later a quiet little figure groped its way into the room.

"Are you there, Constance?" asked the bird-like voice.

"Yes, Nan."

The child's figure grew strained and still. Then she moved toward the voice. She raised her hand and stroked the loved cheek.

"Never mind, Constance," she murmured, "never mind."

It was the childish comfort the little sensitive-plant always offered.

CHAPTER III

THE Herriotts' drawing-room was large and pleasant to sit in. Continual usage had deprived it of many of the semblances of dignity which, in some degree, the room of state usually possesses. The soft carpet on the floor was beginning to lose its delicate shading; the piano, more often open than shut, was generally strewn with loose sheets of music; the heavy, rich furniture, into which a far-sighted economy of long ago had woven a saving fibre, but which now savored of the past like a magnificent, well-seasoned coat, had a faculty of arranging itself in odd groups of twos and threes, as if possessed of a fundamental taste for cliques. The beautiful lace-curtains were often ruthlessly thrust behind a chair, to admit a full flood of sunlight; at times, hastily thrown-down books complacently disported themselves on chairs; now and then a newspaper sprawled over a divan; and visitors, entering, found themselves laying aside all formality, as a foreign wrap altogether out of season.

There was generally a breath of flowers in the air, as herald to the exquisitely arranged blossoms in pretty bowl or dainty vase. There were several fine engravings and two or three etchings on the deep, creamy walls, from among which peeped one perfect bit of French water-color, like a touch of worldliness in a sunny country field. A slender rosewood cabinet containing a few

3

valuable pieces of porcelain and ivory, and many oddities
and incongruities to which Grace's botanic - geological
turn was always adding, smiled in neighborly congeniality upon the pretty tea-table. As social judgment is always passed on circumstantial evidence, the Herriotts
were dubbed, from the appearance of their drawing-
room, careless as Bohemians. But Bohemianism holding
in its appellation a covert suggestion of happiness, the
stricture carried a spice of pensive jealousy interlarded
with its stately disapproval.

The children were all there. Marjorie, whose little
nose was pressed against the window - pane, and Grace
beside her, were watching the sun setting in a flood of
flame. It bathed the spire of the church in a stream of
blood, painted the windows of the city in tattered
splashes of crimson, and fell upon the little one's golden
curls like a band of rubies. Nan, nestling among the
cushions of the divan, listened to Edith's animated account of a tilt she had had at school. They were enjoy-
ing a lazy happiness when Eleanor's entrance scattered
the brooding peace of the room.

" Play something, Grace," she called. " You are forever mooning out of windows, as if your home interior
were of no account. Play a waltz, and we'll have a
dance. Eh, Nansie ?"

Grace seated herself compliantly at the piano. She
struck into a low dream waltz. Nan, who loved the
poetry of motion, was presently gliding about with Eleanor. When the music changed into a stirring galop
Eleanor stopped, after a pace, and seated Nan, quite
breathless, in a chair. Edith, in a fervor of animal spirits, sent the chairs spinning as she flew through the

room, regardless of Marjorie's plaintive appeal to stop, as the child was whirled about in the girl's tenacious hold. It was only when Edith noticed that Grace's music had again changed that she paused to take breath.

She was playing a minuet. At the sound of the quaint, stately measure, Eleanor stepped from the shadowy corner, her lithe figure in pale, vapory gray, slowly advancing to the rhythm of the music ; advanced and retreated, swayed, and was gone ; courtesied deep and stepped a measure, met her imaginary courtier, and parted again, in the mimic pace of life—the joy of coming, the grief of going, the music fainting and flowing, staccato and sustenato, in the stateliness of grave prose, the grace of sensuous poetry.

The others watched with lazy pleasure — they were used to Eleanor's graceful vagaries.

It was Grace who first saw the tall dark figure on the threshold, and her playing stopped with a crash as she sprang to her feet.

" Is it you, Mr. Kenyon ?" she asked, coming forward uncertainly.

" Yes," he answered, taking her hand. " I begged the maid not to disturb you while I stood there with the impertinence of a snap camera. You are Miss Grace, I remember, and you are Miss Edith." He held out his hand to the tall school-girl, who put hers in his with the straightforward movement of a boy.

" Just Edith," she acquiesced, with a friendly nod which brought an involuntary smile to Kenyon's eyes. " There is Nan."

" I know little Nan," he responded, patting the child's hand softly. " And this is Marjorie. You see," he explained, as he picked up the little one, putting the young girls at their ease with his frank ingenuousness, "that cousin of yours has made introductions quite unnecessary. I knew you all long ago."

"Do you know me, too?" asked the other girl, moving from her shadowy retreat. She had been startled at sight of his face—beautiful, yet clear-cut as a piece of chiselling in the dimming light. He took a quick step toward her.

"You are—ah, we have met before!" He held out his hand. "'Had we never met so blindly'—" he began, but stopped abruptly. "I fear I hurt you that first time. Do you cherish animosity?"

"No; I shall forgive you, if you promise never to do so again."

"I never hurt voluntarily; things will move round, you know, willy-nilly. All we can do is to relieve ourselves in a grumble, and—let things pass."

"Molt, as it were," she observed, as their glance fell upon Constance standing in the curtained doorway.

Eleanor, watching him narrowly, saw the easy self-possession of his aspect change curiously. The warm blood surged to his temples as he moved to greet his hostess. The filmy black gown, which she wore without ornament of any description, suited her peculiarly. While dressing she had had a vague, unaccountable desire to add a ribbon or a rose, something light and feminine, but Eleanor's words had routed the unspoken thought.

"What a difference there is between us!" she had exclaimed, almost petulantly. "All you have to do is to put on your gown and you are entirely dressed. Your complexion and hair are always to be relied on—they are as unchangeably perfect as those of a transfiguration; a rose in your hair would be as much out of place as upon your magnificent Venus, who is perpetually clothed in her own marble chastity. I don't know what I lack, but I always have to add stucco-work to my essentials to give the effect its proper character—just as bits of paint on the cheek designate a certain class of women."

"What a comparison!" Constance had laughed. "You do not need your roses—they are only lines of emphasis to the fact that you and they are akin."

Kenyon might have echoed Eleanor's words, without the petulance, as he approached her.

"Good-evening," he said, as their hands met.

"Good-evening," she made answer, as their hands fell apart. Such was his advent into the Herriott family.

There were certain things about the dinner and evening which, being individual, Kenyon never utterly forgot. The bright girl-faces gathered about the circular table held an element of home-light which was new and charming to him.

"I am one of those vagabonds," he commented, with friendly confidence, "whose name has never belonged to a home-list. I was thrust into the world with but one tie, and that was broken as soon as she saw me comfortably started—that is, as soon as my systole and diastole apparatus were in conventional running order. I grew up among strangers, and in my club-quarters have retained mostly masculine associates. Actually, I could count upon my fingers the number of times I have dined, as to-night, exclusively *en famille*. When asked to dine it has generally proven that I was one of a batch of other guests. At such times, dining is assisting at an entertainment. It takes the presence of a child, I see, to rob the pleasure of all formality." Marjorie had refused, with a species of childish infatuation, to be separated from him, and was seated beside him monopolizing him with her favors.

"Marjorie has adopted you," observed Constance, with a smile. "But should we pity you? You seem to have flourished under the privation."

"Weeds also grow strong and lusty without care." He noticed how, almost unobserved, she had placed the fork in Nan's hand, and arranged everything for her within comfortable reach.

Later he could not restrain his look of absorbed interest when Constance carved. She noticed it.

"You do not regard this as a woman's right," she said, glancing up for a second, and then looking down as the sharp steel slid through the brown meat.

"You are an artist," he said, with simple force.

"It is the art of necessity," she replied. It was not the dexterous use of the knife which arrested his admiration ; his eye was held by the manner in which she poised the fork in the bird's breast. The firm, white hand, the rounded, satiny wrist, with the nicks in the corners, did not stir, the supple finger resting on the guard looked strong and nerveless as the steel. It would be a steady finger on a trigger, he thought, by an inexplicable analogy.

"Constance has served her apprenticeship," laughed Eleanor. "The first time she had fowl to carve she was confronted as by a blind alley—there seemed no way through. Unfortunately, our cook, a new one that day, was as conversant with the biped's ligaments as we. We contemplated it for a while in irritable imbecility until Constance was inspired. 'Run for Geoffrey, Grace,' she said. 'Tell him we must see him on the instant. Tell him it is a matter which menaces life and limb.' That was six years ago, when Mr. Brunton was keeping bachelor's hall two blocks from here. Grace and he were back in ten minutes, and that day Constance took her first lesson in carving."

"You were fortunate in having such a convenient ally."

"Oh, Geoffrey is a sort of alarm patrol for us," put in Edith. "Constance has only to touch the button and he is here."

"Mr. Brunton calls us his conscience," explained Constance quietly, her still gray eyes meeting his. "We are quite as troublesome—calling him up sharply at the most unexpected moments. He comes now without demur, and generally at his leisure ; we never expose him to any danger."

"Danger is inviting," observed Eleanor, in a low tone of challenge.

"That depends on circumstances," answered Kenyon, turning quickly toward her.

"Of time and place ?"

"No ; on the degree of vanity."

"Of personality, you should say, and be more exact."

"Pardon me, I said and meant of vanity."

"Your judgment is pessimistic, and, therefore, only half true. Everybody is not brave through vanity."

"*I* believe the contrary."

"Indeed! You are perhaps only following a divine precept—conceiving man in your own image."

The quick interchange of comment, the two bright faces, were dangerously alike. Both their pulses beat warmly as their eyes held each other. Presently he laughed, boyishly throwing back his head.

"Miss Eleanor," he said, "if there were not a child between us I am afraid we might come to blows. It is always good for me to have an olive-branch between my opponent and myself. I am rabid when struck."

"And I," retorted Eleanor.

Afterwards he heard them sing Abt's "Evening." Scott had often expatiated on the harmony of their voices. Constance played and took the alto, Grace contralto, Edith and Nan soprano, and Eleanor mezzo-soprano. Kenyon, sitting a little removed, with Marjorie on his knee, half closed his eyes. He heard almost unconsciously. He was wholly possessed by the form and face of Constance Herriott rising in the midst of her younger sisters like a queenly water-lily among its neighboring buds. The moment was peaceful and beautiful.

Then he asked Eleanor to sing. Scott, he said, had told him she was quite the prima donna. She hesitated capriciously. Her face was deeply flushed, the red rose in her glinting hair drooped in heavy languor toward her tiny ear. Presently she placed a sheet of music before Constance and began to sing. It was a dramatic ballad; the words, somewhat intense, depicted the sensations of Sheba at the sight of Solomon, and began with, "He stood a king." Her voice was full and rich; but it was the power of passion which colored it that astounded Kenyon.

"Thank you," he said, as she finished and Constance arose. "You have a beautiful power in your throat." She smiled. She was slightly pale, as if exhausted.

"Now," said Constance, coming toward him, "you must excuse me one minute while I put this little lady to bed. Kiss all around, Marjorie."

His gaze followed her curiously as she left the room holding the child's hand. Were such attentions necessary?

"Geoffrey will be here soon," observed Nan, in a pleasantly anticipating tone; "won't he, Grace?"

"Yes; Geoffrey always comes Friday night," she explained. Even as she spoke he came in. Kenyon was conscious of a twinge of jealousy as he noted the quiet pleasure with which he was greeted.

"Ah, Kenyon," said Brunton, holding out a hand to his client, and shaking it as if the personality of its owner were somewhat vague. Then he strolled over and sat down by Nan, taking her hand in his. The child's face flushed with delight — the sense of contact is very comforting to the blind.

When Constance came in again she carried a violin in its case.

"I found this in the hall," she announced. "I was afraid you had forgotten it. Will you play — anything — for us? Oh, Geoffrey."

"As usual," he answered, shaking hands and seating himself again, "Kenyon, Nan is quivering with impatience; I, with doubt. Do you know what you are evoking, Constance?"

"I think so. May I accompany you, Mr. Kenyon? I see you have brought your music."

It was a dance of Dvořak, quaint, wild, fantastic. It held them charmed. The violinist himself seemed possessed with a half-barbaric spirit as his bow cut and flashed and danced upon the strings in the flow of singular melody.

"And now," he said, before they could speak, "I must go," and he moved toward the door. They looked up at him in startled wonder.

"You don't know the value of a pause," remarked Brunton.

"It is my way," laughed Kenyon. "To pause with me means to become stationary. I must go at the first inspiration or not at all." He shook hands with them all. Constance accompanied him into the hall.

"I have not had time to speak with you. You are off like an arrow."

"I shall come again," he said, gravely. "I—I promised Scott I would read the first chapters of my book to you. He values your literary opinion highly. May I?" He looked diffident as a big handsome boy, standing before her and glancing down at her.

"Ah," she smiled, her heart giving a painful leap, "you touch my vanity. I am going to take the undeserved honor—like a sneak."

"Don't," he said, his brows contracting.

"Well, come some night next week," she answered, lightly, and he was gone.

When the younger girls had retired, Brunton broached the question of Eleanor's departure.

"Have you come to any conclusion, Constance?" he asked, glancing over toward Eleanor, who appeared otherwise absorbed.

"Yes," replied Constance, clearly. "When the Vassaults go, Grace will have graduated. I think it will be a good opportunity for her to go, and I shall like to know that Eleanor has her with her. Mr. Vassault is very fond of Grace, and will not object, I am sure."

"But," interposed Brunton, with raised eyebrows, "have you considered the cost of Grace's tour? It will require a good sum, you know."

"I have it. I have never used any of my own capital. How does that plan strike you, Eleanor?"

"What? That?" drawled the girl, with a yawn. "Don't trouble yourselves. I am not going."

Constance looked at her in mute inquiry. To Brunton the inexplicable words were like a cold douche after a steam-bath. His eyes, wandering aimlessly from Eleanor, fell upon Kenyon's violin. He had forgotten to take it with him.

CHAPTER IV

MY DEAR CONSTANCE,—No doubt Kenyon has presented himself long ago with a verbal recommendation from me which was valueless, he being one of those fortunate sails who carry their own breeze with them. What do you think of him? Like him, eh? Women have such a marvellous faculty of arriving at correct conclusions without a trace of reasoning. However, it is preposterous to imagine your caring for his forebears, an artist's pedigree being overshadowed by his work. As to his own credentials, a writer paints two men in his hero—his model, imaginary or taken from life, and himself. But genius, you know, is democratic; one never knows what may be picked up with it. Kenyon, however, is of excellent stock and breeding, if you wish testimony as to the animal. His father was one Gilbert Kenyon, an architect, almost an artist, of distinguished repute, whose family dates back to Adam, than whom none prior sat. His mother was a Carter, one of the loveliest of women, who gave to her son all her Southern fire and charm, and, having none left for herself, departed a month after her husband. The record has its parallel, we know. Kenyon is thus free of all family entanglements. He shines by his own light, without even the advantage of an ancestral background—a sort of detached central figure which arrests attention wherever it moves. The world is pleased to call his curious faults eccentricities. A great deal of his success would be accounted the result of his unusual physical attractions, if he allowed himself to be the puppet of the many social queens who have sought to inveigle him to their salons as an additional superb ornament. But he is to be measured by a different measurement. He is singularly indifferent to adulation of that kind. He burns feverishly with strong literary ambitions. He has made some bright showing, but has not yet attained apogee. His powers are all in their incipiency. My conviction is that he requires to go through the mill, especially the "dem'd grind" of another sort of misery than that of the body, before he will stand. Meanwhile he has been put in the way of new material. Give him a little wholesome, unspiced home-diet to act as bromide to his ardor. My love and a kiss to the chickens and their ultra-devoted mother-hen.

Severn Scott.

The foregoing letter came one morning when Constance and Eleanor sat together, rocking and sewing. Constance had smiled over its contents, and Eleanor, reading over her shoulder, remarked that Severn's punctilious solicitude was not to be disdained.

"Does he think us disposed to accept a man merely on the *prima facie* of his good looks?" she asked, mockingly. "Does he account us such barbarians of the West as to suppose we would take into the bosom of our family a man without prenatal advantages and authorized archives that he owns a dust-heap somewhere worthy of distinction from the common dirt of a Potter's Field?

Dear Severn, we are not utterly lost to the survival of the fittest! We are diffident about honoring the most artistic signature without the identification of Eastern approval. Bosh!"

"Not altogether 'bosh,'" Constance decided, with a laugh. "Blood will talk sooner or later, and very often it is later than comfort would direct. These records of the past serve us socially as a sort of reference agency. Half the time we trust to our impulses, which are about as reliable as weathercocks."

"That royal 'we' is generous. You know quite well that all your emotions are tied up with endless, tiresome red-tape. You impulsive! Then I am irresponsible."

They were all in the library in the evening, when the maid brought Kenyon's card to Constance.

"He asked for Miss Herriott," she explained.

"Yes? Very well, Betty. Mr. Kenyon has called," she added, turning to Eleanor. "He promised to come with his book, and read parts of it to me. I—I wish you would come in, too, Eleanor."

"I?" The rising intonation, with its undertone of surprise and disappointment, was of exaggerated duration. "Thanks; it was never my ambition to enact the rôle of fifth wheel."

Constance moved from the room in silent dignity, but with her brows deeply contracted. Eleanor suddenly became absorbingly interested in her book. During the whole evening she did not glance up once—not even when the children said "Good-night." Had Grace been a tease, she might have remarked that the page was never turned; had she been a physiognomist, she would have observed that the set jaw of her silent sister indicated clinched teeth.

"Did I intrude?" asked Kenyon, after they had exchanged greetings, and he had seated himself at some little distance from her.

"Not at all. I was particularly at a loss to know what to do with myself this evening. I was indulging in a bit of dreaming."

"If it was a good dream, I am sorry I broke it; if otherwise, I am glad."

"Good or bad, they are worthless things—dreams," she assured him, lightly. "They serve for the moment, and then, thin as air, pass on. It is better to live in active, substantial materialism."

"That passes, too, happily for the luckless dog who finds no meat on his bone. I knew a fellow once who rowed through life easily with this oar: '*Tout lasse, tout passe, tout casse.*' But, unfortunately for most of us, we have not attained the contentment of seals. To lie in the sun and bask is not the common ambition. I have desires which prick me out of all ease." He touched with his hand an oblong package which lay on his knee. It was a nervous gesture. His face, too, showed in its slight pallor his inward perturbation. He looked across at her with shy eagerness as she leaned back in her chair and listened with gentle interest.

"Of course," he laughed, "this is the most troublesome. I am going to tell you the story if you feel in a listening mood to-night. Do you?"

"I am very anxious to hear it. But why not read instead of telling it?"

"Because its claims for excellence, if it have any, lie

more in the matter than manner. I shall read you a page
here and there to show you the style of the animal ; you
may find it either too dull or fantastic for the characters.
I do not think I should put a black gown on a negress,
but I might put diamonds in her ears, and make her as
much out of drawing. Look out for the weaknesses, but
don't be finical, please."

"It is bad policy to begin with a plea for clemency,"
she smiled. "I assure you I am singularly open to the
conviction of its charms."

"Entirely unprejudiced ?"

"Quite," she returned, with guilty promptitude.

"Well, I won't bore you," he said, untying the cord.
"I shall make it as short as possible."

"Don't," she protested.

"Oh, yes," he insisted, fingering the manuscript nervously. "You will notice that I am experiencing a species of stage-fright just at this moment. I am new to
this sort of thing."

"So am I. I appreciate the honor."

"Honors are easy in this instance. Well, here goes."

Straightway he began to read, his voice somewhat un-
steady, the flickering color gradually mounting to his
temples. For several minutes she did not hear a word
he read. All her being hung upon his presence : his perfect head and countenance ; his easy figure, graceful and
manly in the becoming evening-dress ; his long, supple
brown hands, with the well-formed, finely-kept nails. She
recalled her attention with an effort, and presently his
deep voice reached her with meaning.

The style was straightforward and with little embel-
lishment. He grouped his characters clearly ; then drew

them out, and let them speak for themselves more in action than conversation. After reading enough to introduce the plot, he commenced to tell the story, referring now and then to the MS., so as not to lose the finer points. She grew interested. It was exciting, almost tragic; but whenever he neared the verge of a catastrophe, something intervened to outwit misery. It was exhilarating as a race, the favorite always winning the heat. Presently he again took up the book, and read the last two chapters which he had written. Then he looked up with a faint smile.

" It is splendid !" she exclaimed, wishing to bring back the happy glow to his face as quickly as possible.

" Honestly ?" he cried. He put his hand across his eyes and was silent. When he looked up he wore a questioning smile.

" Where is the dissenting ' but ' ?"

" The beginning is all wrong."

" Why ?"

" That girl would never have loved at first sight."

" Why not ?"

" She was too old. Make her younger — make her twenty."

" No ; she would lose all interest for me at that callow age."

" Then make her love more slowly."

" That would not be love, that would be affection—a dull, insensate feeling, comfortable, perhaps, but one such as animals feel for their furs. They grow used to them, and cannot do without them."

" It is a good feeling."

" You say that as I have heard some women draw at-

4

tention to the lack of beauty in another by saying, ' She
is so good, you know.' No, Miss Herriott, love—what I
call love—is a sudden brilliant flame, alike for man and
woman. It needs no arranging of dampers to make it
burn. And my heroine could easily love like that."

" Do you wish my ' candid criticism ?' "

" Certainly." He reared his head and met her eyes
dauntlessly.

" You have invested a woman of twenty-five with the
attributes of a girl of twenty. Your imagination has deceived you. Beware of imagination, Mr. Kenyon."

His face turned a dark red. He sat silent, without
stirring. Suddenly he leaned forward.

" Do you know," he said, speaking slowly, in a low
voice, "that I do not believe you ? Neither do you believe yourself."

She drew back haughtily, her face white in its indignant pride. He sprang from his chair and took a stride
across the room. At the farther end he turned and regarded her.

" Let me explain myself," he began, swiftly. " You
say an older woman does not love at first sight. Do you
not think some women at that age love as fatuously as a
girl of twenty ?"

" No."

" Then concede that certain types of men might incite
love, the passion, in the heart of the most self-contained."

She considered a moment, looking thoughtfully before
her, not meeting his eyes.

" Perhaps," she answered, finally.

He took a step forward, then turned and leaned his
arm on the piano.

"And do you think Carruthers—fills the bill ?"

She smiled involuntarily, the words of the letter she had read that morning recurring to her on the instant.

"You are better able to judge than I," she said. "You have painted yourself, I think."

"Do you think so ? But I cannot help myself, you see. I need the heroine's insight. Can't you put your self in her place—for to-night ?"

"Impossible. I am not Protean. Let the point go, Mr. Kenyon; you know the girl better than I."

"I shall not change it," he said, laughing and reseating himself. "I ask you to criticise, and after you have done so I cling like a leech to my own opinions. I want things to turn out my way, whether in the course of nature or through my distorted fancy. You read things more profoundly, or, rather, they converse with you. I am not like that. I see only form and color ; a yellow primrose to me is nothing but a yellow primrose."

"You are mistaken about me. Eleanor has a fine subjective mind—not I."

"Yes, you have," he insisted, inflexibly, "through your perfect balance. You are in subtle touch with what is hidden. Now my mental epidermis is thick, and I miss a great deal of the beauty of the occult."

"And the misery. That is why your stories are so happy."

"Perhaps ; but it is a compensation which I don't value. It leaves me at a disadvantage in my work."

"You might remedy the loss."

"How ?"

"By stooping to listen."

"I don't know how. I am provided with a sort of

buoy which keeps me afloat. I can't dive. Miss Herriott, I know there is something lacking in my work. It
is like the faun—wild, happy, but elusive. You could
help me." His voice sank to low beseeching.

" How ?" she asked, her broad gray eyes meeting his
wistfully.

" By pointing out its frailties more in detail."

"Indeed, no. I am not a reviewer — why should I
make myself disagreeable ?"

" On the plea of friendship — not disagreeable, but
kind. Shall we make a compact, and agree to give and
take, without asking pardon, without giving thanks, on
the broad, unquestioning understanding which binds perfect friends ?"

He stood before her with outheld hand. She put hers
into it hesitatingly, yet irresistibly.

"It will be all take for me," she said, with a grave
smile.

" *Quien sabe ?* You will give more than you can understand," he returned, in an uncertain undertone.

" It would be pleasant having such a friend," she
thought, when she was alone. Yet she was not a woman
of easy friendship. With her strong, inward life and
necessary self-reliance she was not prone to make a confidant of any one, and thus she maintained the sover-
eignty of herself. Yet one must be utterly unworthy if
he cannot count one friend; also he is much to be pitied.
Constance, in the truest significance of the term, allowed
herself one great friend; but in that instance she had
always known that she must take more than she could
ever give. With Hall Kenyon friendship would mean
something less grave, something lighter and more in-

tangible, yet bright and alluring as a will-o'-the-wisp. It would be pleasant to feel herself in touch with his eager ambitions.

And yet, as she lay in her bed watching the star-beams reflected on the curtains, a bit of worldly sophistry passed like a cloud through her memory: "I have little belief, as a rule, in friendships between man and woman—I mean when both the people concerned have youth and imagination. One or the other gets generally more or less than was bargained for."

"I am not youthful," thought Constance, "and—" She had told him to beware of imagination. She now reiterated the words over and over to herself as she strove to sleep.

CHAPTER V

As the weeks slipped into months Kenyon's affairs began to adjust themselves, and Brunton announced to him that his presence in the city was no longer required —he could leave whenever he so wished. Kenyon, however, evinced no hurry. He was knee-deep in engagements, doing the coast conscientiously. His trip to the Yosemite with Joscelyn, the artist, occupied several weeks. He had Monterey, Santa Barbara, Coronado, and the Geysers to explore, all of which cut into his time, and made his dropping down upon San Francisco, his headquarters, intermittent and uncertain.

Constance, however, usually knew when he had come to town. A bunch of flowers, a book, or a note soon became recognized *avant couriers* of his evening's advent.

Generally she received him alone. He had made a fine distinction in asking for "Miss Herriott" whenever he could summon the shadow of an excuse for her attention exclusively. At other times he walked in upon the group of girls in the library with the sunny assurance which was part of the secret of his geniality. He met, half - way, the people for whom he cared, and, if necessary, finding them shy, more than half-way. It requires a fund of self-confidence and freedom from any doubt of the desirability of one's society to acquire the ease. Kenyon would have been keen to detect the moment he began to bore, and have governed himself accordingly. His perceptions were too sensitive to allow his inclinations to carry him where congeniality would be set at defiance. Only an ass is sure of himself under all circumstances. But the happy smiles and voices, the little gusts of joyousness, and movements of satisfaction with which they greeted him, were not to be misunderstood. Formality was not long an intruder in his presence. The Herriotts gradually began to regard him as a family friend, though of a caliber which made the friendship totally different from their relations with Geoffrey Brunton. The latter's coming had long ceased to incite any excitement in their midst. He was one of them. A stranger, seeing him enter, might have thought he had stepped in from the next room, or returned from a few minutes' walk, for all the disturbance he occasioned. Often he brought his book, and they would resume theirs as though there had been no interruption. They knew that Geoffrey was comfortable, and had found what he wanted in sitting with them.

Hall Kenyon's personality was too restless to provoke such a calm. Brunton acted as valerian, Kenyon as vigorous massage ; he rubbed and pinched and kneaded their wits to animation. Grace and Edith would have described the feeling his appearance produced by saying, " We are going to have a splendid time." He could tell them much. He had travelled a great deal and in many odd by-ways. He had had thrilling as well as ludicrous adventures and misadventures. He could typify vividly with an adjective, explain sensations by an eloquent pause or odd facial expression.

Eleanor alone met him with nonchalant indifference, a

fact which at first disconcerted him, but which he finally accounted a bit of affectation — the desire of a young girl who has seen a little of the world to appear *blasée* and worldly tolerant. He even laughed over it when he noticed how quickly her real self came to the front whenever she saw a chance to throw in a wordy missile and make him enter a discussion of battledore-shuttlecock rapidity. The attack was always spirited, both having the courage and vim of their convictions. Eleanor never called a truce; it was left to Kenyon to retreat with a laugh, or, occasionally, with a flashing eye and savagely compressed lip. Then Constance's quiet voice would be heard offering amnesty in a change of subject.

It is hard to make clear the older girls' feeling for him in those first months. Not long before, a gloomy winter day had come to an end, and, in the west, in the region of the setting sun, there suddenly appeared a great glory. Billow upon billow of gold was massed in marvellous splendor; it shot a pulsing flame throughout the sombre heavens, it illuminated and enraptured the earth in tumultuous warmth; and Constance, as those who feel such things, with her back to the desolate, dying day, lifting her eyes to the glory, would have hugged the radiance close within her arms. There is a language which has no words.

He had written Constance a note, asking her to allow him to take her and Eleanor to hear the great pianist who had eventually arrived in the music-hungry little city.

Constance handed Eleanor the note.

"Shall we go?" she asked, easily, when Eleanor had put down the missive.

The latter was leisurely swinging in a rocking-chair and did not pause, as she answered: "You can go. I shall not."

"Why not?" Constance looked at her anxiously. She felt a great longing to go with him.

"Because, as I have told you a hundred times, I never go anywhere on toleration."

"You have no excuse in taking such a stand in this case. What do you mean?"

"Why, simply that Mr. Hall Kenyon wishes the pleasure of accompanying Miss Herriott to the concert, and asks her sister Eleanor along for mere form's sake."

"I could say the same with the names reversed."

"It would be a lame rejoinder. You know otherwise. Mr. Kenyon does not send you flowers and bonbons and marked paragraphs and other minutiæ because he admires your sister Eleanor, my dear Constance. He is not such a roundabout man. Nay, nay, take your music and your man without dividing; one likes a monopoly when it comes to an escort. I shall leave you to write your most gracious of responses." She went into her room, singing blithely.

"It is plain enough," she thought, sitting with locked fingers—"plain enough. I am a fool. Good heavens, what a fool I am!" She bit her lip till the blood came; she could feel her temples throbbing at a wild gallop; she sat crouched together in a tense attitude. Pride and jealousy were having a sharp tussle with her. The instinctive conviction that she was only an afterthought stung her with its truth. Had she been indifferent to him this consideration would have had little weight;

but as it was, she rose in arms at the slightest hint of
her unimportance.

Yet, as she recoiled, a sinuous little reptile wound
itself about her heart, and made her sick and chill.
"They will be alone all that time," she thought. "Constance will look beautiful, and he will have eyes and
ears for nothing but her. I can prevent it. If I go he
will be forced to pay me some attention, and I shall, at
any rate, hear all he has to say to her. I wonder if the
statue has some Galatean emotions. I believe I am beginning to hate her. Yes, I'll go."

She arose, hesitating for only a second. Constance
would regard it as another mark of caprice ; yes, she
would make capital of her reputed failing.

"After all," she called, putting her head in at Constance's door, "I believe I shall go to that concert.
Might as well take a gift without noticing the manner
of offering. You will have to enjoy it with me."

"I should not have gone without you," returned Constance, quietly.

So they went. To Constance, music was always a
grave joy. There were some strains, she had told Hall
Kenyon once, which would make dying a rapture. And
Kenyon had taken up his violin and played a certain
passage which made her start—she had been thinking
of the same sublime movement.

To Eleanor the music was but an accompaniment to
her own intoxicated sensations. Young Love is an auto-
crat ; like the king of egoists it cries, " I am ; and while
I am, there is no one else." Eleanor could never clearly
recall the music she heard that evening. A great wit
once wrote that, on his first visit to Paris, he went to

the Opéra on the evening of his arrival, and sat behind a woman with a large pink tulle hat; he thus saw the Parisians for the first time in a rose-colored light, and the illusion never altogether left him. So, ever after, when Eleanor heard a certain marvellous polonaise, a great, confused pain drew her silent.

But quite suddenly one day a disturbing element entered the happy household. Little Nan complained of great weariness and lassitude. When the trouble had continued for two days, Constance called in the physician.

"Bring her to me every day," he said. "I shall try what electricity will do for her. Also keep her in the open air a good deal, and give her a sea-bath three times a week."

"It is foolish to worry, Constance," Brunton had said. "The summer is lasting too long, and the child is enervated. When the rains set in she will be all right. Let me give you an idea: take her over to my vineyard at Napa. Moore and his wife will be only too glad to make you comfortable, and Eleanor can take care of the others."

"The doctor said electricity," she reminded him, with a shake of the head.

When she went in to meet Kenyon that evening he started and changed color. He had never seen the great blue shadows about her eyes, he had never seen her look quite so grave and sad. She was not given to moods, and she had always met him in the same even manner. With him it had been different; he had come to her when he needed her, and it was not always when he was happiest.

He held her hand for a moment without speaking. Then:

"Shall I go away ?" he asked, softly.

"No, no," she murmured. "I—"

"Hush," he said. "Do not try to explain. It is about one of the children—little Nan, perhaps."

She could not understand why his voice, his presence, should make her suddenly feel so weak and womanish; her figure drooped as she sat, her eyes were suffused with tears. No one had seen Constance cry since her mother's death.

"She is so tired," she faltered, shading her eyes with her hand, "and the doctor speaks so doubtfully. I have very little courage. I cannot do without Nan; she is my shrine."

"She understands without seeing," put in Kenyon with another touch of the intuition which always made her fearful. "But I do not think she is going to be taken from you. Trust me; I often augur right about these things. And then with such care as you give—"

"It is not a mother's care."

"It is more—it is a devotee's. That is where you almost err—in being too kind. Relax a little; think of yourself, and every small ill will not prove a great scourge. Love is not blind in trouble; it wears a magnifying-glass. You see things in distorted largeness. Will you not take care of yourself too, for—all our sakes ?" He looked down at her in serious pleading.

"You are so insistent," she said, reproachfully.

"It is my prerogative. And now shall I go, or do you wish me to stay ?"

"Don't go," she said, putting out a hand.

When he left he exacted a promise from her to come with all the children to his Sausalito home on the following Saturday.

"My tenure of the place expires at the end of the month. Let us make a holiday as a souvenir," he said.

The soft October Saturday was in a charming mood, and they all seemed to have caught the infection.

Kenyon met them at the pier with a roomy wagonette. The hills were too stiff and held themselves too high, he said, to be walked over with impunity.

"A fig for their assumption!" scoffed Eleanor, as she started gayly off by herself, with Edith soon after her heels.

Mrs. Granniss, fanning herself down the central garden-path in a plump, downy fashion, announced her chaperonage, and made them each at home with a kiss.

"Regard me as a mere figure-head, my dear girls," she said, with a round-throated, gurgling laugh, as they laid off their wraps in the cool, bamboo-furnished little parlor. "Flirt as much as you want with Mr. Kenyon, because I know he is the most charming fellow in the world. There is safety in numbers, I suppose. My dear doctor will be over as soon as he has finished his sermon. He would rather miss his chance of a mansion in the skies than the opportunity of a talk with you, Constance dear." She was a woman who dealt in superlatives. The sweet old lady's imagination seemed to have expanded to keep pace with her superfluous stock of flesh.

Wong, the Chinaman, was in touch with the day, and outdid himself in the dainty feast spread under the autumn-leaved trees. The gold and crimson leaves underfoot were a soft, rustling carpet for their feet; now and then a single, glowing leaf fell upon the snowy cloth like a whisper—a reminder of departing glory.

"It is a day that sings," said Eleanor, leaning back in her chair, the flickering shadows of the boughs over-head swaying over her face and hair. "It is one of those that we remember years after through a touch of perfume in the atmosphere, like a song which we recall inexplicably days after we have heard it sung. I wonder what it is like to be a bird. I'll be one." She laughed gayly at her own words, sprang from her seat, and the next instant had climbed agilely to a high branch in the old, deep-limbed oak at the side of the house. A few minutes later Edith and Grace started off arm in arm. Kenyon, noticing Nan's eyes closing, picked her up and moved with her toward the hammock.

"She wants to be lazy, Miss Herriott," he called back, "and she shall be whatever she wishes to-day. Eh, Nan?"

Mrs. Granniss toddled good-naturedly after him, and seated herself in a deep, cane-bottomed chair on the clematis-empurpled porch. Kenyon placed the child in the hammock, and, swaying her to and fro, began to sing in his soft, rich voice a Tyrolean lullaby. His eyes followed, for a moment, Constance Herriott strolling about with Marjorie and Dr. Granniss. A smile played over his mouth when he noted the reverend gentleman's court-liness; he held his hat in his hand as they walked under the shadowy trees, the sunlight sifting in rifts upon his silvery hair. `

"Look at my ·dear doctor, Mr. Kenyon," said Mrs. Granniss, in guileless, childlike pride, speaking in a low tone as she noticed that Nan slept. "Do you observe how he holds his hat in his hand when he talks to Constance Herriott? That is to show. his deference. He used to do the same when he met her mother. He would actually stand bareheaded on Market Street while he talked to her, until the dear lady begged him to cover his head. He worshipped that woman, and he showed it; but as to being jealous, I should have as soon thought of being jealous of his worship of God. And he has passed on the feeling to her daughter. I verily believe he would do anything short of crime for that girl. And no wonder—just look at her."

His eyes turned with a slow, tender light toward Constance disappearing at a turn with the child and the old man. A shower of leaves startled them. Eleanor had slipped from her perch and vanished like a flash.

"That girl is a veritable Jack-o'-Lantern," observed Mrs. Granniss, in a perplexed tone.

"And she—she is like yonder peace," thought Hall Kenyon, raising his eyes to the broad, tender blue overhead, where a single, slow-moving gull soared into the distance like a dream of infinity.

"It has been a beautiful day," said little Nan, when he kissed her good-bye.

"And in a few days," he said to Constance, as she turned to join the others, "I am coming to read my last chapters. I have come to the end of the story."

CHAPTER VI

I⊤ was the first rain of the season. It had been coming down all day with the mad fury which follows long
restraint. As night set in the storm gathered in intensity; or is it only the stillness of the night which
brings into such powerful prominence the clamor of the
elements warring with dumb nature and the silent mani-
festations of human creation? The weird grandeur was
reminiscent of Wagner. The Herriotts, singing in their
firelit drawing-room, raised their voices to the utmost
volume to drown the tumult without.

Eleanor, sitting near the fireplace, wrapped in a fleecy
white shawl, appeared relieved when the singing ceased.
Her face was pale, her eyes heavy; she was suffering
with a severe cold which she had brought home with
her from Sausalito.

Edith had thrown herself at full length on the hearth-
rug, Grace had picked up a volume of Tennyson ready
to read an exquisite fragment from the " Idyls," and
Constance was just about going up-stairs with the children when Brunton came in.

" No, I won't sit down," he said, in answer to their
vociferations. " I just came in to tell you that I shall
call for you to-morrow evening for the Ferris dinner, if
you have made no other arrangements." He stood near
the door in his heavy water-coat, and looked at Constance. .

"I had made no arrangements. Thanks, Geoffrey; it will be pleasant going with you. But why do you venture out in the storm merely to deliver a message when you have no intention of staying?"

"I have an engagement with a fellow at my club. You *do* look snug and cosey." His eye swept about the group. "What is the matter, Eleanor?"

"I have a cold."

"Well, coddle it. Nan has a pretty winter rose in either cheek, I see. I assure you this room is a powerful antithesis to the unhappy night. I hope you don't depreciate your good-luck in being all safe together."

"Stay and 'reminisce' with us, Geoffrey," begged Edith.

"I should like to, but I am dragged from you by the teeth of my appointment. Well, good-night."

In the hall he stopped to put on his mackintosh.

"Go back into the room while I open the door, Constance," he said, picking up his hat and umbrella.

"Geoffrey," she replied, with a little pucker of the brows, "you are looking ill. What is the matter with you?"

"Eh? Want of grit, I suppose." He opened the door hurriedly, and stood on the step to open his umbrella.

"I wish you would take half as good care of yourself as you do of others." She held the door open, the flickering gaslight from the hall falling upon his thin, plain face as he looked into her earnest eyes.

"Do you?" he asked, with a sudden, unexpected, hard laugh. "What for?" Before she could reply he had lifted his hat and gone down the steps.

5

"Let us go to bed, too, Edith," said Grace, after a little, when Constance had gone off with the children. "I love to lie in bed and listen to the rain. Come along, Ede."

And presently Eleanor found herself alone. The stress of the storm had beat her into apathy, and her heavy eyes closed.

A few minutes later Kenyon came into the room. The maid, recognizing him, had told him that the family was in here, and he walked in without ceremony.

He was disconcerted when he found himself alone with the sleeping girl; but she would waken soon, he thought, and Miss Herriott would probably be in in a few minutes.

He picked up the volume of Tennyson which Grace had thrown down, and seated himself at some distance. The book was open where the girl had been reading. Glancing casually through the lines, he lingered with a smile over the closing stanza, where the poet's pen had rounded the picture with an irrepressible note of passion :

> "A man had given all other bliss,
> And all his worldly worth for this,
> To waste his whole heart in one kiss
> Upon her perfect lips."

Dreamily his eyes fell upon the face of the girl before him. Her red, flower-like lips were slightly parted; the heat of the fire had flung a velvet rose upon her cheek ; her bright, bronze hair, loosely braided together, fell soft about her face. The words of the poet echoed subtly as he suddenly felt her witching beauty; yet the feeling was simply appreciative — something had gone from him to make the sensation a temptation. As he looked her eyelids fluttered, and his eyes fell quickly again upon the page. When he glanced up he saw that she was intently regarding him. He arose at once.

"Are you not well, Miss Eleanor?" he asked, coming toward her, and holding out his hand deferentially.

"I caught cold over at Sausalito the other day," she replied, letting her fingers touch his for the space of a second.

"That is too bad. It seems as though I were always to be the cause of some discomfiture to you. I am heartily sorry for it. You will end by avoiding me as you would the plague."

"My mental constitution is in good sanitary condition. I am not afraid of you," was the rejoinder. "And as to plagues, the only ones to be avoided are those which leave one unsightly."

"And those which hurl you away without warning?"

"Good and welcome. They are the most considerate of friends. The best deaths are like dawning — early, and soon over."

"Very well and young people feel quite brave in making grimaces at death—it is a remote contingency with them. Now I feel rather diffident about going hence. I like novelty, but not shocks. If I am going to entertain the kingly stranger I should like to be prepared. I should wish the feast to be in keeping with the guest. Fact is, Miss Eleanor, I believe I'm not good enough to die." He was laughing down at her, amused with her moody talk.

"Pooh! Good enough?" she retorted, cynically. "For what? to turn to dust?"

"Listen," he said, swiftly. As he spoke, the low, rumbling thunder approached like a mighty voice, rolled into the distance, and died in the incessant swish of the rain. Eleanor turned pale.

"The Valkyries are making a night of it," he observed, lightly, and just then Constance entered. At sight of Kenyon she started in surprise.

"I did not know you were here," she said, meeting him with gentle composure. "I am half glad and half angry to see you. Only extreme friendliness or extreme carelessness would bring you out on such a night."

"I told you I was coming," he replied, in a low voice, drawing up a chair for her.

"Ah yes, with the last chapters. Have you them with you?" She looked up at him eagerly. She noticed that he was pale, and her heart smote her with an inexplicable foreboding. "Sit down," she added, quickly.

"This is a good seat, Mr. Kenyon," cut in Eleanor, rising, as he turned for a chair.

"Where are you going?" asked Constance, hurriedly.

"To entertain myself. I have been inconsiderate too long already."

"Don't go," said Constance, putting her hand on her shoulder impulsively. "Mr. Kenyon will postpone his reading. We must amuse Eleanor to-night," she added, turning to where he stood resting his hand on a chair. "She is not well."

"Nonsense," asserted Eleanor, with a harsh laugh. "I draw the line at being the party of the third part. Besides, I would not postpone Mr. Kenyon's reading for the world. Let go, Constance."

"Do stay, Miss Eleanor," said Kenyon, with abrupt earnestness. His glance swept past Constance with studied nonchalance. He meant her to stay now, and his voice was almost commanding. "If it will not be too irksome for you, I should like to have you listen. Will you?"

"You put it so that one cannot refuse," she said, reseating herself somewhat dazedly. She was dimly conscious that she was being made a cat's-paw of, that she was to be used as a blind wall between two forces which threatened to meet.

"Will you give your sister the points of the plot, Miss Herriott?" he asked with marked carelessness, as he busied himself with his note-book. His tone cut Constance rudely. She looked at him in fleet reproach. He did not return the glance. Eleanor's narrowing eyes were upon them with instinctive bitterness. In a low voice Constance commenced to tell the story. Kenyon's hands ceased to turn the leaves while he listened to her full voice, repeating his thoughts, his play of imagination. She spoke concisely, but with the clearness of perfect knowledge.

"Do you quite understand, Miss Eleanor?" he asked, when Constance paused.

"Quite," she returned, with brilliant, excited eyes.

"Then I shall finish." He picked up the manuscript, the beat of annoyance dying out of his voice as he read. Constance sat quite still. His manner had silenced her effectually. Only Eleanor, roused to feverish excitement, seemed to vibrate under his words.

"Well?" he demanded, when he had finished. He regarded Eleanor unseeingly; he was conscious only of Constance's statuesque face beside her.

There was a long pause. Eleanor's fingers locked and unlocked themselves as if struggling to say something.

"It is clever," she said, in a slow, restrained manner which belied her face. "And you are kind to give it a happy ending, but it is not at all natural."

"Why not?" He shifted his position, partly turning from Constance, and getting a fuller view of the younger girl.

"Your heroine could not have married Atwyn and have loved him, as you lead us to infer."

"Why not?"

"She loved Carruthers."

"But Carruthers was dead."

"His death is nothing. A woman can love only once."

"Is she as poor as that?"

"Yes, and as strong."

"I think you must admit that example goes to prove that a woman can love and forget, if put to the test."

"Not if she really loved. Real love is not a possibility with every woman, you know. She might marry another, but not love him as you say that girl loved. Love has no duplicates. There is the original. All the other forms are something paler and less."

"But," he insisted, "women marry for love after a disappointment."

"There is a slight distinction. You do not make it. They may marry *for* love, but not *out* of love."

"That is sad. Is there then no cure for love—unrealized?"

She looked past him dreamily.

"Shall I answer with a bit of fantasy?"

"How?"

"Listen." She flung her arms over her head in a manner peculiarly her own. She was intoxicated with the knowledge that she was holding his attention for almost the first time without the fractious sparring into which they had always fallen.

"I'll put it in the form of narrative. Let us call it 'Love's Antidote — for Women.'" She paused for a fleeting second, and then dashed on. "This is how it was discovered: There was once a beautiful woman whom I shall call — well, the Lady Margaret. One day her people noticed that she had grown strangely weary. Quite suddenly it dawned upon them, and they put out their hands as if to stay her, for she had grown frail as well. Then, because they loved her, they called in physicians. They shook their heads and departed — there was no ailment. But one, more wise than the rest, said, 'This is not of the body! I cannot minister to a dying heart! You must wean her from herself — interest her, distract her.' It was easily said, and they thought to carry it out as easily. But all their efforts proved unavailing. Daily she grew more listless, more intangible, more removed. And one day, through chance, they discovered that it was the shadow of a great love which hung over her — a love for one who had proved unworthy. Then, by hints and innuendoes, by open tales of his egoism and profligacy, they strove to dispel the charm which invested him in her heart. But she looked at them with sad, indulgent eyes and the shafts fell at their own feet. So one day, when she sat in the midst of sunshine and roses, there came up the sunlit path a peddler with his pack. He was brown as a bronze, slim and straight as an arrow; around his head was twisted a red silk scarf, and she knew he was of the Orient. Silently his pack slid to the grass, and he, beside it, opened to her view his store of treasures: silks soft and lustrous as the sun, broideries stiff and gorgeous with gold, dimities fit for a fairy, ivories carved as with a lace needle. But she only looked, and said nothing. And when he had come to the end, still silently he put them back, and rose and stood before her like a gleaming bronze, and looked upon her spiritual beauty. Then, stooping, he laid something within her hand, and, like a dream of mysticism, passed down the sunlit path. Curiously, then, she looked at that which she held. It was a dainty ivory box, upon the face of which were carved the words: 'Love's Antidote — for Women.' With a look of wonder she lifted the lid. Within, exquisitely wrought in ivory, lay — a tiny skull and cross-bones. The Lady Margaret let her hands fall in her lap. She smiled, and—waited."

Eleanor ceased to speak, but did not look at Kenyon.

"You improvise admirably. That is a pretty conceit, but the ending is too sad," he remarked, finally.

"I said she smiled. Is that sad?"

After a pause he spoke again, glancing swiftly from Constance's slightly flushed face to this new interlocutor.

"I wonder how many women would agree to the truth of your conception. I am going to ask you a pertinent question. Do you speak from experience or imagination?"

"From neither. I speak from conviction."

"Ah! But convictions are relative, not to be taken as axioms. Will you let me criticise now? The inscription on the box was too wordy."

"In what respect?"

"You unnecessarily added 'For women.' It holds as well for men."

"I do not think so. It is woman's one coffer. Man's love has departments."

"Pardon me, you know nothing about it."

"And you?" she asked, rising and regarding him rather defiantly. "Do you speak from experience or imagination?"

His face flamed hotly, he caught his breath hard. "From neither," he replied—"from conviction."

Whereupon they both laughed. It is a strangely accommodating thing, a laugh; it covers many an awkward heart secret. Under its cloak Eleanor left the room.

She sped up-stairs to her own room, shut and locked the door, and leaned against it as if some one were attempting an entrance. She became conscious that she was breathing heavily, and she strove to quiet herself by closing her eyes; the effort was useless. She moved over to her bureau and groped for a match. Finding none, she stood still in the dark.

"Why did I tell it?" she muttered. "Why could I not control myself? Why could I not cover my heart by keeping still? Must my mouth always betray me? Does he know? Does he surmise? Is he laughing at me—or pitying me? Oh, merciful oblivion, don't let me think!" She brought her fist down fiercely against the bedpost. It was merely another woman groaning over impulsive words spoken past recall; it was merely tardy pride upon the rack of remorse.

Presently her face ceased to quiver; a listening, stealthy stillness enveloped her from head to foot. "What is he

saying to her?" was the slow thought which took possession of her. " I know. I could see it in his face. And
she ! What will she answer? I must know—I *shall* know."
The stealthy stillness communicated itself to her movements. She drew the shawl over her head, carefully
unlocked her door, and passed out. Like a noiseless
somnambulist she glided down the stairs, the stealthy
stillness rising to cunning care in her young, impassioned
face. Still creeping, she passed down the long hallway,
entered the darkened library, and drew near the heavy
folding-doors dividing it from the drawing-room. A
line of light escaped between the locks. Slowly sinking
to her knees, she looked in. It was the first low act
Eleanor Herriott had ever committed. Passionate, ca-
pricious, vain, she may have been ; but hitherto she had
been too brave to stoop to tell even a childish lie. And
yet, as she crouched there, she was utterly insensible to
the fact that she was debasing her finer instincts. She
was in torture, and torture, whether of mind or body,
means distortion.

 She saw the two, still seated where she had left them.
She could distinctly discern their every movement, distinctly hear their every word. Constance was speaking
with unusual volubility.

" So I decided to let her remain home to-day. You
have no idea what a boy Edith is. Happening to glance
out of the window during the morning, I saw her making
her way through the mud on little Teddie Barlow's stilts,
looking as happy as the first bird who has espied the first
leaf of spring. She is so happy when she is mischievous
that my reprimands always sound cruel. But what can
I do ?"

No answer. She hurriedly continued :

" I have never seen it rain so steadily. Listen. It seems to be slackening."

It was; the sound came fitfully now like a tired child sobbing wearily in his sleep; the wind wailed eerily in a witch-like interlude.

Constance moved uneasily. The watching girl on the other side of the door noticed, with the keenness of jealousy, the queenly head, the full, perfect figure, the white symmetry of the firm hands. Kenyon sat quietly before her, his dark, clear-cut face bereft of its warm underglow.

" And will you send the book off at once ?" she asked, desperately.

" That depends."

" Upon what ?"

" Upon you."

" Oh, I beg of you, do not burden me with the responsibility. What more can I do than to hope that others will look upon it as favorably as I ? Have I not criticised and made myself as disagreeable as the most dispassionate of reviewers ? Have I not told you wherein I find it fine, interesting, and moving ? What more can I possibly say ?"

" Constance."

At the low call, so full of intensity that it seemed lifeless, the light left her face—it was waxen. She put up her hand.

" Hush !" she commanded.

" I have spoken. I am waiting for your answer."

She looked at him fearfully. She knew that all had been implied when he spoke her name. They had both reached that stage of intuition where higher thoughts require no verbal medium to make them understood.

"You must not," she breathed, almost mechanically.

"You speak too late."

"We were friends."

"Never."

He arose, the restraint he had put upon himself well-nigh suffocating him.

"I have never been your friend," he said, the hot blood rising to his temples, his eyes dangerously bright. "I have loved you since the moment I met you. Let me confess. I did not want your friendship. I did not need it. Men could suffice me there. I wanted you, your love, your tenderness, your womanhood. Friendship? Are you so utterly blind to yourself as to think any man could be to you as I have been and not become your lover? Must I tell you that you have become my very life and senses? that I walk, talk, think, sleep, breathe, with but your image before me? Answer me. Did you not know this?"

His imperious, impassioned voice ceased; there was a breathless pause. The girl crouching, sick and numb, behind the door put her hand to her throat—she was choking.

"No," answered Constance, in slow, painful precision, "I did not know! If I had known, honor would have forbidden me to look upon you long ago. Was it not clear to you, did no one ever tell you, that I am — pledged?"

"Pledged!" he echoed.

"Yes; pledged to these children."

He looked at her without comprehension.

"Did *you* not know," she went on, in gentle quiet, the effort of making herself quite clear bringing out the words in strange slowness, "that years ago I made a promise to my own dear mother never to leave them? That they are my children now? That Constance Herriott's life is not hers to give to any man?"

A smile lit up the pallor of his face. "Ah, Constance," he said, "the age of martyrs is past. You take your promise too severely, surely not as the mother who loved you intended. They can still be your children — you need never leave them."

"It would not be the same," she said, drawing back unconsciously. "They would be pushed aside by—another. Forgive me—I thought you knew. I meant to be your friend."

"No," he said, moving nearer, "no. You know that is false. I know—and you know—that you love me."

She sprang to her feet, her chair rolling, from her violence, to the other end of the room. She confronted him, white and forbidding.

"You are mistaken," she said, with the hauteur of a queen. "Your own—conceit—has deceived you. And I must ask you to leave me."

He made a movement toward her, but the icy chill of her attitude, the calm, menacing eyes rooted him where he stood. His face was ashen.

"Tell me," he said, through parched lips, "are you a woman, after all? You lead a man to love you with the desperation of life, and then calmly stand there and say you have nothing to do with his love. You are as hard as granite. You have no pity. You look at stars, and trample the flowers under your feet. Your virtue is so high that you have ceased to be human. You should not tamper with the earthly heart of a man—you, who are of stone."

She stood quite still under his mad revilings, her bloodless, dispassionate face never flinching. Suddenly he held out his hands in agony.

"Constance," he entreated, "consider. You will not wreck my whole life for me. I—I shall make you so happy!"

She stood white and moveless. "I have told you already," she uttered, in almost a monotone, "that I could not and I *would* not be your wife. You say you love me. It is fancy, an infatuation. I am older than you—at least, through circumstance. You are a boy to me. It would be like tying a kite to—a stone. You would have soon tired. I am sorry that we ever met. I can never be more to you than I am now." She held out her hand. He looked at her still in agonized incomprehension. She met his eyes with sad, immovable firmness. Suddenly divining her attitude, a sneer escaped him. The next instant he sprang forward and caught her to him. For a second, as his lips touched hers, Constance Herriott's life ceased to be. Then, with the strength of a man, she pushed him from her.

"Go," she muttered, hoarsely.

"God forgive you," he whispered, incoherently. "I shall never look upon your face again."

He turned from her. A moment later she heard the outer door close. She stood with bowed head under the gaslight, moveless as if carven.

"I hate her," murmured Eleanor, watching her breathlessly.

Suddenly, in the intense quiet, down through the halls there floated a soft, bird-like voice:

"Constance," it called, "Constance dear."

From the still figure there came a shuddering moan. She raised her head as if regarding something, her lips moved as if in prayer.

"Forgive me," she murmured, "forgive me. I forgot; but only for a second—only for a second, mother."

"Constance, Constance," called the voice.

"Yes, Nan; yes, my child; Constance is coming."

Up the stairs she moved quickly.

"Were you frightened, Nan?" she asked, bending over the little one.

Nan did not answer. She lay in a listening attitude for a moment—she had heard something besides her sister's low words. And the little hand went up to stroke the cold, white cheek, and the well-remembered words were softly whispered, in great trouble as in small:

"Never mind; oh, Constance, never mind."

Five minutes later a white, creeping shadow entered the room beyond.

CHAPTER VII

THE clouds had beat themselves empty. The next day dawned rainless and dull, though the wind still blew stiffly.

"Eleanor is late this morning," said Constance, at the breakfast-table.

"She came into our room before we were up, to say she had a headache and did not wish to be disturbed," said Grace, looking curiously at Constance. "But I confess, Constance," she exclaimed, uncontrollably, "you look fully as bad as she did."

"I did not sleep well," replied Constance, turning to pull down Edith's jacket as the latter stood drawing on her gloves, ready for school. She had known that the blue shadows about her weary eyes would not pass unremarked. Members of a large family must always hold themselves in readiness for this sort of inquisition.

"Put on your overshoes, Edith," she said, looking the girl over carefully, "and ask Miss Temple to send me a report of your progress in mathematics. There is no necessity for me to call just now, is there?"

"No," replied Edith, hastily dismissing the subject, "none at all. What is this queer little book? I found it on the cabinet in the drawing-room this morning."

She held out a small brown note-book, which Constance instantly recognized as the one from which Kenyon had read.

"It is Mr. Kenyon's," she returned, taking it from her and placing it upon the table. "He must have forgotten it," she continued, as she opened an egg with a steady spoon. "I shall send it to him this morning."

"Wait till to-morrow," Grace laughingly advised. "He will surely be around for it." Constance salted her egg and said nothing.

After breakfast she softly tried Eleanor's door. The key was turned, and, receiving no answer, she surmised that she slept, and went away. Twice during the morning she repeated the attempt with the same result. Toward noon she became alarmed, and decided to waken her.

"Eleanor!" she called, shaking the door. "Eleanor, wake up!"

"What do you want?" asked a muffled voice.

"It is almost noon, dear. How are you?"

"Better."

"Won't you open the door? I want to see you."

"Don't bother, please. All I want is to lie still. Do go away."

"Open the door, Eleanor. You speak as though you were ill. Besides, you must eat something."

"Tell Betty to bring me a cup of tea, then."

At the ungracious words Constance turned and went down-stairs. She returned soon after with a tempting salver, and, finding the door unlocked, went in. The tray almost slipped from her hands when her eyes fell upon her sister's face. It was sallow and worn, as though she had been through great suffering.

"I shall send for the doctor, Eleanor," she said with determination, while she carefully arranged the table at the side of the bed. "You look wretched,"

6

" It is nothing but my cold," replied the other, shortly, without looking at her. "And you need not send for the doctor, as I shall not see him. I'll lock the door if I hear him coming. I'll drink this tea, and then try to sleep again. You need not wait."

" Let me sit beside you. I promise not to talk."

" You annoy me. Please go."

She had not glanced at her. A wondering chill overspread Constance's body. Rebuffs are hard when one is seeking comfort. She looked at her wistfully, and bent to kiss her. Eleanor turned her face away.

" You might catch the cold," she murmured.

Constance straightened herself. "You are very cross this morning," she said, half tremulously, half playfully. " Well, I shall not tease. Eat the toast, and perhaps you will feel more amiable after you have slept."

She got Nan ready in the afternoon to take her to the doctor's, as usual.

" What are you going to wear to the Ferris dinner to-night?" asked Grace, before they went. Constance started. Was it only yesterday that Brunton had been in? The tragedy of one moment had dimmed what had immediately preceded it with the distance of years.

" Oh yes," she replied. " Tell Betty to lay out my gray crêpe."

They had been gone about a half hour when Grace, who was seated in the nursery with Marjorie and Betty, was startled at the sight of Eleanor standing in the doorway in hat and jacket.

" Why, Eleanor !" she exclaimed.

" I'm going down to see Mrs. Vassault," returned Eleanor, in a low, cool voice. "She has not been very well since her return."

"But with your cold!" remonstrated Grace, utterly taken aback. "It is very unpleasant out. If Constance were home she would forbid your stirring from the house."

"I am able to take care of myself," was the cutting reply. "Good-bye." She walked swiftly over to where Marjorie sat on the floor surrounded by toys, and gave her a close but hasty kiss.

"Take me with you," begged the child, throwing her doll aside and scrambling to her feet.

"No, no, Marjorie; little girls don't go where I am going. You be good, and play house—with Grace—and Constance."

"Constance is out," averred Marjorie, in a puzzled, resentful voice.

"Oh, she'll come back—she always does. You can always count on Constance. But give Eleanor a kiss. Good-bye, sweetheart."

The next minute she was gone. Marjorie resumed her doll and Grace her book.

"Miss Eleanor walks like the wind," remarked Betty, standing by the window with her sewing in her hand. Grace came to her side, and watched the graceful figure in sealskin jacket and simple brown dress moving fleetly up the street. "She's here and gone, and you're never sure of her. When you think you've got her tearing at your back, she's laughing in your face. Well I mind me of the day your blessed mother went, when Riley and me—Riley was the coachman, my dear Miss Grace—you kept a coachman then, along with other good things—

when Riley and me found her sitting in a corner with her little apron over her head, crying, and rocking backwards and forwards as if her little body were like to burst with the storm inside her, like a balloon that's blowed too high; and then of a sudden, when Riley downs on his knees before her and begs her to stop, saying, ' Don't, now — don't, little lady,' she takes her apron down from her head, and looks at him, and bursts out laughing, because, 'Oh, Riley,' she cries, 'you've got the funniest nose I ever did see ; it's just like the top of a crutch !' And she laughed and laughed, and Riley was mighty proud to think he had such a handy nose as could make a girl laugh when she was nigh to dying of sorrow. And I says to him, ' Riley,' says I, ' that there hitch in your nose is a Godsend.' And I suppose every hitch we meet is put there a-purpose to bring somebody up short on the road they shouldn't be taking."

" Eleanor is quick," said Grace, " but she's all right."

" Oh, her heart is in the right spot," acquiesced the old nurse, as she creased a hem. " But sometimes it's out walking when it should be in—just as she is doing now."

Eleanor walked like the wind. Turning the corner, she kept straight ahead. Under her veil her eyes and mouth looked stern and repellent. Had she been commanded to divulge her destination she would have been compelled to reply, like the weary worldling of old, " Anywhere—out of the world." She longed to get as far from the reach of people and observation as she could. Wretchedness and crime are alike in this—isolation is their desired goal. She walked westward, regardless of the space of time and ground she was leaving

behind her. Only to get away—to get away, in the vain
hope of getting away from herself! And now she had
passed out into the country. Sandhills and trees, nature
unmolested travelled beside her. Still on she went, the
trees growing more frequent, more regular, and presently
she found herself near the entrance to Golden Gate
Park. Three hackmen and a mounted policeman stood
in the gateway. They arrested her attention. The fact
of the distance she had reached assailed her grimly.
"I'll go to the end," she thought, and she turned toward the beach cars. Five minutes later the salt breeze
struck sharply into her face—she was steaming along to
the ocean. On sped the cars; past trackless stretches
of sand-dunes, swept smooth and white as the hand by
the winds of yesterday, the young pines and eucalypti
rising along their embankments in stripling slenderness.
And ever the salt breeze lashed her face and stung her
eyes, and the whistling steam harked eerily back to her
as she sat alone in the open tram. She alighted with a
sense of freedom. She walked quickly down the rocky
road, and at last—at last she had reached the sands of
the ocean. How it boomed!

She stood alone. The Cliff House rose at her right,
silent and bleak; to her left, along the sinuous sweep
of sand, not a living thing was in sight; before her was
the dim, misty stretch of limitless ocean. Now and then
the hawking of the seals from their distant rocks reached
her dimly through the thunderous clamor of waters.
The slow, heavy billows swelled toward her, seething
far above her head, and as they broke madly at her feet,
curled backward, hissing like angry serpents which were
swallowed like froth in the cavernous depths of the mon-

ster breakers foaming to the shore. Roar and boom and swish, as the boiling waves dashed themselves in continuous fury against the cliffs and rocks toward the north. And presently she forgot the noise; its wild diapason no longer had meaning for her. Only before her, as far as eye could travel, north, west, south, spread the great ocean, meeting the gray horizon in a line of silver.

As she looked the fever left her; the stern, repellent look in her eyes changed to one of weary sadness. "Oh," she thought, "to be free like that, to expand like that, and still be sentient. To float into an infinity without limitation, without end, free from fret and care, rid of humanity! To comprehend and to be uncomprehended, a soul, a spirit, asking nothing—for nothing should be wanted. To know no longing!" Unconsciously her feet moved to the tide. It drew her like a magnet; she moved as if asleep, her eyes on the line of silver. Almost, and Eleanor Herriott would have passed out. Something crossed her line of vision — the dark figure of a man moving along the sands. She knew him on the instant. It was Kenyon.

"No, no," she murmured, shrinking back in wild revulsion. "Not while he lives!"

She stood still, out of the reach of the waves, and looked with a pale, wondering face upon him. He was not three yards from her. He stood looking out, a tall, strong figure with folded arms. What was he doing here on this dark, blustering day? Why had he come? The question was confronted by another: why had she come? Her heart gave a wild bound. She felt herself growing intent and still. The next minute she had approached to within a foot. She looked at him with quick comprehension, yet never had she seen such change wrought upon the human countenance in the space of a night. He was quite ghastly — with the ghastliness of cold ashes where a glowing fire had been alight. His eyes were dark as dead embers, the corners of his nose pinched and drawn, his lips close-pressed and dry, his chin looked hard and resolute as a bulwark. There was not the shadow of an emotion upon him, only the cold, indelible imprint of a great tragedy.

She had known he would take it hard ; they were too much akin for her to delude herself with a contrary belief. She had known he would revolt as only those who have never been denied anything will revolt when a great demand is ignored ; but she was not prepared for the devastation of all hope upon his beaten face.

He was quite unconscious of her proximity ; not a sound, not a movement escaped him. She longed yet feared to have him make some sign of consciousness. She was startled when the sign came—the cold, deadly sneer which drew out lips and nostrils was an agonizing sight. Presently, as she before had glided down the sand, he moved toward the waters with apparent, deliberate purpose, in the momentary bravery of reckless cowardice.

"Mr. Kenyon ! Hall ! Hall !"

The sharp, clear call, the sudden grasp upon his arm were an unforeseen shock in his disordered mentality. He paused abruptly, turned toward her, and reeled. Her arms went about his shoulders. He leaned unconsciously against her in vertigo. The blood rushed in a torrent to his brain and receded as rapidly.

"Come," she said, her voice rising like a command

above the deep roar of the sea—" come away from the waves !"

At her voice a flutter of consciousness sprang to his face ; he moved mechanically with her.

"You—" He faltered as she paused breathless under his weight. " Why did you come ?" A painful, miserable hope had leaped into his eyes.

" I—I was here," was the simple answer.

Revulsion overtook him at once. His eyes closed, he swayed against her. A man on the upper balcony of the Cliff House, sweeping the horizon with a field-glass, suddenly perceived them and let his gaze rest.

" Two lovers," he conjectured, with a half - smile, " having it out—with the breakers. The woman seems to be supporting him, though ! Perhaps he is ill ! Tempted by the waves—" He made a hasty movement as if ready to go to her assistance, but paused and continued to observe them with interest. " They are moving away," he commented to himself. " They look like aristocrats, too. A queer situation ! But then one can never be sure of a woman."

Her skirt trailed along the sand as she led him on. He was giddy—in an unconscious whirl; the vertigo had left him weak and helpless. Eleanor Herriott's face was calm and steadfast. She was called upon to help him, and her soul could hold no further thought.

They made headway toward a cab near the house, the driver of which had just emerged from the bar-room wiping his mouth with the back of his hand. The sun was lowering to the ocean, a huge, blood-red ball, surrounded by black, volcanic clouds.

The man touched his hat as the girl accosted him.

"Will you drive us to the Sausalito ferry at once?" she asked.

The hackman looked from the calm-faced girl to the handsome, death-like face above her.

"Yes'm," he said, with alacrity. "Gent sick?"

He received no answer, and he lent an assisting hand to Kenyon.

As he closed the door upon them the sun's ball of blood sank to the waters, staining them with crimson, flushing cliff and house and sands in rosy incandescence, and lighting the heavens with marvellous splendor. But the human actors were no longer in sight.

CHAPTER VIII

"Good - night, dearies," Constance was saying that same evening. She was standing in the dining-room doorway, and smiling upon the little group about the table. "Don't forget anything I have told you. Nan and Marjorie may stay up till half-past eight, and—"

"Say till nine, Constance," broke in Nan, eagerly, laying down her fork. "We are going to pop corn and tell stories. Half-past eight would be just at the beginning of the fun."

"No, Nan, I have given you a half-hour longer than usual; you must be satisfied. Otherwise you would be worn out to-morrow, and Marjorie would be cross all day."

"Oh no, we wouldn't! Truly we wouldn't!" chimed in the two childish voices, half in promise, half in entreaty.

"There, there, I said half-past eight. And you must see, Grace, that they are both in bed at just that time."

Brunton, leaning against the sideboard, looked quizzically from the disappointed little faces to that of their guardian in the doorway. She was ready to go; upon her head and crossed under her chin was a black lace scarf, from the filmy shadow of which her face looked out in calm austerity.

"Why so—impregnable?" he ventured, in an undertone.

A quick contraction fluttered her nostrils. " It is necessary," she answered sharply, moving to leave. She
turned back, after making a step.

"Girls," she said, "tell Eleanor when she comes
home that I brought her a volume of short stories from
the library; they are on her table. Tell her that I said
that they are *very* clever and amusing. And, Betty," she
added to the maid hovering over the children, " see that
Miss Eleanor has a good hot drink when she goes to
bed. I am sorry Mrs. Vassault kept her for dinner.
Good-night all, again."

" You see, Eleanor went out this afternoon when I had
gone off with Nan," she explained, as Brunton stepped
into the carriage after her and the horses started off
briskly. " I am afraid her cold will take a relapse. The
air is anything but dry."

"Taking a homœopathic cure," suggested Brunton,
easily, leaning back in the opposite corner. " Eleanor
is a fantastic creature, but her little lapses are pardonable
on the plea of being committed without premeditation.
She reminds me of Kenyon. You remember Kenyon,
the writer?"

" Yes."

" Ah, of course! He has developed into quite a house-
friend, hasn't he?"

" We have seen him very often during his stay."

Brunton looked at her curiously. Was it merely the
jolting over the uneven street which caused her quick,
short tone?

" A most unaccountable fellow—Kenyon. Makes an
appointment—rushes in on the tag end of it, or forgets
it entirely in the overwhelming absorption of other in-

terests. But he invariably remembers soon enough to bring a breathless apology which knocks out the rating I have in preparation. It is impossible to do more than swear in the face of his contrition. His personality is magical."

" Do you ever swear, Geoffrey?" she asked, lightly, curving the subject adroitly.

" In my better moments. For instance, when I waited a half-hour for Kenyon to-day to come in and sign a deed; it should have been mailed this evening. He never made even the ghost of an appearance. There is no excuse, as he was in yesterday, and in a fever-heat to have it consummated."

" You men always forget to be human when your interests are retarded. Do you ever remember that illness or accident might prove a possible hinder-ance ?"

" Seldom, when dealing with a man; never, with one put up as Kenyon is. Now, if I had made the engage-ment with you for to-morrow and you should not mate-rialize, I should hold those dark rings about your eyes to account. Where did you get them ?"

" In a mental prize-fight. Don't laugh at them ; they are sometimes inseparable parts of the spoils. I suppose we shall have a pleasant evening."

" Indeed !" he responded, closing his hand tightly as it rested upon his knee. He was barred out ; he was turned from the door of her confidence in a manner curiously unlike herself.

This was the first invitation he had ever accepted from Mrs. Ferris. He did not like the woman, but he held a genuine admiration for her daughter, which no amount of maternal propagation could stifle. Looking at Gertrude Ferris next her mother, it had always remained a wonder that the girl had continued unspoiled. She was gentle, refined, and full of that sweet charity which is the root of as many feminine omissions as commissions. Her mother's small, sharp eyes were like so many antennæ, to which no social morsel was too microscopic to be unworthy her interest and publication. And yet he had to admit that Mrs. Ferris understood the art of entertaining to a fine degree. Her dishes, decorations, service, and guests were chosen with a refinement of knowledge which showed great study, sharp adaptive powers. She told off her guests with a nicety of discrimination which proved her something of a diplomat. Brunton felt a complaisant pleasure in the fact that Miss Ferris fell to his lot. Had she been a mere pretty girl whose best points were her facial features, she would, of a certainty, have been placed opposite him in the light of an attractive picture, instead of next him in the position of an entertaining companion. Constance, he remarked, was neither within sight nor hearing. She had been apportioned to Garth, the young portrait-painter who had done Mrs. Ferris's head with the accuracy of truth and all the art which discovers extenuating possibilities of beauty in the plainest subject—the refutation of the libel that portrait-painters are independent of fancy.

Young Garth had been standing near his hostess when Constance entered. His eye had been held on the instant by the odd contrast of her pale olive complexion and the pale gold of her hair. Upon being introduced he had addressed some remark to her which arrested her. They had drawn somewhat aside. It happened that Constance, standing talking to him until they went in, paid no attention to the other guests.

But as they seated themselves at table Constance gave a start; for there sat Mrs. Vassault, radiant and lovely— Mrs. Vassault, Eleanor's friend, opposite, in lively converse with her escort! And the next instant she found herself nodding to Mr. Vassault, a few seats farther on. She looked at the wife and the husband in dismay : if they were here, where was Eleanor?

She felt her heart beating anxiously. She tried to compose herself with the thought that Eleanor had waited to be driven home in the Vassaults' carriage on their way to the Ferrises'. She succeeded in lending an attentive ear to Garth, who, being a voluble talker, found himself as much at ease in addressing this statuesquely beautiful woman as if she had been a model whom he was warming to the desired expression. But she listened as idly to his conversation as to the music. Yet Garth found her extremely entertaining, his monology requiring only a good listener who showed no sign of weariness.

She had to wait. But at length the ladies had filed into the drawing-room again. Quickly Constance approached Mrs. Vassault.

" Tell me," she began, with a half-smile, " did you not find Eleanor looking rather miserable to-day ?"

" Eleanor !" repeated Mrs. Vassault, raising her eyebrows and fan at the same time, and wafting a breath of violets as she spoke. " I did not see Eleanor to-day ! I believe that fickle girl is beginning to abandon me ! I have seen *so* little of her since our return."

" Ah," returned Constance, feeling her limbs suddenly grow heavy and cold beneath her. " I thought she said she was going to visit you this afternoon. I must have misunderstood her."

There was some mistake — some accident or trouble. She must see Geoffrey at once. She glanced around; he was not in sight. And now she felt herself growing white and excited. Ah! there was Geoffrey, at the other end of the long room. She would go to him and tell him her anxiety. With a murmured word of apology to her companion, she turned into the near conservatory.

The perfumed air enveloped her languorously as she moved over the floor. She had almost reached the door when it was flung open, and Charlie Ferris stepped in. He was a young, bright-looking lad of seventeen, clad in an old shooting-jacket and spattered leather breeches.

"Oh, Miss Herriott!" he exclaimed with a laugh, as he started back. "Don't look at me, please! Just stole in —to get a package of cigarettes I left here this morning. Been shooting over at Mill Valley; bagged some great birds. Oh, I say, I saw your sister."

"My sister!"

The palms, the flowers, the boy, the music from the next room, danced fantastically about her.

"Yes, the pretty one; had on a seal-skin jacket; saw her walking up toward the heights at Sausalito with Kenyon, that handsome fellow who writes. I met him at my brother's club one night—"

"When did you say you saw her?" came the low words, accompanied by a strained smile. She had suddenly become conscious of a heliotrope gown near the dividing portière. She recognized it at once as Mrs. Ferris's; it stood intently still. The wearer was listening.

"Let's see," calculated the boy, "it must have been about 5.40, because I was hurrying toward the station to take the 5.45 boat home."

"Yes," said Constance, slowly—was she talking to the heliotrope gown or to the boy?—"perhaps it was about that time. I suppose she took the next boat home."

"Couldn't do that," exclaimed Charlie Ferris, with a grin. "I took the last boat over myself. There's no boat after the 5.45."

He stood with his hands in his pockets, and regarded her like a young mastiff of superior wisdom. In his careless, boyish face there was no trace of the hideous thought which assailed the woman standing stonily before him. Finally a peculiar little laugh escaped her. The gown was waiting for some further comment.

"I am so forgetful," she explained, carefully, as she regarded the boy. "Of course. She thought of passing the night with May Turnbull; the Turnbulls are living over there now, you know. How foolish of me to forget!" There are moments of confused agony when the bravest will seek to escape in the shadow of a subterfuge.

"Yes, I know Tom Turnbull," nodded Charlie, picking up his cigarettes from a small rustic stand. "Don't give me away, Miss Herriott!" And with this cavalier adieu he disappeared. The purple gown moved away.

Constance stood alone. What did it mean? She put her hand to her head as if to brush aside the cloud of blood which blinded her. Geoffrey! That was it—she was going to call Geoffrey. She took a step forward. No, not Geoffrey now. There was no one—no one in all the world—to help her. There must be no gossip.

Eleanor Herriott was her sister—hers, and the sister of those four girls at home. She belonged to no one else; hers—her mother's child.

"Ah, Constance, what are you doing here alone?"

The blood rushed madly over her brow as she faced Brunton.

"I saw you leave the drawing-room hurriedly," he said, approaching her with quiet concern. "Is anything wrong?"

"Wrong!" she repeated, with such exaggerated vehemence that he drew back. "What could possibly be wrong? I—"

"Excuse me, Miss Herriott," interrupted Gertrude Ferris's voice, as she stood, somewhat flushed, near the portière, "but mamma sent me to ask you if you would please play something for us."

"Certainly," asserted Constance, moving swiftly to her. "I shall be pleased to play for you, Gertrude."

There was something like entreaty in the smile she gave to the girl. Gertrude, who had an almost idolatrous admiration for Constance Herriott, touched her arm timidly. Constance involuntarily shuddered. Gertrude drew back, blushing violently.

"Forgive me," said Constance, with an indrawn sigh. "I believe I am slightly nervous to-night."

"Then do not play," begged Miss Ferris, hurriedly. "I'll sing, if you would rather stay here."

But Constance stepped into the drawing-room. As she seated herself at the piano her hands felt like insensate lumps of ice. But she must play. Everybody was looking at her, and nobody must know. She felt as though it could be read all over her figure—her back,

7

her hair, upon her white neck. She must play to hide it, play to show that nothing was wrong. Like a criminal on the verge of being discovered, she gathered her wits in one supreme effort. She played a quaint mazurka. Her fingers moved like excellently drilled waxworks. How the notes tripped, tripped—mocking, jesting, happy-sad notes tripping over a grave ! Only one among all her auditors knew that the stately, calm-faced girl was in a delirium of suffering. Brunton, standing in the doorway like a sentinel, regarded her with the assured conviction that she would suddenly break down ; only some great physical or mental pain could have made her act as hysterically as she had acted a moment before in the conservatory. He was on the alert to give his assistance. It was not needed.

From then till the moment when he unlocked her door for her she appeared quite self-possessed.

"Can I do anything for you?" he asked, as she stepped over the threshold.

"No, thank you ; I have everything I wish."

"Then good-night ; sleep well."

"Good-night, Geoffrey."

She closed the heavy door softly behind him. Then, with a wild movement, she rushed up-stairs into Eleanor's room, over to the bed, feeling convulsively for the young form she loved so well. Nothing.

She put her hand to her throat ; her heart was strangling her. "Eleanor!" she called. No answer. She lit a match and groped about the room—perhaps there was a note. She lit the gas. Nothing. She must search the house. From room to room the still, misty gray figure passed, making no sound, no outcry, no call for help. And at last she stood again in Eleanor's room with empty hands.

She was utterly bewildered. In the irresistible rush of opposing thoughts her mind wandered strangely. Kenyon! The man of whom, for months, she had thought but as of something beautiful and strong— something purer and more wholesome than any personality which had ever touched hers outside of childhood and adolescence! Quick, passionate, dauntless, she knew him to be ; stubborn and selfish, perhaps, but not— vile ! And if he were vile, what was Eleanor? What was her sister? The shame and wretchedness of the question were pitiable.

It was significant of the horror of the situation that she gave no tender thought to Eleanor. One supreme question rang eternally in her brain : What would people say? What would people say? Always, always— came the answer—at the sound of the name of Herriott, that the sister of those innocent young girls was— No, no! It was too awful, too pitiless. It must not be— God help her, it *should* not be !

The demoniacal shapes filed slowly out of her mental portal. She felt herself gaining a peculiar, moveless power. Emotion, weakness, femininity, fell from her. She grew cold, hard, relentless as a commandant before a deadly enemy. Something was to be done, and she must do it. There was no man, no father, no brother to turn to in this sickening crisis. It was man's work, but there was no one but herself—no one but Constance Herriott; and the father, the brother, was at hand.

She stood wrapped in a hood of strong thought. Finally she turned and walked down-stairs. Her step was

deliberate, sure, masterful. The woman in her was routed; she strode like a man. She lit the gas in the library;
she found a newspaper. With strong, nerveless fingers
she turned it till she came to the railroad guide. The
first ferry left San Francisco for Sausalito at 7.30 in the
morning. The first ferry from Sausalito arrived five
minutes before; she would be in time, if they had not
gone farther north. She looked at the clock; it was half-
past two. There were four hours to wait.

She mounted the stairs and entered her own room.
She did not glance toward, did not see, the child Marjorie sleeping in the bed. She began to take off her gown.
She replaced it with a plain, dark, tailor-made garment,
whose severity but augmented the severe aspect of her
bearing.

" There is only one way," she thought, as she pinned
on her hat. " I must go to them. People must never
know. Only one way "—her eye, travelling toward the
open bureau drawer, encountered a small derringer, which
always lay there hidden—" or," came the cold, emotion-
less thought, " perhaps two."

Then, taking from the closet a dark, straight ulster,
she sat down and waited.

CHAPTER IX

"You want him tea velly stlong?" asked Wong, standing, caddy in hand, and looking with an odd expression upon Eleanor Herriott. Eleanor stood near Wong in the tiny kitchen.

"Yes, please. And if you will arrange the tray, I shall take it right in."

"Misser Ken velly sick man?" asked the Chinaman, his slender yellow hand deftly spreading the small tray with a white cloth.

"He is better now."

The slanting brown eyes regarded her with the cool, intrepid, Mongolian stare as he placed the tray in her hands. She did not notice it. There was a serenity, an indescribable lack of self-consciousness upon her face such as one sees upon the clear, chaste countenances of some nuns. She passed quietly out with the steaming tea, Wong following her; but he went on to his broom on the porch.

She entered the sitting-room. Kenyon still reposed in a partly reclining attitude upon the lounge, where he had half-fallen, half-thrown himself the night before—after that scene upon the beach at sunset. His elbow was sunk in the soft cushion which Eleanor had managed to place under his head. His face looked gray and thoughtful. He received the tray from her hands without a word of protesting thanks. While he idly stirred the spoon, his wandering gaze travelled from her hat and jacket on a chair to the slim, graceful form beside him. A puzzled look gathered in his eyes.

" Will you tell me," he asked, gently, " how I happen to be lying here ?"

" You were ill," she replied. " I brought you here. When we came in you sank down there. At first you were in a sort of stupor; then your breathing changed. You slept all night."

He listened attentively, swallowing the while a little of the hot tea. When he replaced the cup in the saucer he shot a quick look of consternation at her. She stood with her hand on the head of the couch watching him with simple solicitude. He raised his cup again to his lips without a word.

They remained thus in silence until they heard Wong's voice suddenly raised in colloquy upon the porch. There was a slight movement in the hall. A hovering, dark shadow appeared in the doorway. The next minute Constance stood before them.

The cup and saucer fell with a crash as Kenyon rose to his feet and confronted her. His face and lips were deathly. Eleanor had drawn back in surprise. Constance's face was covered with a still, mask-like composure. It was not a pleasant expression.

" Are you two married ?" she asked, in a hard voice, meeting Kenyon's eyes.

A stifled cry came from Eleanor. The sudden flood of consciousness the words bore to her was brutal.

Kenyon's unswerving gaze did not turn to the girl, nor did Constance's; they regarded each other dumbly.

" I asked if you two are married ?" she repeated, in deliberate, heavy precision.

"We are not," returned Kenyon, in an unnatural tone.

"How dare you, Constance!" The cry came from Eleanor, as she sprang forward with burning eyes and cheeks, and hand upraised as if to strike. Constance turned easily toward her.

"You are not responsible for your inspirations," she said, "but you had better put down your hand. I have come to see that Mr. Kenyon repairs the wrong he has done you. Please stand back."

"What wrong?" demanded the younger sister tersely. "What wrong are you insinuating, pray?"

Constance heard her without a change of expression. She looked again toward Kenyon.

"Mr. Kenyon, you must marry my sister to-day—before you leave this house."

"Marry Miss Eleanor? Your demand is hasty," he replied, with a laugh. "Had we not better control tragics? Why should I marry Miss Eleanor—now—at any time—I beg?"

"I had not thought you a scoundrel," she returned. "But in any case—"

"In any case you would marry your sister to the scoundrel." His teeth were set now. He understood. He would offer no recriminations to her.

"Mr. Kenyon, listen to me. A woman has only her good name. She may be forced to maintain it at the price of her happiness. If you have one spark of manliness left you will make right in the world's eyes what has passed since yesterday by making my sister your wife." Her figure seemed to tower over the quivering younger girl. Her face was as relentless as that of an Atropos. "I can trust you to do this, as the friend of

my cousin, Severn Scott." She chose her words carefully. Kenyon drew himself up haughtily, his nostrils
quivering with repression. Constance, mistaking the
movement, drew nearer, regarding him with stern meaning.

"There is one way out of it," she added ; "but it is
a more melodramatic and disagreeable one."

"Oh, there is no need for violence," he returned, understanding her. "If you stop to consider, shooting
would only aggravate scandal. And really I am ready
to make all amends for an unforeseen adventure—since
you are so insistent."

"But I—I—" Eleanor's voice came sharply.

"Miss Eleanor, it is better so," interrupted Kenyon,
with sudden sternness. "Your sister is right. She has
a cooler finger on the pulse of the world than we. Let
us submit. I promise that it will be better—for you."

"You will allow me to send your servant for Dr. Granniss ?" broke in Constance's calm voice.

"Certainly. My house and all in it are at your dis-
posal. But there are certain preliminaries—"

Constance had already left the room.

Fifteen minutes later Dr. Granniss came in. His
cheeks showed a faint wintry rose of disturbance as he
looked about him.

"You sent for me, Constance ?" he asked, in surprised
gentleness.

"Yes, doctor. I want you to do me the only favor I
may ever ask of you. My sister here and Mr. Kenyon
are to be married this morning—now. I want you to
marry them. Will you ?"

There was a deep silence, while the clergyman considered her unexpected demand. His wrinkled hand trembled as it rested upon the table.

"Have you a license?" he asked, turning to Kenyon.

"No."

"The State law requires one. I cannot honorably perform the ceremony without one." There was another painful silence, during which Kenyon contemplated him with folded arms.

"Dr. Granniss," said Constance, clearly, "I know I shall not appeal to you in vain. I ask you to go through this ceremony—this form, *now*, for my mother's child—for my mother's sake."

The pastor's delicate old face flushed painfully. He turned to her and looked at her questioningly.

"Is this haste really so necessary?" he asked, sternly.

"It is."

He bent his head in thought.

"For your mother's sake," he said, finally; "and because I know you all so well, I will do my part there. Come a little forward, please."

The binding words were soon spoken. Without many words Granniss drew up a certificate.

"You are man and wife," he said, picking up his hat and stick, and moving to leave. "You have vowed it before God and in the presence of man. There is your voucher. And I pray you will be happy and true to each other. Good-morning. Good-morning, Miss Constance."

He was man enough of the world to understand that the occurrence had had a peculiar forerunner. He shook their hands earnestly but rather curtly. As the gate clicked behind him Constance moved toward the door.

Kenyon was leaning silently against it. Eleanor, white to the lips, watched her blindly.

"Good-bye," said Constance, coming toward her and holding out her hands.

"Don't touch me," breathed Eleanor, drawing back. Constance's hands fell to her sides.

"Will you allow me to pass?" she said in a low voice to Kenyon, his powerful figure barring her way. He stepped aside without a word.

"Good-bye," she said, looking for a moment at him. In the single word lay a world of command and entreaty. He bent his head in silence. He had always understood her thus.

"Stop one moment," called Eleanor, huskily, as Constance's hand turned the knob. "Will you tell me now why you have done this thing to me — to Mr. Kenyon? What reason, what right—"

For a second Constance's waxen face looked toward her, a subtle nobility emanating from it like a white flame.

"Why?" she repeated, in a clear, passionless voice. "Because, Eleanor, there must be no shame attached to the name of your mother's children. If you do not understand how it could come, I cannot teach you now."

A minute later the elder sister had passed quietly, swiftly down the hilly road.

CHAPTER X

It was bitterly cold, despite the dazzling sun overhead. As Constance neared the station she looked at her watch; it was twenty-five minutes past nine. The next ferry would leave at five minutes to ten. She began to walk slowly up and down near the wharf. A belated school-girl, bound for the other side, forgot her irritation over having missed her boat while watching the marble-faced, regally-moving woman. She was surely " somebody," thought the girl, or a " woman with a history." An Italian fisherman, drawing in his nets, lay idly rocking in his boat with his eyes upon her. A tall, stout, well-groomed old gentleman with white side-whiskers and an eye-glass scanned her curiously and with a start of recognition as she turned and her hair came into view. He looked searchingly at her, and was about to approach her when he saw the small crowd moving toward the boat, and he moved with it. Constance, quite unconscious of being noticed, mechanically mounted the ferry steps and seated herself in the corner near the boiler, resting her elbow on the railing and her head on her hand. The throbbing of the steam, the easy sweep of the boat, soothed her insensibly. Her gray eyes rested wearily on the blue, white-crested waves. She felt old and dreary in this moment of relaxation. But it was all arranged now; there was nothing more for her to do. And yet —would he be good to her? Habit overrides change;

Eleanor was still to her one of her children. Would he be good to her? A rush of memory brought his face and figure before her as she had last seen him—stately, white, and grand. A rush of something else almost simultaneously obliterated every other sensation. But she shut her eyes and pressed her lips hard. A cold, stern, inner voice reiterated, "He is your sister's husband now! Remember! Your sister's husband!" She was dumbly trying to learn the "never again" of the stoic, the death in life which is an endless death-scene. She was painfully startled when she heard herself addressed.

"Good-morning, Miss Herriott; I thought I could *not* be mistaken." A well-groomed old gentleman was standing before her with a beaming face and gloved hand outstretched. As she put her hand into his a wave of color flushed her face.

"Did you stop over at our little plateau last night?" he asked, seating himself beside her with an air of comfort. "I saw your sister with my distinguished neighbor, Kenyon, coming over, too, on the ferry last night. Where did she stay? May was expecting her when I told her I had seen her."

She had not thought of the explanatory contingency. Her wits worked rapidly. Presently a conventional smile curved her lips as she spoke.

"Why," she said — "well, I have a little surprise in store for you, and others. You did not know that you were travelling with a pair of elopers! My sister and Mr. Kenyon—can you believe it?—they fairly ran off together last night. They were married by Dr. Granniss, over at Sausalito."

"Miss Herriott! Really? No?"

He veered his huge bulk slowly around in order to get her more completely into view. Ah! she had said it well; there was only one meaning to be taken from her words. She thanked God that she could say them even so.

"Yes," she nodded, still smiling as one does when delivering happy news. "Geniuses are romantic, you know; and my sister, Lydia-Languishwise, preferred the excitement of an elopement to the conventionality of an ordinary wedding. So they just took hands and ran off." Another good sentence — she must learn it. The next time it would come more glibly.

"Well, I am astonished! You don't say so! Well, well! I must make a note of it, so as not to forget to tell May this evening. She does take on so when I fail to tell any piece of news I have been carrying around with me all day. And this *is* a piece of news." He had taken out his little alligator-skin note-book, and was jotting down a word or two. Then he made an excited gesture and laid his hand upon hers.

"But how are *you* taking it?"

"With a smile."

"Exactly. That's wise. Tell you what, Miss Herriott, there's a good deal more sense than nonsense in an elopement; saves lots of time, money, and flummery, which would be spent in mere show. But I am astonished! Your little sister gone and married to the young literary lion! Do you think the couple will settle down here?"

How easy and jolly and natural it sounded!

"I can't say," she answered, with a little laugh, which was almost a sob of thanksgiving. "You see, it was all so hurried, Mr. Turnbull. They have not told me their plans."

"Ha, ha! you'll hear them after they are settled, I suppose, in order to maintain the consistency. When did *you* get wind of it?"

"I? Only late last night. Absurd, wasn't it?"

"Wired, I suppose."

"How else does news travel?"

"So you came over to give them your blessing and a godspeed! You're an early bird. Well, business is business. Boss can't lie calmly abed when the cashier's run off with his treasure. Remarkable-looking man, that Kenyon. Stands out and over every one wherever you put him. Suppose he is pretty well fixed through his uncle's will. Don't go much, however, on the stability of a Bohemian's bank-account. Genius is apt to be either erratic or erotic. Don't be surprised if you find your brother - in - law. surprising. So Dr. Granniss did it. Queer! The old gentleman is a great stickler for regularity. But better so. Well, here we are. I think I'll telephone to May. Then she won't have to go ferreting her out, as she intended doing this morning when I told her she had come over on the last boat with Kenyon — look out for those steps, Miss Herriott. Good-luck to them! They're taking a risk — getting married; but what's fire - proof nowadays? Which car do you take?"

"The—the Market," she answered, after a slight hesitation, as they walked around the noisy pier. If she took the more convenient car she would be liable to meet other acquaintances.

The old gentleman saw her fairly seated, paid her fare,

saluted, and was gone. The car started off. It was quite empty—a fact for which she was grateful, as she felt feverish and uncanny. Several men were seated on the dummy, but no one came in till they reached Lotta's fountain. She dimly saw the waiting crowd, old Father Elphic's white, uncovered hair, and the baskets of violets and chrysanthemums held by the importunate little boy venders. A few women got in. Some one touched her slightly on the sleeve and took the seat beside her. It was Mrs. Ferris.

"Good-morning, Miss Constance. Lovely morning, isn't it? Been shopping?" she asked, with that airiness which makes a question a mere formula, and which takes no cognizance of an answer. "Haven't you lost your bearings by taking this car?" There was a steely brightness in her eyes—a covert curiosity, well-spiced with some anterior knowledge.

"I shall transfer to the Powell Street line."

"A little roundabout, I should think. I had some business to transact on Market Street, and as I am due at my dress-maker's, make the connection this way. Did you hear the news last night?" The sharp, ferret eyes were upon her; the slight, abrupt change of expression which flitted over Constance's face was not unobserved.

"I scarcely think I know to what you refer," Constance ventured, almost naturally. "One hears so many rumors. I generally wait before I consider them confirmed facts."

"As some people wait for the evening paper before they pronounce the morning news verified. Don't you think life is too short for such long *entr'actes?* It must make the play rather slow, as it were. I was referring to Mrs. Vassault's proposed fancy-dress affair. By-the-bye, I suppose your sister Eleanor—"

"Ah, here we are at Powell Street," interrupted Constance, with a motion to the conductor to stop. Crossing Market Street at mid-day is not a careless affair. With its numberless cable-cars thrumming up and down, horse-cars interspersed *ad libitum*, trucks thundering over the rails and cobble-stones, carts whizzing by without regard to life or limb, car-bells ringing incessant warnings to the thousands of intrepid foot-passengers darting in and out in alarming proximity to revolving wheels, it is a hazardous undertaking, and one is always thankful when safely over the slippery, well-watered street.

There was a prolonged pause in Mrs. Ferris's and Constance's conversation, during which time Constance steeled herself to make the best front before this consummate female barterer of all privacy. As soon as they were safely seated again, Mrs. Ferris picked up her broken sentence and rounded it.

"I suppose your sister Eleanor will go. There are so many charming characters she could personate. I suggested to Mrs. Vassault that she ask the girls to represent different courts. For instance, there is Elizabeth's, Louis Fifteenth's (the women of the Salon), and those of Martha Washington's time. Now, in regard to your sister Eleanor, I think that her vivacity would suit the French—"

"One minute, Mrs. Ferris," put in Constance, with successfully forced *sang-froid*. "I have been endeavoring to tell you another piece of news ever since we met. Did you know that my sister Eleanor is married?" Her words were followed by an overwhelming thought:

"Thank God—thank God *now!*—that my sister is married!"

"Your sister Eleanor? Married!" The intense color in Mrs. Ferris's sallow cheek attested to the force of the sensation. "Heavens! what do you mean?"

"She went gayly off with Mr. Kenyon yesterday—was married to him over at Sausalito."

"An elopement then!" Mrs. Ferris was off her guard. Constance recognized the knowledge of which this exclamation was an outgrowth.

"Exactly. These—these geniuses are romantic, you know, and Eleanor, like another Lydia Languish, always said she preferred the excitement of an elopement to the more conventional, ordinary wedding. So they just took hands and ran off—like children!"

The news had robbed Mrs. Ferris of her presence of mind. Her eyes looked ready to start from their sockets. She glanced in uneasy bewilderment from Constance to the window. They had reached a corner, and she motioned hurriedly to the conductor.

"I forgot," she murmured, putting a flurried hand upon Constance's. "I must get out here. You have *so* surprised me, too! But—but—I congratulate you—good-bye—I'll see you soon again."

As her tall, thin figure disappeared on the car-step, Constance looked out of the window. Down the street before a millinery-shop she plainly discerned Mrs. Vassault's carriage, with its rather prominent coachman in green-and-white livery. She understood. Mrs. Ferris's ruling passion had claimed her.

"The ball is set rolling," she thought, in grim weariness. "It was a little turn of luck that enabled me to give Mrs. Ferris the news first-hand. It may not come out altogether distorted now."

The sight of her own door-step was a welcome greeting. When her foot touched the first step she felt as though an elegant robe of state had slipped from her and left her free to clothe herself as she would. The sense of the familiar is always peculiarly soothing and comforting to all solitary, thoughtful souls. She stood in her rightful realm, alone in the arched doorway. The marble under her feet, the oak panels behind her, knew her and recognized her as theirs in a silence like that which distinguishes familiar loves from the noisier contact of the less intimate.

Before she could ring, the door was flung open. Grace and the two children stood in the doorway, excited and red-eyed.

"Oh, Constance," they cried, "we have been so upset! Where—"

Constance closed the door quickly as she stepped in. "Come into the library, dears," she said. "I'm cold."

They followed her silently. The mark of years was upon the new-comer. She drew off her hat and coat, and went to the fire.

Marjorie burst forth, in sobbing excitement, "Edith isn't at school. A girl came and said she hadn't been at school for four days. Miss Temple wants to know why, and Eleanor didn't come home—you were out before we got up, and Grace hurt me when she dressed me, and—and—it's all so uncomftafiddle!" The shrill, childish voice broke in a flood of tears as she rushed to Constance and hid her head in her gown. The wretchedness of disorder had penetrated even to the baby. Constance turned a questioning face to Grace.

"What is this about Edith?" she asked, in a harsh, quick tone.

"I don't know," answered Grace, in pale affright, regarding the changed, haggard face before her. "Miss Temple sent one of the girls to find out why Edith had not been to school for four days. She *did* go, didn't she, Constance? And, Constance, what—what is the matter, that Eleanor does not come home?"

"Wait," answered Constance, sharply. New mystery! New misery!

"I shall go over to the school now. Stay in-doors till I get back. What time is it?"

"Eleven o'clock."

Still morning! Would the day never end?

Constance was out in the street again, her temples throbbing hammer and tongs, her limbs, stiff and numb, almost crying out their pain as she walked on to the large private school on the heights. Miss Temple greeted her visitor with marked deference. She had little to say except that Edith had been absent, and she had made it a rule to inquire after the fourth day.

"She was seen each day but the day of the storm by a number of the girls, apparently on her way to school with her books."

"Yes. She started at the usual hour and has returned as usual," replied her sister, imperturbably. "Do not let me detain you, Miss Temple. Thank you for informing me. I shall have to punish her accordingly. Good-morning."

Miss Temple was somewhat abstracted after the quiet

woman had left. "She looks ill," she reflected. "She must have a great deal of trouble with all those girls!"

Constance turned again homeward. She passed houses of all descriptions, from quaint Queen Anne and feudal-looking castles to simple, old-fashioned cottages with old-fashioned gardens, like country-girls astray in town for a holiday. She halted suddenly, as if to find her inner bearings, at the corner of Fillmore Street and Broadway, whence an almost perpendicular declivity descended abruptly, sloping gradually in billowy undulations to the bay. She leaned against the low, rickety fence which surrounded the lupine-grown lot, and let her eye sweep over the soft harmony of colors beyond : the deep blue of the bay, with its still, white sails at anchor; Angel Island, stretched like a slumbering, dun-colored dream-god; behind it the foot-hills, rising gradually into the purple, starry-pointing Tamalpais, which the tender cheek of heaven seemed to touch—all parts of a poem of divine inspiration. But again her gaze fell to the water, and swept around the curve where Golden Gate opens like a neck of silver into the head-waters of the great Pacific—a cramped little soul bursting its bounds. Constance, too, reached out for immateriality. Cares and frets dropped from her like frail rose-petals in the breeze. For five minutes, at least, she ceased to think.

At that moment a man descending the steps of the house opposite was attracted by the leaning figure of the woman. He paused and peered carefully, shading his eyes with his hand in the manner of the near-sighted. Then he crossed over with an air of uncertainty. As he approached his step gained in alacrity.

"Well, Constance Herriott, the Abstracted," he said,

before his foot had touched the sidewalk, "where are your thoughts?"

She started violently as she turned toward him.

"I can't locate my thoughts just now," she said, with a wandering smile. "Where did you spring from, Geoffrey, at this hour of the day?"

"From yonder," he replied, nodding toward the dark, imposing mansion, his penetrating eye silently taking in the sad discomposure of her face, but seeming to take no cognizance. "Been aiding Stephen Gage to deliver himself before the Highest Magistrate with a clear conscience. His charities are all posthumous, so I suppose his beatitude will be coincident. At the present moment he is dying a very miserable, lonely death. You see, giving up anything is hard for a miser, and when it comes to life and fortune, the moment is better imagined than described. I'll walk home with you."

They crossed the street, passing the darkened house whence Brunton had just emerged. Before the next door stood several carriages. Just as they came near, the chords of Mendelssohn's "Wedding March" pealed out exultingly. As the pæan of joy reached them, Brunton remarked, grimly:

"Life! Here—good heavens! Constance, what is it?" She had grasped his arm and hurried him on breathlessly, her face working with anguish.

"Hurry," she whispered, hoarsely, "hurry, I can't hear *that*—I can't bear it!"

When they had got out of ear-shot of the music, she looked up at him with a painful smile.

"That march—that march, Geoffrey," she faltered, "always affects me strangely! It depicts happiness so confident, so solemn, that it is heavy with pain. It exults so, Geoffrey. Whenever I hear it, it excites me almost to delirium, and, before I know it, tears are in my eyes. And, Geoffrey—you don't know it yet—but Eleanor is married."

It escaped her with resistless force. Brunton turned pale.

"Eleanor? Nonsense! To whom?"

"To Mr. Kenyon."

"When?"

It was not coming out right. What was it she had said to the others? Oh, why could she not remember! Yes. She had it now.

"They ran off together yesterday, and were married over at Sausalito—by Dr. Granniss. You know old Dr. Granniss—you have heard of him, Geoffrey? It is just out—of course. Even you—you—"

"Hush, Constance." Her excitement was painful to witness. The excitement to which a calm personality so utterly submits must have a mighty cause.

"You think it odd for a girl like Eleanor to elope," she pursued, unheedingly. "But you see, Geoffrey, Mr. Kenyon is—is a genius—and these geniuses—and Eleanor—Lydia Languish—it couldn't—you know it is different—they—"

"I understand, Constance. I beg you to say no more."

She had bungled sadly. Before Brunton's truth-compelling, kindly gaze the stereotyped phrases melted into incoherency. Her brain was in a whirl. Excitement, fatigue, and want of sleep and food had undermined her wonted equanimity. Brunton walked beside her, helpless in his yearning strength. He dared not question her, he could neither congratulate nor console. He stood before a wall of mystery which hid, he knew, some tragic occurrence. She made no further attempt to speak till they reached her steps. Then, she held out her hand, and raised her heavy eyes to his.

"I assure you, though, it is all right, Geoffrey," she said, simply, in a dull, even voice.

He held her hand in a strong grasp. "Constance," he said, quietly, "there are things that only a man can do. Are you quite sure you *don't* need me now?"

She looked at him with a sad shake of her head, the deeper meaning of his tender words and tone unheeded in her numbed senses.

"Not now," she answered.

"God help you," he said, with the submission which knows no alternative—"God help you! since you will give no one else the right. But you are wrong."

She did not answer him, and he turned silently away.

At about half-past three that afternoon Edith Herriott came in with glowing cheeks and sparkling eyes. She threw her books upon a chair, and was about to run upstairs when Constance arrested her.

"Where have you been?" she asked, in stern deliberation.

The girl quailed and turned a guilty red. The words struggling to her lips found no utterance.

"Do not lie further, Edith," continued her sister. "You have not been at school. Answer me at once, and truthfully. Where have you been?"

Edith turned like a stag at bay. The other children listened breathlessly.

" I—I—well, if I must tell, I was bicycling at the park.
You know, Constance," she rushed on, recklessly trying
to exculpate herself—" you know I have begged and
begged you to let me go; and now that Jennie Under-
wood is learning, I thought I would just take the chance
at last. You said you didn't believe in it; you wouldn't
try to think it might give me pleasure; there was no
harm in it; it was only that you are so immovable and
unreasonable. I *did* want to go, so I went without, asking you—it was my only way."

Constance listened to her stonily. Suddenly they
witnessed a marvel: her head sank to her knees, her
form shook with dry sobs. They looked at each other
in consternation; the little ones began to cry. Edith,
white and conscience-stricken, approached her wretch-
edly.

" Oh, Constance," she cried, " Constance, forgive me !
I didn't mean to hurt you so. Constance, darling, won't
you ever speak to me again ?"

She had sunk to her knees before her in abject misery.
After a moment Constance raised her head.

" Tell me," she said, bitterly, " am I so unjust and
hard that you cannot trust me ? Am I so cruel that you
have to be underhand to escape my tyranny ? Have I
only made you hate me, after all ? And yet, children, I
cannot rid you of me."

The words died on her lips in a storm of caresses.
Little hands smoothed her hair, sobbing whispers implored her to forgive, clinging arms pressed her in love.

" Get up, Edith," said Constance, finally, in a tired,
gentle voice, to the crouching girl. " I don't think you
will ever deceive me again. Will you, dear? No, I am

sure not. Kiss me, child; I only meant to be kind to you."

After a pause she spoke again. "And now please listen, dears, all of you, for I have something to tell you *all*," she said, in grave seriousness. "Eleanor is married. She is married to our good friend Mr. Kenyon. Isn't *that* news? That is why she did not come home last night. They were married over at Sausalito by Dr. Granniss. It has all been a secret. I do not know what they are going to do just yet. They are over there now. I saw them this morning. It is to go into the evening papers." And so the news was told to Eleanor's sisters.

Night closed in. The surprise was over. The younger ones crept off to bed. Grace laid her hand upon Constance's, and said, in a low voice:

"Constance, is Eleanor going to be happy?"

And the quiet answer was, "Let us pray so, dear."

What other reply could be more practical and safe?

CHAPTER XI

I AM quite alone, Constance dear. The sea is grave and gray, reflecting the smileless sky which looks into it. The steamer glides on almost imperceptibly, leaving in its wake a long black shadow, a momentary record that something has passed. Nothing is without shadow. Over the waters sweeps the flying image of two sea-gulls, winging heavenward like soaring seraphim. Nothing is without meaning — when we breathe there is a mist upon the glass. Yet who can rightly interpret the flying shadow of a soul ?

Constance, I want you to understand. I want you to know me as I am, not as I seem to be, but stripped of all the flimsy little charms which hid my weak and baser instincts, and left me at least tolerable. I wonder if there are many as I—if, under all the suave smiles and apparent indifference, beat hearts as vain and selfish and passionate as mine. God help the sad old world if it is so. And yet, perhaps, such a vast hypocrisy is better in the long-run—though it is like a fair building built over the ugly crater of an apparently extinct volcano, but holding forces which some day will rise in one tumultuous upheaval and lay the pretty conventionality low.

I am at your feet. Look down, Constance, with your indulgent eyes, and when you have heard, will you not try to forgive ?

You know my childish faults; there is no need to recapitulate or excuse. But do you remember what our German governess said the day I shattered the Sèvres vase because my sash was narrower than yours? " The apple," she said, " falls not far from the tree." I did not understand then, but I do now. She remembered that I had a father. Men and women who expect to be fathers and mothers some day owe a grave duty to the helpless victims they will bring into the world—the duty to be noble.

It was only after I met Hall Kenyon that you ceased to know me. Because from that moment I was changed. I saw him. That was the end — or, the beginning. I never learned the nursery rule of counting ten before acting; I never reason. Neither can you drive me with a whip. Good or bad, my words, my deeds, must be the result of some impulse which seizes and binds me, and rushes me madly on.

I should have been content enough to love without being loved. I was happy, in a dreamy fashion, just in thinking of him, in looking forward to the time when I should see him again. I did not long for his love at first. It was only after I saw that it was given to another that it became to me the one desire of my being. The fairest things in life are those which belong to others; that is the creed of the egoist and the hungry.

Suddenly, one day, I hated you! There! It is out. I could no more retard my pen from writing it than I could withhold my soul from feeling it in that moment when I saw his eyes look love to you. Constance, Constance, my heart grows faint with the weight of the hatred I held for you. If you had fallen dead as you stood before him it would have been but the consummation of my unspoken imprecation; and if not dead, hurt, maimed, made ugly — in his sight, at least. Do you turn pale? Do you understand my blackness now? God has been good to me in this: in my worst moments I held no weapon. Yet wait. All this was as nothing to what I felt when I, Eleanor Herriott, listened at the door when he offered you the most sacred gift in his keeping. Yes, yes, I listened—let me hurry in the telling. I desecrated the scene, perhaps, but not as I desecrated my own womanhood. Sometimes I think my self-contempt will eat holes into my heart.

That night—are you indulgent now, my angel?—that night I drugged myself to keep my hands from doing that which my passion prompted. Yet they say love ennobles; there is another side for such as I: an epigram is never always true. If there are many like me, there are more assassins out of jail than in. When daylight came I wanted the night again. Thank God for night, Constance. The sun is an ugly searchlight to the heart which knows its guilt. I wandered off; I wished neither to see nor to be seen. I came to the ocean. It is great and wide and cool; it lulls many a fever. But before I reached it I was withheld.

He stood before me on the shore. I am not a fatalist, but sometimes the parallels of consequence run strangely close. He was gaunt, miserable, wretched. That form upon the sands made the world beyond a sickening void. Love has much to answer for: it not only makes humanity miserable, but keeps it from flinging off its misery. And, Constance, he was—mad. He was desiring death. In one frightful second I kept his feet from slipping from the verge. I think he had wandered about, almost insane, the whole preceding night. He was ill—so ill that he scarcely knew me. I held him back. There was but one thing for me to do — to take him home. I decided it in a flash. I saw nothing else, like the photographer who, looking into the camera darkened on all sides, sees nothing but the one spot where all rays converge. He was helpless in my hands, and I — I loved him. I brought him home ; in that wild hour the world held no place for me. He could not deter me, I could not leave him. There was little I could do for him. Once home, he sank into a stupor. I sat and watched him through the night without a movement. When the first signs of waking came to him I caught my breath as though it had been suspended in his sleep. And so you found us.

Do you know how your implication struck into me ? I had been in heaven—a heaven as pure as can be found on earth. You stepped in with a warrant of arrest from the world — from the breeders of scandal. Whether you wronged him then in thought, I do not know ; but *now* you must believe how guiltless he was. You know he was blameless, don't you, Constance ? Whatever wrong was done, I did it. I could have choked you with your words. Did *I* wish to be foisted upon a man for the mere sake of gossip — upon a man whom I loved to the exclusion of all else, and to whom I was—but your sister ? But presently, when he had spoken, I saw something else ! It flashed upon me. Let me be frank. It was not fear of slander which made me acquiesce. It was another phase of love—the selfish, jealous phase. He would be mine, not yours !—in name, at least ! Perhaps—, O hope,

hope, what a Fata Morgana you are! As his wife, he could not slip entirely from me; as his wife, I had a chance of winning him to me. And yet when you left I hated you doubly, because in that moment when you bound him to me he still loved you more than he ever had or would. That was the beginning of the wall which grew about my heart. Because he loved you, he must never know that *I* loved him—I, his wife.

. . . . . .

I think it was a half-hour after you had gone that morning that he came over to me and said, with an attempt at playfulness:

"I am sorry for the *contretemps* which provides you with a *roué* of a husband, Eleanor! But we may as well make the best of a bad job and do it up brown. We may as well go across and have it recorded civilly. It will not put you to any further inconvenience or publicity. What do you say?" He held out his hand. If I had put my arms about his neck I would have been following my bent. But I neither took his hand nor answered.

"It will be best for both of us," he went on. "The ceremony just performed has been binding enough, but as a sop to our consciences it will be well to go through the full conventionality. After that, if you wish, I need no longer annoy you by my presence. But I think we could become good comrades, if nothing more. Are you willing to make the trial?" I cannot explain to you the eagerness of his tone; it was more dauntless than pleading, more stubborn than deferential.

"It can make but little difference," I answered, listlessly, but with feverish pulses.

He looked at me almost triumphantly as he added: "Good. That is brave. Let us put on a happy front. We may even come to deceiving ourselves if successful in deceiving others." After that I understood that he was going to meet the situation—you, to speak by the letter—with a sort of bravado. And I fell in with the scheme, knowing that I was, as I had always been, but the undesired yet inevitable third party, of no consequence to any one but myself. There is little dignity to my love.

At twelve o'clock we came across and went to the Lick. After which he went to the City Hall.

So we are bound. Let me not desecrate the term "marriage" by calling a few meaningless words by that name. He and I now, this minute, are no more married than are two trees which happen to be planted next each other! Marriage means something deeper—it lies in the roots of both; when they reach out to each other, then the trees are wedded, and one cannot tie the knot alone.

When we were again alone he looked at his watch. I have never seen him more business-like.

" What do you say to our going abroad ?" he asked, as if he were asking me to go out to dine with him.

"At once ?" I questioned. My face was burning with excitement.

" Yes."

" I am not prepared."

" You could easily get, this afternoon, all that you would require till we reach New York."

" At what time does the train leave ?"

" At half-past six."

I thought quickly. Then I decided to send for my

trunk. I directed the message to Grace, as you know. I could not regard you as a friend of whom I could ask even this slight favor—you were to me only the love of the man I loved; therefore, my enemy! *You*, dearest! Oh, Constance!

We left that night. A few days later I saw a *Chronicle*, in the society news of which I read: "Hall Kenyon and his bride left hastily last night for New York *en route* for Europe." He passed me the paper himself, and I could feel myself pale as I read. "It reads smoothly," he said.

We paint the landscape with our mood. I could tell you little of what I saw. It was all unreal to me—the flying country, the other passengers, and the man who sat opposite me. The fevered remembrance of what had passed was too much like a sensational play to seem to pertain to my life, though my surroundings were the outcome. At times he would enact the part of cicerone in a kindly, off-hand manner, as an experienced traveller might to a young student who happened to be thrown in with him.

He is not unkind to me, Constance. He is a gentleman, you know, and to one of that caste every woman calls for courtesy and consideration.

Sometimes when he passed through the car I noticed the men and women turn to look after him with admiration. It was a painful ecstasy to know that he was mine—according to the bond.

The evening before we reached New York he told me in a few words about Griff. You remember Severn mentioned the name in one of his letters. "He is a little fellow," Hall said, "who has lived with me for the past two years. He is a cross between my secretary and my conscience. This trip was the only one which has separated us for any length of time, and I don't know how he has weathered the interval. He has had charge of my rooms at the club during my absence. I wonder what you will think of him."

We drove directly to the Savoy. After luncheon he went out to get passage for us on the steamer which sailed the next day.

"You won't be lonesome, will you?" he asked. As I told you, he is very conscientious in his kindness.

"No," I said. "I can look out of the windows or read the newspapers." I had long since made up my mind never to act as a chain or weight to his inclinations.

"I'll send Griff to you," he said, with his hand on the door-knob. "Perhaps, when I return, you will like to do some shopping?" But there was nothing, and he left.

About half an hour later there came a knock at the door. I opened it expectantly.

"I am Griff," said a low voice. I looked down. I asked him to come in. The unreality of my sensations was not lessened as I looked. He is very small, something over four feet, weighted down by a cruel hump. His head is large, and covered with fine, straw-colored hair; his skin is a dull white; his eyes are preposterously large, and of a clear, green hue. His appearance was so unexpected, so gnome-like and ugly, that for a moment I was quite bewildered.

"He did not tell you, then?" he questioned, in a sweet, gentle voice. I started, conscience-stricken. What had

9

my eyes betrayed? He was regarding me with his peculiar, limpid eyes, in which lay the patience of a St.
Francis.

" Will you sit down ?" I asked, and he took a seat
somewhat removed, with an air of reserve which was
quite distinct from humility. And presently we were
chatting in low, peaceful voices ; his own voice is like
the approach of an incense-bearer—it hushes all unseem-
liness.

Once, in a pause, he said, quietly, " If there is ever
anything you should want me to do for you, command
me. My life belongs to you now, as well as to Hall."
He called him " Hall," though the familiarity had a curious intonation—almost such as accompanies the word
" Jesus" on the lips of a devotee.

" Belongs ?" I repeated, uncomprehendingly.

" Yes. You know he saved my life."

My breathless attention drew him on.

" The river, you know. It is Lethe. He drew me from
it. When I revived, before I could reproach him, he
said, ' I promise you a surer happiness than that which
you sought.' He has kept his word. The reproach can
never be uttered. And he did not tell you ?"

I shook my head. The tears choked me. He had
told it so simply, yet with a depth which could not be
fathomed. I stretched out my hand and laid it upon
his—he had had a sympathetic listener.

After a while there came another knock. It was Severn. He carried in his hand a bunch of red roses. He
had just met Hall, he said. He looked at me curiously
while he spoke, asking after you all in turn. Griff had
meanwhile vanished.

"It was a blow straight from the shoulder," he said. "It knocked me out. Why didn't you wire the news? Not very cousinly, Eleanor—to say nothing of Kenyon's remissness."

"We had no time," I answered with dignity.

"I might have sent you a fitting send-off. All I could do was to get you these roses—you used to resemble them. But, confound it! I can't offer them to you now."

"Why not?" I asked, quivering with fear.

"Consult your mirror," he growled.

When Hall came in I made some excuse and went into the next room. Presently I heard their voices somewhat raised.

"What have you done to that girl?" I heard Severn say, in a menacing tone.

"What do you mean?" Hall responded, with a mixture of surprise and haughtiness.

"I mean," retorted Severn, "that when last I knew her she was a charming, high-spirited young girl. She is now, after a week's marriage, a sad-faced woman, whose light-heartedness seems to have vanished with her maidenhood. I warn you, Kenyon, that you have to do with a high-bred animal. She is Philistine to the backbone. You cannot break her at once into Bohemianism."

There was a pause, during which I felt a bitter smile creep over my lips at Severn's ignorance of all details.

Finally Hall spoke. His voice was cold and restrained.

"I cannot understand," he said, thoughtfully, "by what right you presume to call me to account. Let me beg you to remember that I want no interference between me and my wife."

"Pardon my bluntness," returned Severn, in a queer

tone. "I forgot the change in our relationship which your benedictine state has wrought."

"My dear Scott," laughed Hall, in easy affectation, "you must remember that a man's *amour-propre* resents the insinuation that he has been derelict in his attentions to his wife of a week. Your growl really was indelicate."

"Oh, to the devil with your evasions," was the snapping rejoinder. "I hate palaver between friends. But I understand that perfect frankness is incompatible with a married man—there's a woman behind the screen. I respect your resentment, but for Heaven's sake, Kenyon, bring the laugh back to that girl's eyes! You can do it if ever man could."

A moment later the door was banged to. I regretted that I had no rouge-pot; it is a gay mediator between the resentful pride of a man and his wife when her pallor might bespeak his cruelty or neglect.

He came in shortly after, and I could see by his drawn brows that he was extremely irritated. It is not his way to dissemble.

"Are you very unhappy, Eleanor?" he demanded, with a peremptoriness which may have been meant for consideration of my welfare, but which held no trace of tenderness. He eyed me sternly. Probably for the first time since our marriage my appearance meant something to him. If I had not had myself under guard I would have blushed with trepidation. As it was I answered, flippantly:

"Happiness is relative. Once, when I was a young girl, I was reading Balzac's *Lily of the Valley*, and crying over it as though my heart were breaking. My sister Edith asked me why I read a book which could make me so sad. I answered that I was having a splendid time."

He looked at me as if he did not quite comprehend.

"I am not clever enough to catch the analogy," he returned, with a shrug, as if my words had come from a silly school-girl. "But if there is anything you wish or that I can do for you, I wish you would tell me. We may as well be frank with each other. You will, of course, have to put up with my society to some extent, more as a matter of prudence than of choice—on your part. I have endeavored not to bore you unnecessarily. But if there is anything I can do to make you more comfortable, don't hesitate to tell me. Else where's our pact of *bon camaraderie?*" He took both my hands with a pale smile of persuasion; he was nerving himself to his duty. At that moment my poverty almost made me turn sick. Never had he seemed more cold and distant than when he stood so close and held my hands.

"What are the considerations of the pact?" I asked, nonchalantly, as I withdrew my hands and he seated himself astride a chair. "We have not made them clear, I think. Better let me know to what I have bound myself before I put the ocean between myself and a chance of retraction. There might be some impossibilities among them for me."

"I don't think I shall exact impossibilities," he responded. "But it would make your enforced position more congenial, I think, if you would try to regard me as a brother. Do you think you could?"

"I do not know what the relationship entails. I never had a brother."

"Nor I a sister. But I can readily imagine that all it

requires is perfect frankness, friendly confidence, favors asked and given as a matter of course, and all done with a spirit of toleration and good-will. Do you think you could manage it?"

"It may be worth trying."

"I think so. Neither of us is blind to the fact that the great sentiment did not make the tie; and neither of us expects the extravagances of the feeling. We can get along in a practical, pleasant fashion, I believe, if we trust each other. I know that I have no right to ask, but I hope no former attachment is making this life bitter for you. I can thoroughly appreciate its strain upon your whole being, but without the past to hold you I think you will not find the present formidable."

"And you?" I asked. "How are you going to meet it?"

"With you," he said, with a courteous inclination and a smile from the lips. "And now let me explain my standing to you. I am not a rich man, but my income will easily provide our creature comforts in a civilized way. It is somewhere between six and seven hundred a month without that which comes in from my work. Not a princely fortune, but an assured one. So start in, Eleanor, and make out a list of wants."

"There is nothing," I replied, feeling hot and uncomfortable.

"That is not fair," he said, earnestly. "Why, Eleanor, just forget what is past, and come down to an easy-going, common-sensible view of the present. Are you not my wife? There, don't look so defiant. Perhaps I can find another way to make you get what you want."

I found a packet of money on my table that evening.

But I cannot take his money. I want Geoffrey to send my allowance regularly to our London address.

Griff was waiting for us on board. He is always with us. At sight of the stunted little figure and ugly, peaceful face a feeling of calm possessed me, and not only calm, but comfort and respectability ; do you know what I mean ? It was as if his presence made my position less false, as if a chaperon had been provided, and all was more proper and as it should be. In my cabin was a huge bunch of chrysanthemums and some dainties which Severn had sent. There were many comforts in the way of cushions and rugs which made me very uncomfortable, a feeling with which I am battling and bravely trying to overcome.

Griff seems always near me. I do not know whether the charge was self-appointed or whether Hall suggested it. I only know that with him within reach I could go to sleep as fearlessly on deck as in the privacy of my own cabin. Yet he is a man scarcely older than I. There are souls so pure that they clarify the air about them, and keep those within their reach out of all harm. Hall has been busy with some writing which he prefers doing below ; the sea, he says, distracts him. Still, I ought not to be lonesome, if to be surrounded by friendly-inclined people is to be accounted an antidote. There are some charming English people, a handsome girl and her brother, who seem to have formed an agreement with each other that I am never to be left alone. The girl told me that she took my "husband" to be a brother; she thought there was a striking resemblance between us. "But, then," she added, naïvely, "husbands and wives often grow to look alike ; sitting opposite each other so often makes them adopt each other's facial expressions, just as people often in converse assimilate each other's opinions." There is a young medical student *en route* for Germany, an attaché of the French legation, and a widow with two daughters about Grace's and Edith's age. When I look at them I say to myself, "Grace," or "Edith." I never knew before what pretty names they are.

We were approached, as we stepped on board, by a Mr. Talford. He is a distinguished-looking man of about forty, a member of Hall's club, to whom I was introduced. I did not like him at the first glance; I think his regard would bring a blush of resentment to the face of any woman. He is a brilliant talker, in a satirical, sceptical way—has rather courtly manners. I always turned to look for Griff when he drew near. He has kept his distance, however, for the last few days. The English girl had just gone below one morning and I had reopened my Shelley, when this Talford made his way over to me, and sat down in the chair she had just vacated. I glanced around for Griff; he was not in sight. He had possibly gone in to do some copying for Hall. I assumed the defensive at once.

"Shelley?" he said, taking the book from me. "Will you allow me to divine the bit that has charmed you most of late?"

"You are not a mind-reader, I hope," I said as pleasantly as I could, looking beyond him to the water.

"Only sympathetic," he replied in a low voice, as he turned the pages. I could feel my heart flutter ominously, but I thought it best not to answer. Presently he was reading, in a gentle, significant tone. You know the lines, perhaps:

"I can give not what men call love;
But wilt thou accept not
The worship that hearts lift above
And the heavens reject not:
The desire of the moth for the star,
Of the night for the morrow,
The devotion to something afar
From the sphere of our sorrow?"

I had turned my face as far from his view as possible.

"There comes a void, a desire like that to every one once in a lifetime," he went on, easily. "The humility does not last long, however. It is only distance, the unknown, which exalts the vision. The nearer we get to the stars we lose the sparkle in viewing the component parts which made the glow. Knowledge is disappointing."

"Not if you are clever enough to catch the comical side," I murmured.

"The bathos of pathos, do you mean? It's the one side I see. But I believe it has entirely escaped you. After the manner of women, you conceive the melodrama of life to be a serious tragedy, over which you find it impossible to smile. And yet that, too, will pass."

"What?" I asked, staring stonily at him.

"Your disappointment. Women — young women — expect too much; they are grieved when their imagination does not materialize, and they either enjoy the unhappiness or consider it frivolous to relieve themselves. Let me tell you, Mrs. Kenyon, when a man finds himself neglected in one quarter he will set about to find the means to fill in the chink. And though you must remember that art is a jealous mistress, I think it is ex-

cusable and philosophical if one were to seek some—
diversion for one's self."

"When I *am* seeking diversion," I said, slowly, "I'll
call upon you for a plan, Mr. Talford. But at present
I do not need your assistance."

He laughed lightly and leaned forward. "Is that
meant for a dismissal?" he said. "Don't be rash. One
suddenly needs a knight sometimes."

It was too much! I could feel myself turning white.
At that moment Hall's head appeared above the com-
panion-way. With a gravely ironical bow Talford turned
away. Hall, catching sight of me, came across. He
looked at me curiously, and interposed his figure between me and the passengers moving about.

"What is it, Eleanor?" he asked. "Are you ill?"

"No," I managed to answer; "I have been insulted,
that's all."

His face turned red.

"Talford?" he questioned. I pressed my lips hard.
I was shaking miserably.

"What did he say, Eleanor?"

"Oh, it was nothing much, I suppose," I almost
sobbed. "He was only offering his sympathy for—for
my 'being alone.'"

His hand went quickly to my shoulder and rested
there.

"Forgive me," he said, in deep earnestness. "It was
my fault. I brought it upon you. But I'll show the
fellow that he has some one to answer to!"

"No, no," I protested, hastily. "Don't say anything to him. He is not worth noticing—and I am all
right."

Hall's writing has been neglected since then. And still I am sorry he saw. One of my most passionate desires is not to hamper him in any way.

Last night they decided to give a dance. The medical student has musical fingers, and promised to play until we grew tired. Hall excused himself from attending, as he had some letters to write anent our landing to-morrow. The Townshends—the English people—begged me to come in notwithstanding, and I went. The salon looked bright and pretty—everybody seemed gay and happy. At the first chords of the waltz I could scarcely keep the tears from my eyes. When one is unhappy the gayest music is sad. But I danced. I was always accounted a good dancer — my brains in my toes; a good place to keep them in a ball-room. I could feel Talford's eyes upon me from the first. He soon began to annoy me, and finally I slipped out of the doorway. I was feverish and excited. The dancing had affected me like wine.

Without a thought I hurried to Hall's cabin and knocked at the door. He opened it immediately.

"You! That's right; come in," he said, looking surprised as he held the door open. I stepped quickly past him, and he shut the door.

"Grown tired already?" he asked, drawing up the chair for me and seating himself on the bed. He looked pale and weary, and my heart was filled with a yearning tenderness.

"No; but I thought you must be," I answered, wistfully. "Can't you leave your writing for a while and come in and dance? Miss Townshend is so anxious to measure steps with you."

He smiled quietly as he leaned slightly back against the pillow. "Sit down," he said. "I'd rather talk than dance."

I glanced at his writing materials, longing to stay, yet hesitating oddly.

"I finished some time ago," he said. "The music has disturbed me too much." As he spoke the melody changed. The musicians had begun that minuet Grace played the first time I met Hall Kenyon to know him. I started and looked toward him; strangely enough, his smile showed that he remembered, too. The old mood took possession of me. I made him a deep courtesy, laughing as I did so. Once started, I entered into it with my old-time nonsense. By a curious coincidence, I had on the same pale gray gown. As I swayed backward and forward in the narrow space I could feel my hair loosening from the gold comb with which I had loosely gathered it up. Suddenly, just as I neared him, it tumbled about me, and I stopped on the instant, putting up my hand to gather it together.

"Don't," he said, staying me, and reaching out his hand towards it. "What beautiful hair you have!" He was standing close beside me, and I made to draw back; but his hand still held the mass of loosened hair, and at my movement he drew my head to him—and kissed me. It was the first time my husband's lips had touched mine, and I sprang back as though he had offered me an insult. So might he have kissed a Nautch girl—anybody.

"How dare you!" I cried, shrinking against the panels as far as possible from his reach. The flush of admiration still lit his eyes as he answered:

"Ah, Eleanor, you were too beautiful just now! Excuse the impulse on that plea," he demurred.

"Well, don't do it again," I said, not meeting his eyes, and rubbing my lips with my handkerchief, as a child shows its distaste for the same unasked token.

Seeing that I was more than indignant, he added, "I shall try to remember." He handed me my comb deferentially. I knotted up my hair, wished him good-night, and left him.

I was trembling violently when I reached my cabin. I felt so common—so wanton, Constance!

I had *meant* to attract him. But I did not know what I was doing till I had achieved the result. I wished I were home with you, safe in my little white bed. Oh, Constance, angel, why am I not like you? No one would dare make you feel as I felt then. He does not understand, of course. He does not know that I want something higher than mere beauty-homage. We get what we deserve. Help me to deserve something better. I am going to try. I thought it all out last night. I have found a model. Do you mind much, dear? I am going to try to be like you. I am going to lock the door upon my selfish, passionate past, and begin over again. Pray for me.

ELEANOR.

CHAPTER XII

AGAIN I take up my self-centred diary, this egoistic record of a heart which asks for no answer—only for a hearing. My postal-cards and letters have been for all; this is for you and myself alone, for you have become as my confessor.

I jotted all the observations of our travelling in those other communications; in this—to you—I need speak only of the incidents that befell me in these far-away lands, where the surroundings were but shadows to me, where the only reality was the man beside me. It is of these memories, which would have been as dreams but for his presence, of which I tell you.

To-day I have little recollection of the beauties and wonders of museums, galleries, and cathedrals, or even of the great Abbey; small memory of movement from place to place in the London immensity; I only recall an impression of grandeur and strangeness, and always that Hall has walked beside me.

It was afterwards, when we were loitering through the Surrey country and had settled down in a Kentish village, that I began to realize my entity and know that this was my—life! But it was a life so different from the past that I seemed to have gone into another existence —a period of peace as after death, before which all had been delirium. Perhaps I was emotionally weary, for nothing soothed me more than the sound of the children's voices—the two little maids of the kindly English gentlewoman with whom we had taken rooms. One of them has a bird‑voice just like our Nan's; when she talks and I close my eyes, I can see a little American girl with— Do you know, these little ones grew to like me! I did not think I cared much for children, but I am glad I do; their little hands and caresses fill out the hollows of both cheek and heart. I am gladder still that they can love me. Child-love is so true; it is all spontaneity, a spontaneity which is seldom misled; there must be something good in me if children turn to me. But I have never seen a man more passionately fond of children than is Hall; they knew it, and were as happy as he when with him. Those were good days.

Passion is love's vanity. I am endeavoring to drop it; it wants too much and gets too little. I think we both grew gentler in the quiet English country. We had some walks and talks, in which we each showed the other some of self, without the fever and turmoil of emotions. We put our quicker, warmer beings behind us, and met as kindly friends. It was a difficult task at first, Constance, this seeming; but under it I felt myself growing broader and more self-respecting. In the country time lounges, and our pulses beat more slowly in consequence.

But I knew it could not last; I felt him growing restive. One morning I heard him among the trees with the children; they were shouting merrily, and, as his deeper tones reached me, I was glad to feel that I could listen so calmly. Presently I saw him making his way towards me across the sunlit grass, his hat pushed from his brow, his face warmly flushed—such a picture of vigorous man-

hood as one seldom sees in life. He seated himself on
the railing of the porch where I sat in the shadow of the
rose-trellises, and looked at me with a slightly quizzical,
slightly hesitating smile in his eyes.

"Something new in view?" I asked, returning the
smile. I had overcome much of my self-conscious awk-
wardness in his presence, and our conversations had
fewer angles and empty spaces.

He laughed lightly in turn. "Is my face placarded?"
he questioned. "You read me very accurately."

"It is not ambiguous to me," I returned. "You are
contemplating a move."

"Right. I felt rather paralyzed a few minutes ago.
What do you say to Paris? Does the shock upset you?"

I laughed with him. "No. When do you wish to
start—this evening?"

He looked at me with bright satisfaction. "Could
you get ready?"

"Certainly."

"You *are* a good fellow," he cried, bringing his hand
heartily down upon my shoulder. I winced under the
spirit, not the manner, of his approval. "That is where
your congeniality comes in, Eleanor; you don't find it
necessary to protest and be coaxed in order to give your
final agreement more value, as most women do in every
trivial affair. You practise a splendid nerve economy."

"And then it flatters your good judgment. I have
merely learned to hurry noiselessly."

He gave me a quick look, as though reminded of something. "Can I help you with your packing?" he asked.
"You look so leisurely, sitting there on that settee. I
feel as though you needed pushing."

" I have plenty of time ; my belongings are easily put together. It is only yours that are scattered all over the place. You had better begin to gather them up."

" I intend making a holocaust of most of my papers ; Griff is sorting them now. Want to witness the sacrificial flames ?"

I followed him into the little sitting-room, where a small wood-fire was burning. Griff had arranged several piles of MSS. upon the table. Presently he was passing them, one at a time, to Hall, with a word of explanation concerning their material. Most of them the latter tossed carelessly into the fire, watching them burn and blacken, with a comment of indifference or depreciation. Others he hesitated over and consigned to the folding-desk, alleging that he might " work them up " for posterity or—the edification of his library drawer. When near the end Griff passed him a rather bulky package. As Hall took it from him, his face and figure lost their easy complaisance at once.

" That is the story you were engaged upon while in the West," Griff explained, mistaking his silence for confusion of memory.

I looked towards him with a start. He had drawn nearer the fire with the manuscript, and I moved swiftly to his side.

" Is that that novel ?" I asked, in impulsive bravery.

" Yes. What do *you* know about it ?"

" Why, you read the end in my presence ; the beginning was—"

" Yes, yes. It's worth nothing now. It is fit for obliteration. Just move a little, please."

" Wait ! don't !" I exclaimed, grasping his arm. " Put

10

it with the others. You will read it over some day when
you will be able to acknowledge its power."

"Never is far away. Take your hand off, Eleanor."

"No, I shall not. You must not do it!" I cried, with
sudden vehemence, keeping a tight hold on the papers.
"I tell you it is too good to be lost. I recall it perfectly. Some day you will thank me for having saved it."

"You tempt me to rudeness," he said, with restrained
annoyance. "This thing is especially hateful to me. I
don't want to see it again. Loosen your fingers, Eleanor."

"Please give it to *me*," I entreated, in compromise,
steadily meeting his angry eyes. "You shall never be
annoyed by sight of it. But I beg it of you. It is the
first favor I have asked you."

The blood rose curiously to his face, which has never
regained its warm glow; he hesitated a second, and then
let go. "Well, if it will make you happy," he observed,
with cynical weariness, "take it."

I thanked him quietly, and went away with it. There
is an old folk-lore tale of a house which was built from
the pinnacle downward — you know, or can imagine, its
length of endurance. I am doing better—I took for a
foundation a bundle of papers.

A week later we arrived in Paris, travelling, as you
know, down through Normandy and Brittany. As we
approached the city I could feel the delirium of expectation attacking my pulses. After a day here I had left
the long peace of the country and the sweet breath of
the North far behind me.

Paris holds a strange incident for me. I have endeavored to lead up to it gradually. I wanted you to
know that under different circumstances and surround-

ings our characters work out different histories. In Paris life knows few deep pauses. To withdraw into one's self would be to miss part of the spectacle which provides the Parisian with his inexhaustible *esprit*. We caught up with the pace. Hall ran across some old artist and literary friends, and is acquainted with our American Minister ; they all seemed anxious to honor him and his wife. This constant social ferment must be what keeps Paris laughing — aloud ; she is a coquette who ridicules the trace of tears.

I cannot explain how it happened, but we had been here two weeks before we put foot into the Louvre. Ah, Constance, it is such a strange thing that I must relate to you ! I had thought—had hoped— Love, love, you know him better ; you will understand, perhaps, that it could not have been otherwise—for him.

"I am going to satisfy a long-felt curiosity," I told him, as we sauntered on, "in seeing the Lady of Milo. From the casts and photographs I have seen I have never fully appreciated, or even understood, her. She has always been a mystery to me—she seems too grave for love. Heine's ecstasy over the original is incomprehensible to me as yet. But his poem portrays the sublime passion with which she evidently inspired him."

" Which poem ?" he asked, with interest.

"Don't you know it ? I think I can repeat a part of it. In reverting to the last time he looked at her he said : ' Though she looked down on me with compassion, it was compassion without comfort, as though she would say, " Seest thou not that I have no arms, and so cannot give thee help ?" Even with arms a woman may be helpless as—' "

"Yes," he interrupted, roughly, "as a goddess whose feet rest on a pedestal. What was that poem?"

"It is an ode. I recall these lines:

> "'O perfect form of perfect woman, clad
> In that sweet light not born of earth, but drawn
> From those high realms that bend above the gods,
> Whose sun has lent the softest of its light
> To cling forever round this splendid form
> That cares not for our worship, nor the love
> Of pilgrims drawn by unseen links to lay
> Their highest love—highest, since no desire
> Can ever mingle with it—at thy feet!
> Thou wert to me as sunshine to the day,
> The presence by whose side I knelt, and saw
> The shadowy curtains of the land of dreams
> Lift, as a morning mist takes to the hills,
> And thine the voice that, soft as April rain,
> Bade me rise up and enter! . . .
> But thou who standest with no arms to clasp
> Thy worshipper, nor tears to dim the light
> In those pure eyes of thine! how can I say
> Farewell—and pass from thee?'

Would you call it an exaggeration?" I asked, after a pause, as he did not speak.

"No," he answered, shortly. And then abruptly added, as though wishing to forget the subject, "You interpret poetry as you sing—intensely. Your voice grew as deeply sad over those closing lines as though you had felt such a farewell."

"Oh," I laughed, easily, "haven't you suspected that I was meant for an actress?" He looked at me curiously as we passed in.

When we stood before her in the long gallery I felt a

singular awe. I do not know how long I remained there in silent contemplation. But I know now the meaning of her majesty; she is Love that is sure of itself, thoughtful without passion — deathless! Not that little Love which desires return, but that greater Love which is self-sufficing.

I was about to turn to him when something, a flickering sunbeam upon the sculptured hair, arrested me. I felt a surprised start of recognition. In a moment the cold, still woman was no longer a chiselled idea. Constance, it was *you!*

I cannot explain the resemblance. It is less in form and feature than in the soul pervading it; but it is there unquestionably. Quickly the thought flashed through me, "Has *he* seen?" Was the statue to him the embodiment of his lost love? Ah, the old, overwhelming jealousy had seized me!

I turned to look at him. He was gone! Then he *had* felt it! *You* had come before him! He had not wished me to see its effect upon him. I walked from sculpture to sculpture, standing still before each, but seeing nothing. An eager voice accosted me. Helen Glynn came up with beaming eyes; she is studying in X——'s studio, you know. She had been sketching, and had just caught sight of me. I wonder what she thought of my abstraction. But her attendant soon came along, and she left, promising to visit me.

I looked around for Hall. He was not in sight. I felt cold and uncomfortable in the strange crowd. Perhaps an hour later I saw Griff making his way toward me.

"We have become separated," I explained to him, almost with a cry of relief. "Did you see Hall as you came along?"

"Yes, Mrs. Kenyon. Shall we go home now?"

"Why, no; I must wait," I said, regarding him with wonder. "He — Hall will be looking for me, of course!"

"No," returned the boy, earnestly; "he will not look for you. I met him on the street a half-hour ago. I stopped him. He told me not to deter him. He said he had been called hastily away. He did not look well, by-the-bye."

I stood still, understanding but imperfectly. My pallor did not escape Griff.

"Do not be frightened, Mrs. Kenyon," he said, with a reassuring smile. "I have known him to run away like this before. It was once when greatly disturbed over the return of a manuscript. It is a mood, a whim, which he allows as a sort of hair-shirt to moderate strong pain. It's part of his temperament. I don't know what has disturbed him to-day, but he'll turn up all right soon. Shall we move on?"

His words gave me some assurance, and I went out with him. He is like a great silent watch-dog. We reached home, but Hall was not there, nor did he come. Think, Constance! Days succeeded days, and yet he did not come! The days grew to weeks. Griff told me to be calm, not to be frightened, or I should have been crazed. In fact, I think I was very quiet and gentle in my bewilderment and fear. Perhaps I caught a little of Griff's patience. Griff and I are very sympathetic, and, alike, we make little noise, and sit or move out together in perfect understanding and unison.

Yet I received no word from Hall. I did not expect
it. Griff gave me a hint—kindly, reassuringly. Such a
flight is only one of those sharp peculiarities, untrained
idiosyncrasies, which Hall's solitary, independent life of
leisure has had no domination to uproot. I shall grow
used to them, perhaps, as Griff has; they are weaknesses,
not vices, Constance. As such they do not make me
love him less. "I tell you, absolutely, he will turn up,
and that all right, soon," Griff had said, and I clung to
his words as to an oracle.

And then, one day, as I sat with a bit of sewing in my
hand, Hall came home! Will you understand how I have
changed when I say that I did not start, that I could
even look up with a quiet smile into his face? It was
worn but calm.

"Good-afternoon," I said, with a nod, continuing my
sewing.

He came and stood by my side, silent for a moment.
He struggled to say something. "Eleanor," he murmured, and his hand touched mine. I did not repulse it.
Several seconds passed before he went on in a self-
angered tone. "I've been a brute," he said. "I can't
ask you to forgive me! And—and—I can't explain myself."

"Then don't try," I returned, hastily, looking up. "It's
all right!"

He looked at me as though scarcely understanding
me. "I forgot everything. I forgot—that afternoon!"
he went on, as if goaded to explain. "I left you like a
madman!"

"No," I remonstrated; "you had not grown used to a
wife's presence, that was all."

" It can never happen again," he said. " I lived alone too long, Eleanor. I have never had to account to any one for my actions. I am egoist to the bone. Heaven help you, my poor girl, with such a protector !"

I laughed softly and shook my head. He sat down wearily. I continued my sewing. The restrained excitement had made my cheeks burn and my hands feverish. I could feel his eyes intently resting on me for a long, silent time.

" I have never seen you sew before," he said, presently, leaning back with half-closed eyes.

" I sometimes do," I returned, without looking up.

" It is womanly work, and—pretty. What is it you are working over so industriously ?"

My heart began to flutter rapidly. His voice, so long unheard, possessed a gentle inflection which was almost yearning in its weariness. I felt myself flush as I looked up with a shy laugh. " Guess," I said. " It is dreadfully prosaic."

" Is it ? It looks like—a stocking."

" I am darning. Over and under, and in and out, like life—half on top and half underneath ; but patience will fill out a perfect whole. What an execrable pun !"

He came to my side and looked down with odd interest. " Let me see it closer. Why, this is a sock ! Mine ?" he asked, flushing.

" I had nothing else to do, and I thought you would not mind the bit of interference."

He put it back into my hand without a word. It seems a foolish thing to relate to you, but I am merely telling you the records of my heart—not of my memory—and they are sometimes very trivial to a second person. I know he exaggerated the commonplace Joanesque domesticity out of all proportion. He has never had any one to do for him, and he is unusually susceptible to the smallest mark of interest.

After dining that night we went to the *comédie*. Just before we left he knocked at my door.

"May I come in?" he asked, as I held it open; and he walked into the room. "Will you wear these violets tonight, Eleanor? It is my favorite flower, and they will become you."

Perhaps they were only a peace-offering, but I almost cried out with pleasure. They were such a handful of fragrance and joy for me.

"They remind me of home," I said, unsteadily, while he watched me tuck them into my corsage.

The next day he asked me whether I cared to go down to Italy. "We can make our home in Rome for the winter," he said. "I think you would enjoy it."

He said "home;" it had a beautiful sound. I shall write to you from there.

ELEANOR.

CHAPTER XIII

New York, *March* —, 18—.

Not Rome, you see, dear Constance. I promised to write next from there; but the best plans are only promises which circumstances must sometimes break for us. The one short letter I dropped you all before quitting Venice would have answered for every one of our loitering stoppages on the way to the City of Memories. I can hear Grace complaining of the meagreness of description it contained, but tell her— I was just about to anticipate something. I must proceed more quietly. Do you remember, Constance, how we used to laugh over the honeymoon descriptions some of our girl-brides used to give ? " Perfect !" " Glorious !" " Utterly indescribable !" They never could go any further in their naïve admission. Ask Grace to be as lenient to my discrepancy as we used to be to theirs.

We had been only a week in Rome when Hall received news of Severn's illness. It seemed to draw him up sharply. He grew grave, almost taciturn, on the instant, and I could feel the disturbance it occasioned him, for the mood did not wear off. He was quiet, abstracted, and slightly nervous all through that day, and the next he admitted his concern.

" I think I shall send Griff on to him," he said, pausing in his march up and down the room in the evening. " He will at least then have some one other than paid attendants beside him. Eleanor ?"

" Yes?"

He glanced at me swiftly, bit his lip, and turned abruptly away. "No, nothing," he returned, shortly, continuing his walk.

"Did you — you want to go yourself, Hall?" I asked, throwing my book aside and looking at him expectantly.

He flushed; but you know his candor. "I suppose it is another of my idiotic ideas," he confessed; "but you have guessed it, Eleanor. However, I have no intention of gratifying it."

"Why not?"

"We are settled here for the winter."

"But we are not—married to the place, as nurse used to say."

"That is true," he answered, with a smile. "But, though we are married to each other, I have no desire to make your life a series of jumps."

I laughed merrily. "You could leave me," I suggested, after a pause.

He stood still, and turned upon me quickly. "Do you mean that?" he demanded, quite as quietly as I had spoken. He seated himself upon the window-sill near which he stood. He was perfectly still as he awaited my answer.

"Why, yes," I answered, somewhat uncertainly, though I could go no further in my equivocation.

"Oh!" That was all the comment vouchsafed. He looked straight ahead for several seconds before he added, simply, "You know I would not go without you."

"Then we could go together," I returned, lightly. "After all, you know Severn is my cousin."

"Don't give in to me so easily, Eleanor," he enjoined, seriously, as he met my eyes.

"In the struggle for existence, sir," I replied, "the weaker always goes to the wall."

"Am I such a brutal tyrant?"

"Unconsciously — yes," I laughed. "However, in this instance my will does not suffer complete extinction. New York is—"

"Well?" he urged.

"I have quite finished."

"No; what were you going to say? 'New York is'— what?"

But I had no intention of completing my impetuous sentence, and our eyes flashed as they met; but he let the question go. Two days later, as we cabled you, we left for New York.

And here we have been domiciled in New York with Severn, in this beautiful apartment-house, for the past three weeks. Poor fellow! He could scarcely understand that we intended staying with him till he has fully recovered. He pooh-poohed the idea as vigorously as he could in his weakened state, but with a sort of sneaking pleasure over our obduracy.

I immediately assumed the position of commander-in-chief in the sick-room, and it was pitiful to see how much he made of the fact that one of his own—and a woman, at that—was caring for him. "Nurse Eleanor" he and Hall dubbed me at once; whereupon I twisted a lace handkerchief, cap-fashion, upon my head, to be in character, and they have pronounced it vastly becoming. Hall attends to Severn's important affairs and keeps him in the best of spirits, while I am "seeing to things," I tell

him, with an air of mock importance. The pleurisy was
very sharp, and his complete recovery will be slow. He
gets quite impatient at times—men have not our sex's
inherent submission in physical trials.

While Hall is out I read or talk to Severn. We have
had some beautiful hours. We had been here but a few
days when I received a box of jacqueminot roses one
morning with Severn's card. I was expostulating with
him over the pretty extravagance when we were alone
together later in the day.

"I know you like Kenyon's violets best," he said, putting his hand over mine, as it rested on the sheet beside
him, "but I wanted to condone a former rudeness of
mine. You have grown to look like your rose-cousins
again, little girl, and I wanted you to know how glad
I am."

I was perceptibly startled as the purport of his words
occurred to me, for the blood rushed violently over my
face; but afterwards we had, or, rather, he had, a long
talk about Hall.

He told me many little tales of his independent boy-
hood and adolescence, throughout which he had never
had to account for the gravest indiscretions to any authority closer than his tutors or the college faculty ; of
his recklessness and Bohemian tendencies when he came
into manhood; all of which, added to the charm of his
person and intellect, had provided him an easy entrance
to a brilliant circle of literary and artistic men of the
world. It had spoiled him with adulation almost irresistibly from the first. I knew he was offering the loving critique of his peculiar friend as an apology for
much from which he supposed I had suffered, and I

thanked him—with a look—for his tenderness when he had finished. I feel that he knows us both pretty well, and he wants to ward off all clashing; but I think he realizes that I am not the Eleanor of the past, for he has ceased to quiz me as he used.

Last night—dear Constance, if the writing is illegible you will forgive me, I know, when you reach the end— last night we were all three together. We were very merry, and, to speak truly, Hall and Severn soon became so hilarious that my head began to throb with the un- usual excitement, and I finally grew altogether silent, con- tenting myself with smiling, with half-closed eyes, over their anecdotes and reminiscences.

Hall quickly noticed my silence, and stopped abruptly in a tale he was telling of some preposterous wager. "What is wrong, Eleanor?" he asked, hastily.

"I have a slight headache," I answered. "I think I shall go to bed."

"We were too noisy," said Severn, with compunction. "You do look sort of drooping, lady-rose. Can't we do something for you?"

"No," I smiled, rising wearily. "I shall make myself a cup of tea and sleep the ache away."

I came over to shake up his pillows, and as I bent over him he drew my face down to his.

"Kiss all around, Eleanor, as Constance says!" he laughed, in his big-brotherly fashion, holding my face be- tween his hands. "I wish my kiss could conjure off the pain for you; but perhaps Hall's can."

"Silly fellow!" I returned. "Let me go; tea and quiet are all I need."

"How do you like that, Kenyon?" he questioned;

but I did not hear Kenyon's answer as I closed the door.

I lit the spirit-lamp under my urn, and, while waiting for the water to boil, settled myself on the divan with a copy of Hall's first book. Have you ever seen it?—that book of sketches, I mean. Most of them appeared in the magazines, but two of them are new; you will detect them at once. They are powerful, I think—written with a clear, steady pen. He calls a spade a spade with an almost brutal frankness in places, but he has adopted a style which admits of few trimmings.

I had just grown interested, for the third time, in the one called "Shadows," when he came in. He insisted upon making the tea, and carrying a cup in to Severn; but he returned immediately, and we were soon drinking our own together, as we had done once or twice before in our nomadic hotel life. I love to watch him when he is in that quiet mood, the thoughtful, musing look upon his face evidencing his contentment of mind.

Quite unexpectedly he looked across at me and said, "What does that far-away look in your eyes mean, Eleanor?"—we had been very quiet. "I have noticed it several times in the past two weeks. It's a remarkably hungry look. Anything wanting?"

"Oh no!" I faltered; and, being in a somewhat unstrung state, the tears crowded to my eyes. I buried my face in the cushion, not, however, quickly enough to escape his observation. The unprecedented sight shocked him curiously. I tried to control myself, but could not; and I cried silently for several minutes with my head in the silken pillow. He made no sound or movement, but when I at last turned my head I saw that he was quite pale.

"I—I was only silly," I stammered, sitting up. "Forgive me."

"Have I hurt you in any way?" he asked, bluntly.

"No, no," I protested, hastily, drying my eyes. "Don't you know that a woman often gets hysterical for no definite reason?"

"And you are sure you are quite well but for this headache?" he returned, still unconvinced.

I laughed, though somewhat unsteadily. "Of course. It really was nothing."

"You can't evade me now, Eleanor. There is something haunting you. Out with it!"

But I shook my head.

"Then I'll guess," he ventured, playfully.

"You can't," I said, swiftly, with a burning face. Then, because the anxious regard of his beloved countenance drew me closer to his confidence, I added, "It was all Severn's doing."

"Severn!"

"Yes; he—he is so lov—he reminds me so much of the children—and Constance." I tried to keep my voice brave and steady, but it was altogether impossible.

"Ah, you are homesick."

"No, no," I pleaded, pained by the pain in his voice as he so quickly grasped my trouble.

"But you are. After all, it is not to be wondered at. This hop-skip-and-a-jump existence is not exactly what you have been trained for. What have you been considering, Eleanor?"

"Only dreaming," I murmured, carried away by my wistful heart and his insistence. My eyes were on the tip of my shoe as I drove it in and out the deep pile of the carpet.

"Dreaming of what?" he pressed, with gentle indulgence.

"I have been dreaming—dreaming of a home," I returned, abstractedly.

"Yes, dear?"

"It was a visionary one."

"Perhaps not. Go on. I have an idea you could make a very charming home, Eleanor."

"Have you, indeed?" I asked, with some excitement. "Shall I give you a design?"

"Proceed, architect," he returned, half banteringly, as though humoring me in a whim; half earnestly, as though with serious purpose.

"Well, this is one," I said, slowly, leaning back and clasping my hands over my head, as I do when I let myself day-dream. "It is not a large house, but a broad and sunny one. I should want each room to be beautiful and individual, as though the furnishings were the evolution of some particular motive, graceful or quaint, rich or simple; but each warm and welcoming, like faces that bring peace or comfort at a glance. I should want your study to be full of solid manliness and ease, where you could write without disturbance. Of course, we should entertain somewhat, because friction is broadening and brightening. I think — yes, I think I should make a feature of some 'perfect little dinners,' to which we should have your brightest, most captivating, and congenial friends—not more than two or three at a time, because I should want to 'make economies,' as that little French lady said; and after dinner we can always have

11

some music." I had been speaking excitedly, but I noticed the glow which had slowly mounted to his temples.

"Go on romancing, Eleanor," he said, as I paused to take breath. "It sounds very alluring."

"That is all," I said, with sudden shyness—I had forgotten myself entirely.

"Well, let's go home, as the children say when they feel tired, and go to—such a home."

"To-night, sir?"

"No, madam," he bowed. "In a week or two, when Scott is quite well. Griff can stay and go with him to the mountains."

"Why, I was only jesting," I objected, stunned by his calm decision. "It was only an idle dream."

"Was it? Would you not like it to materialize?"

I gazed at him uncomprehendingly. I could not answer.

"*I* should," he continued, with a grave smile over my bewilderment. "Perhaps the fact that, heretofore, no business or—family ties have ever bound me to a place, or recalled me with a trace of necessity or desire, has engendered this roving spirit in me. But it is different now. Why should we be forever on the wing? I am tired of it, too! The idea of going home to roost for good and all is at last pleasant to me. Growing old and less adventurous, Eleanor! But I—I should like to build such a nest, where we can always find each other. It is good. Where shall it be?" He spoke with singular resolution.

"Could it be in—San Francisco?" I almost whispered, in my intense amazement and happiness.

"Certainly. Why not?"

I strangled a sob before I answered. "Then—I want to ask you something more—may I write and ask—Constance to find us a house—to have it ready to step into—all but the touches which we shall bring and give to it ourselves?"

"Constance? Yes, *she* will know," he answered, quietly and very gently. "Write to her, and tell her just what you want."

Something sang in my heart all night, and early, early this morning—for he would not let me last night—I got up to write to you. Oh, Constance, we are coming home! It is ringing in my ears like marriage-bells—coming home! coming home! So find us a house, love, not large, but cosey, with a pretty hall; a pretty entrance is like a happy promise. And remember, Griff will come later—Griff, who will adore you, Constance. And then furnish it. See, I do not even ask, "Will you?" We come to our mothers unquestioningly. As for the rest? Oh, you will know—did not Hall say so? Buy as for yourself. Engage the maids; let all be ready to receive us on the day when we shall send you word! And then, angel, on the day after our return, when you and I are sitting quietly together, holding each other's hands, I shall have much to tell you!

Constance, Constance! will you be glad to see your selfish, troublesome child again? Pretend you will be! Pretend you love me—because I love you so much. And, Constance—I am coming home, coming home! Dear, I cannot see, I am crying so. . . .

ELEANOR KENYON.

CHAPTER XIV

THE stuffy Oakland local sped eastward. At every whistle a little girl with a piquant, freckled face would spring to her feet and exclaim, excitedly, " Here we are, Grace ! Do get up now."

" Sit down, Marjorie," finally came the pleasant voice from the gentle-faced girl beside her ; " we won't be there for fully five minutes yet."

" Do you think you'll know her, Grace ?"

" Of course, child. It isn't two years since she left."

" But she won't know me ; I've grown so .big since. Grace, you are terribly excited, too ; you are holding my hand so tight that you hurt."

" Because I am afraid you'll fidget yourself out of the door. Let me pull your hat straight. Do you want to look like a little Western hoyden before your distinguished brother-in-law ?"

" What shall I call *him ?*" asked the child, sitting still while Grace retied the white silk ribbons under her chin and pulled a few curls into view.

" Why, Hall, of course ! Now one more station." The flush rose steadily over her face, and her hold on Marjorie's hand tightened. Before the cry of " Sixteenth Street!" had fairly left the conductor's lips they had moved quietly and swiftly to the door.

The " Overland" whizzed into view a few minutes later. As the long train passed, Grace caught a glimpse of a tall form and memorable face on one of the platforms, and, grasping Marjorie's hand, hurried with her toward the car.

Her foot had just touched the step when she felt a hand upon hers, and she looked up into Kenyon's face.

"Grace!" he said, in low-voiced greeting, lifting the child to his side and keeping his arm about her while he shook Grace's hand in silence. "This is kind of you," he added, after a second, his eyes resting with steady friendliness upon her girlish face. "You will find Eleanor inside. I'll come in presently with Marjorie." He nodded toward the door, and Grace moved on.

In some bewilderment she passed with several others down the aisle, scarcely scanning the faces of the passengers, conscious that the one she sought would stand out before all others.

"Grace!"

She stood still. The low, sweet call was unexpected. Standing before her was a woman—one with a soft radiance upon her beautiful face! Grace caught her breath.

"Eleanor!" she breathed, as the slender, gloved hand drew her into the drawing-room. For a moment she felt a lingering kiss upon her lips. Then she found herself seated close beside her, the strangely lovely eyes devouring her in painful ecstasy.

"You have grown to be such a pretty girl!" spoke the changed, slow voice, so deeply happy that it trembled on the verge of sorrow.

The tears rose unaccountably to Grace's eyes. She was unprepared for the change and thoroughly unnerved; she could not speak.

"Are you all alone?" asked Eleanor then.

"Marjorie is outside with your—with Hall," she answered, conquering her emotion. "Edith, you know, is at Vassar—"

"Yes, we saw her there. She is a very happy student. But it seems queer to see you without your chum."

"My demon, you mean—yes, that will be the greatest change of all to you. But Constance thought it best to let her have her way; she thought it a very excellent way—for Edith. Constance was so sorry she couldn't come. The mornings are still too cold for Nan, and Constance seldom leaves her now."

"Then we shall go to them at once."

"No; they are coming to your house directly after luncheon. Nan is so excited that Constance said she would try to make her sleep this morning. She knows every corner of your house by heart, though she has never been in it."

Kenyon came in with the child at that moment. "There is your new sister, Marjorie," he said, lifting her into Eleanor's arms, where she stayed until they reached the slip.

About an hour later Grace came in upon Constance. The latter had turned from the window where she had been stationed for the last quarter of an hour, and regarded Grace in questioning anticipation.

"I did not know her, Constance," she replied, as though still spellbound. "She is simply the most beautiful woman I shall ever see. She is so changed, too! I can't describe her to you. There is a spiritual radiance upon her face which makes it more like a

dream-face than a human being's. She seems to have
struggled out of a conflict into an unfamiliar peace.
She is the same—yet so new. And then her voice—it
is like the murmur of quiet waters. But the change is
wider than on the surface. She is slower in every way.
When we reached the mole she saw that every one was
carefully out before she gave her hand to her husband to
be helped down. You remember how Eleanor used to
jump from a car or a train, and leave others to straggle
after her as best they could. I did not know her; she
is no longer Eleanor Herriott — she is Hall Kenyon's
wife. She has been *tamed*—yes, that is it. Yet why
should it make me sad, Constance?"

"You are excited, Grace. It is only the great happiness of her home-coming which makes her look like that,
and brings these extravagant phrases from you."

"No; you will feel it fully when you see her! I noticed people on the ferry turning to look at her. No
wonder; if I were a man I should fall hopelessly in love
at the first glance at such a face."

"She has her husband for that, dear," she said, gently stemming her romantic dreamer. "Has—*he* changed
much?"

"He has grown older. He has the same striking physique, but his face has lost its glow; so has his whole
personality. There is an air of imperturbability about
him now which makes me wonder what is going on behind his brow. Oh, they looked *so* handsome as they
stood together on the steps of their house! Eleanor
nodding—Hall with his hat raised as we drove off."

For the two home-comers had mounted the steps of
their new home quite alone. Kenyon put into the lock

the key Grace had given him, and threw open the door to Eleanor. "Walk into your own, my lady," he said.

Eleanor stepped in past him. A bright fire was burning in the open grate of the quaint redwood-encased hall, and as the friendly warmth of the blaze burst upon her, she turned hastily back to him.

"Well?" he asked, with a little laugh, throwing his hat and overcoat upon a chair.

"It looks so beautiful," she faltered.

He laughed again, and took her hand in his. They walked from room to room, saying little, but each feeling the experienced, womanly knowledge which had given to the house the atmosphere of a refined home. They came, presently, into the shining, tiled kitchen, full of savory odors of good cheer, where a plump, rosy-cheeked German girl stood smiling and courtesying.

"You are Gretchen, aren't you?" said Eleanor, coming farther into the room, leaving Kenyon standing in the doorway. The girl stammered something in answer, and looked from one to the other in unreserved admiration.

"I hope you will like it here," continued her mistress's sweet voice, "and that we shall get along nicely together."

"I hope you like me!" exclaimed Gretchen, with unrestrained bucolic fervor, impulsively disregarding grammatical time.

Kenyon, with an eye to effects, noted the picture before him: Gretchen, in bright blue calico gown, flaxen-haired and blue-eyed, gazing with humble wistfulness at the beautiful woman in her simple dark travelling-dress; behind them the glowing cooking-range, with its great red eye and steaming pots.

" You will get along capitally," he said, heartily ; and after turning to say a word to the little French maid, they went on up-stairs, but came down again shortly after, and moved into the dining-room, with its table prettily laid for two.

" You should say grace, Hall," suggested Eleanor, glancing with a shy smile towards him, as they seated themselves at either end.

" Your face supplies that," he said. " My lips are overpowered in moments of joy." Eleanor caught a swift, unfathomable look from him. The luncheon passed merrily, Kenyon assuming the honors with exaggerated ease.

" I must go down to the Custom-house directly," he said, just before they arose, and he lit his cigar, at Eleanor's suggestion—she was never averse to the smoke of a good cigar. " There are three cases, I believe, with our effects of travel."

" Yes, *and* the trunks," she supplemented, following him into the hall. " Will you send that long, low one up at once, please ? I want it particularly this afternoon."

" Want it particularly ?" he repeated, as he stooped slightly to allow her to assist him with his overcoat. " Have you found a particular want ? It will be a novelty to gratify one for you." He was looking down at her with a smile that seemed to come from a great height. The smile was quickly succeeded by a faint frown, and he put his hand under her chin and raised her face.

" You are tired," he asserted. " Your eyes have great shadows about them. Lie down and rest for a while."

"I am not tired," she returned, flushing, and drawing from his touch. "It is something quite different. Hall"—her breath seemed entangled before she could continue—"Constance will be here presently."

"That is good to hear." Their eyes met steadily.

"Then—I want you to come home and have tea with us. Will you?"

"I shall surely come," he replied, as he stooped and lightly kissed her wistful eyes. "God bless our home, dear," he murmured, earnestly. And as he picked up his hat and gloves, he added, with a curious, abrupt laugh, "Do you know, Eleanor, that you have never kissed me?"

She took a step forward, but as swiftly drew back before she reached him. "Wait till to-night," she promised, in low indistinctness.

"That's a long way off," he returned, with an irritated laugh. "Many hours between now and then! Better—Well, never mind! I must be off."

When the door had closed behind him she moved up to her pretty violet-hung bedroom. There she quickly made her toilet, gathering her hair anew into the great coil at the nape of her neck, and changing her travelling-dress for a pale heliotrope gown which she had brought with her in her bag. Then she wandered down into the drawing-room.

"It is a graceful room," she thought, moving noiselessly about. "No one but Constance could have arranged it. I shall not move a chair to-day. I suppose it will take the kink of my taste soon enough. But to-day—"

The sound of rolling wheels came to a stand-still before the house. Her hands caught at each other as if for mutual support. She stood still as death, her eyes turned towards the door. Presently the portière was drawn aside, and the grave, noble-faced woman looked in at her. They advanced with outheld hands, which, groping, met in a vise-like grasp as they stood and gazed deep into each other's eyes. Then Constance drew the younger to her in a close embrace. There was the sound of a passionate sob from Eleanor as Constance softly laid her cheek upon hers.

They had drawn apart. Eleanor started with pain at sight of Nan standing in the middle of the room with her hand in Grace's. "Oh," she cried, brokenly, "little Nan!" She sank on her knees with her arms about her, and Nan's small, thin hand wandered over her face. She was very light and frail now. Eleanor lifted her easily in her arms.

"Take off your things, girls," she said, as she unfastened Nan's wraps, "and draw your chairs up close." Her happy eyes glanced in such satisfied joy from one to another that Constance felt her throat swell when they came to rest upon her.

There was scarcely any change in her own peaceful face. Her eyes were, perhaps, filled with a graver light; her mouth had a slight new sadness in repose, but that was all.

"How I miss Edith!" said Eleanor, presently. "Do you remember, Constance, how you used to count us as we all filed out of a car when we travelled anywhere? I've been counting. It seems strange to think of our wild girl as a quiet student."

"She is not a quiet one," put in Grace, noticing that

Constance, too, was struck into momentary silence by an intangible something in the face and voice of their new-found sister. "She writes wild letters yet. Don't you think it was queer that Edith, of all girls, should have developed a reverential bump for anything as dry as mathematics?"

"I am glad you let her go," said Eleanor, thoughtfully. "No matter how incongruous it seems, it is a providential ballast—she was too much like me."

Just as she spoke a yellow envelope was handed her. It was a telegram from the absent one saying, characteristically:

I am with you all.—EDITH.

"Poor girl!" smiled Eleanor, with wet eyes. The current phrase had struck her as one of lonely longing.

"I wired her as soon as we received your despatch," explained Constance, and when, shortly after, another message, this time from Brunton, was brought her, Eleanor knew that her return had been scarcely less indifferent to those to whom she had come back than to herself.

"Dear old Geoffrey!" she mused, aloud. "How is he, Constance?"

"He is well. He had to go to San José. He will be back in a few days, and is coming out at once to see you."

And so they took up the broken threads of their lives, and slowly, by question and answer, knotted them again together. As the sun began to slant toward the decline, Constance made a move to go. "It is getting late for Nan," she said.

"I have been waiting for Hall before making the

tea," Eleanor explained, glancing toward the clock. "I thought I heard his step in the hall some time ago. I must have been mistaken. Perhaps he will come while we are drinking. A waited-for person never comes, you know, till you have stopped watching for him."

She looked so graceful at the pretty tea-table that Constance wished he would come in then, but he did not. The shadows grew longer, and Constance arose.

"It is too late, indeed," she said, "and the cabman is growing impatient."

"I am sorry," said Eleanor, regretfully, "for he can't be gone much longer now."

Nothing could have more strongly marked the change in her personality than the easy patience of her words and manner. There had been no disturbed movements— only the calm of implicit trust. Yet it was a calm that disturbed Constance inexplicably.

"I am so happy," she whispered, raising her face to kiss Constance as they stood on the door-step.

And Constance, kissing her, said, gently, "May you always be so, darling. Be sure to come to-night or to-morrow morning—with Hall." She caught a fleeting glimpse of her standing in the doorway and gazing up the street as the carriage rolled off.

The next minute Eleanor turned and went in. "He has been detained," she decided.

Catching sight of a huge bunch of violets on the hall-table, she caught them up, and buried her face in their fragrance.

"He must have sent them," she thought, with a little intoxicated laugh.

She was singing softly as she pressed her lips to

them and passed into the dining-room. She placed half
of them in a low bowl in the centre of the table already
laid for dinner, and then went into the kitchen for a second to speak to the cook. She was still singing softly
as she trailed up-stairs to her quiet bedroom, and, moving over to the window to draw down the blind, gazed
out upon the gathering dusk, while overhead, in the soft
spring sky, the glimmering stars stole forth in holy loveliness.

CHAPTER XV

For many weeks Eleanor Kenyon had been anticipating every detail of this evening. With the love of an artist who dreams over each line of his secret conception, so Eleanor, with the most magical of brushes, had perfected the smallest accessory to her vision.

Now, as she lifted from the long, low trunk the shimmering white gown in its many wrappings, an expectant serenity attended face and movement. It was the first step toward fulfilment. And presently, when she stood fully arrayed, her head and shoulders rising like a flower from the filmy fall of rich lace, she turned her starry eyes toward the glass, and regarded herself in still pleasure.

"This is my wedding-night," she mused, "and this my wedding-gown." She leaned her elbows on the stand and rested her cheek in her clasped hands. "I am glad that I am fair to look upon," was the long thought, as her eyes travelled over her mirrored loveliness; "it was half the battle. I am glad to know that his eyes must be pleased when they rest upon his wife. Eleanor Kenyon, I kiss my hand to you." She was grateful for the winsome reflection.

The color had risen slowly and softly over her face when she turned away and went down to the drawing-room, the violets in her hair breathing about her their perfume of love. The light from the tall, shaded lamps lent a fairy glimmer to the apartment. She moved about, drawing out the chairs, arranging a fold of drapery, turning a vase, as a mother shakes out her child's furbelows before presenting her.

"I think," she debated, looking around as she stood still, "that *he* will sit there!"—indicating a deep, low chair. "And I shall take this odd little seat, and then"—she moved the smaller chair closer to the arm of the larger—"and then"—she moved it slightly back again—"then I shall tell him—and that will be the beginning!"

While she stood there feeding her happy fancy she caught a glimpse of herself in the long glass opposite, and started in bewildered surprise at the bride-like vision. A playful little smile dimpled her mouth at the unfamiliar aspect of her own presence, inward and outward. "I scarcely know myself," she thought, with a laugh. "I am Cinderella!—Cinderella, who dropped at last her rags and cinders, and put on folderols and happiness. But the prince *is* late." She glanced at the little clock on the mantel. Nearly half-past six, she saw, with vague uneasiness, but a faint smile. "I wonder if he could possibly have forgotten that he is no longer a bachelor, and have gone to dine at some club or restaurant." She recalled, with amusement, the story of a man who, the day after his marriage, forgot he was a benedict, and went, as usual, to lunch at his father's house, to his mother's unbounded consternation.

"I shall give him ten minutes' grace," she said, finally. "If he does not come then, it will be time to grow angry; and if he is not here when the clock strikes seven, I shall consider it a signal to begin to be alarmed." She moved over to the window, pulled aside the dra-

peries, and stood looking out at the falling night. The
lamplighter on his white horse moved, with his torch,
from post to post, and lit the street with mundane stars.
As he passed out of sight, and the flickering lights be-
spoke the night, Eleanor began to wonder.

"It *is* getting late," she thought, with a sick little feeling about the heart. "Gretchen will soon announce that
dinner is spoiling. It's a shame, too, because Constance
ordered a very good dinner. And—pshaw!—I am truly
growing angry!" She ended with an agitated laugh.
Her exuberance exhibited an undercurrent of increasing
excitement. As she turned toward the room the maid
pulled aside the portière, and announced that dinner was
served.

"It will have to be delayed, Marie," replied her young
mistress. "Mr. Kenyon has not come in yet."

The servant dropped the curtain, and flew out to tell
Gretchen that madame was *ravissante*, and while, with
expressive eyes and hands, she proudly described the
Parisian gown for the wonder and humiliation of her
Teuton fellow, the striker of the great hall-clock began to
beat its mellow note of warning.

"I must have that stopped," meditated Eleanor. "I
hate being reminded that I am growing old."

The minutes slipped away. The two servants looked at
each other with some curiosity and unconscious enjoyment over the odd situation. Suddenly Marie started up
as though recalling something. With an unintelligible
exclamation she hurried from the kitchen. When she
reached the doorway of the drawing-room, however, her
glib tongue was, for the moment, bereft of action as
she beheld Mrs. Kenyon seated in a strained attitude,

12

her white face turned, as if in expectation, toward the door.

"Madame—pardon," finally faltered the girl, coming into the room, her fingers twitching nervously at the edges of her apron, "but did madame know? Monsieur Kenyon came home once this afternoon."

"Came home? When?" demanded Eleanor, the color leaping to her cheek and brow as she strove to keep herself in hand before the unfamiliar eyes of her maid.

"I think it was at four," considered the girl, earnestly—"maybe four and a quarter—yes. I was bringing madame the water for the tea."

"Go on," she commanded, hoarsely.

"Monsieur Kenyon—he came in the hall with the bouquet and laid it on the table. He had his overcoat and hat—he looks like he hears something that gives him fear; then he listens a minute, turns himself, and he is gone!"

"Marie," came Eleanor's faint question, "you said he seemed to hear—to be listening? Do you remember hearing anything, any sound, any noise?"

"No," replied the girl, with bright, important eyes, "nothing; that is, only the sound of the voice of mademoiselle, your sister—Mees Herriott."

Without a word Eleanor let her head sink back upon the cushions of her chair. She divined. And she quietly fainted.

When the maid realized what had occurred she rushed out to summon the cook, and presently they were bathing her deathly face with brandy, and forcing a few drops through her locked teeth. Many minutes passed, however, before consciousness returned.

"Has Mr. Kenyon come?" she asked, as she strove to raise her head.

"Not yet, Mrs. Kenyon," returned the German girl, compassionately. The other stood by, curious-eyed, excited, silent, as she watched her mistress's ineffectual effort to speak.

"Leave me," at length came the command.

"But, Mrs. Kenyon," ventured Gretchen, gently, "dinner—you have not—"

"I told you to go!"

The girls started at the passionate voice, the brilliant eyes, the quivering figure, the transformation of the peaceful-faced woman of the morning to this wild-eyed being. Characters suffer change, not death; in moments of strong emotion the old powers rise to confuse and refute the personality which lies but surface deep. The maids had not known Eleanor Herriott. She was again here. They moved from her, half in terror, half in hesitation, as she arose.

"I do not wish any dinner," Eleanor vouchsafed, as though her throat were clinched to keep back the turmoil within her. "Close the house for the night."

The next minute she was alone. She stood motionless for a space; then, without a glance behind her, passed out and mounted the stairs to her room.

She locked the door fast, lit the gas, and again stood moveless under the chandelier. Then, by one of those mysterious impulses of consequence for which there is no conscious accounting, she turned to her dressing-table, seized a hand-mirror which lay there, stood a moment holding it without looking into it; then, with a fierce movement, dashed it violently to the floor.

"Vain fool!" she imprecated, looking down at it; and lifting her foot, she ground her heel into the glass till it lay splintered in bits. She was still very far from being a Griselda.

Her face was vacant now; she sank into a chair and covered it with her hands. She had been but a while ago in the position of one who, struggling from the depths of a profound abyss, finds herself at the top of the precipice, wholly oblivious that hands are torn and limbs weary, conscious only that the foothold has been reached at last! And now, just at the supreme moment of triumph, to sink down, down again to the abysmal depths of the past!

Constance's voice! Oh, it was ludicrous! She began to laugh queerly, but put her hand in affright to her mouth at the strange sound. A little thing like that! Only Constance's voice! Yet powerful enough to bring back to him, with overwhelming force, the love, the despair, which she, Eleanor, had thought long since buried! He had confessed as much to her himself the evening after their visit to Pompeii. He had said: "There are dreams of youth which lie buried under the cold lava of a great upheaval. It is better to travel far from such dead, since they cannot be restored to life! If they rise again, they will be but as the ghosts of dead desires. I prefer the warm clasp of a human hand, Eleanor, to the icy touch of any ghost."

It had been a confession and an admission which she had quickly interpreted. Had he deceived only her? Had he played upon her nostalgia only to bring himself near again to his lost idol? Or had he also been the victim of distance and hope? Was it love or only memory that had throttled him again, and obliterated all else?

A melancholy bitterness slowly overspread her. She seemed to stand off and regard Eleanor Kenyon as a shivering, impotent object, and her lips almost murmured, "Poor wretch!" Self-pity is the weakness of desperation. Now, beside her old jealousy of Constance, there rose the miserable picture of the hungry woman who had had the morsel dashed from her hand just as it had been raised to her lips. And presently there was added to this another maddening feeling. Under her corsage a woman may carry a brutal wound with smiling nonchalance; but let a telltale scratch show itself upon her face, and the vulnerable spot has been found. In Paris, an alien among aliens, her sorrow had been her own. Here, among her people, it would resolve itself into a vulgar scandal commodity. It is easier for a woman to own to material poverty than to a hungry heart. Woman's love must be sought, never go begging; it must wait until called for, else it might find itself, like Eleanor's, wandering in the night. The convention, as are most such conventions, is one of chivalric protection for the sex, and she who cannot abide by it must expect to suffer either pity or ridicule. Pity is pride's rack, ridicule its guillotine. "I hate him!" she said, in the very madness of love.

During the hours which passed while she sat there motionless she endured all the agonies of social damnation, and when she finally raised her head her sallow, haggard face and dark-ringed eyes were eloquent testimony of her torment.

Her gaze fell upon the bridal-gown enveloping her

like a satire. "I am Mrs. Haversham," she thought, with a distorted smile, and as the grizzly vision arose before her, she shuddered and hid her face. "I am afraid of her," she murmured; "I always was afraid of that woman. Oh, take her away, take her away — I don't want to be like her!" She suddenly became conscious that she was talking aloud. She looked about her in horror. "I am crazy," she thought, wildly — "I am quite mad. Oh, papa—" She sat stunned, pallid under the awful fear of hereditary want of mental fortitude.

"No," she said, finally, crushing her hands heavily upon her knees. "Let *him* go mad! One of us is enough. I shall not go mad. But I have had enough of this man's individuality — too much. I shall not submit to it. I shall give him two days to return. Then I will see if *he* can suffer." She rose with menacing dignity, as though confronting an adversary. As she moved across the room the violets dropped from her hair—like withered hopes.

CHAPTER XVI

THE tension of Eleanor's faculties was drawn so tight that the following hours passed with diabolically creeping slowness. Her strained senses, fastened upon one ultimate moment, suffered the hideous torture of the screw, of which her changed aspect gave dumb evidence.

"Mr. Kenyon was suddenly called away," she said, in even, cold precision to the two wondering maids the next morning. "I am not feeling well. I wish to see nobody. I am out to whoever calls—even to my sisters. You will simply say to all inquirers that I am not in, and that Mr. Kenyon is away. Let no one come further than the door."

She was aware of her impotence to hide her misery—feigning would prove so evidently an artificiality with Eleanor Kenyon that her voice behind the mask would cry out the deception. The heart has its seasons with all nature, and, without art, it cannot bear June berries in December. She was maintaining her self-mastery by an unfamiliar dominance of will, but the woman became rigid in her restraint and silence.

The cards of many old intimates were handed to her during the next two days; their owners were turned away with the glib excuse. She looked at the bits of card-board without a glimmer of comprehension.

"Mademoiselle, your sister said they would expect you to-night, as Mees Nan cannot be left," repeated Marie, in the afternoon of the first day, when Constance, after waiting all morning for their advent, had sent Grace with the message. " She was sorry not to find you," continued the girl, curiously, throwing out the remark as a projectile against an iron wall.

"Very well," was the low comment, and the baffled maid left the room.

She would go into the dining-room at meal-time and sit staring at her plate or at the opposite wall, as though she had lost all knowledge why she sat there. But always, by the same unaccountable dominance of will, she would force a few mouthfuls to pass her pale, dry lips. Her cheeks and eyes already looked sunken— a great gnawing void soon sucks beauty out of sight.

On the morning of the second day Constance, in some anxiety, left Nan with Grace, and went herself to investigate Eleanor's tardiness.

"Mrs. Kenyon is out," repeated Marie, like a well-drilled marionette.

"Do you know whether she will be at home this evening?"

"I cannot say ; perhaps not."

"Is Mr. Kenyon home?"

"No, Miss Herriott; every one is out."

Constance looked at the cool, non-committal young face with a slightly annoyed gaze. Not only the maid's tone but her position in the doorway seemed to bar all further inquiry or entrance. A flush of resentful dignity rose to Constance's cheek as she turned away. She had descended only the first step, however, when she came hastily back, arresting the maid just as she was closing the door.

"Tell Mrs. Kenyon that I am waiting for her, please," she said, and, with a kindly nod, she went down the steps.

The day dragged on sluggishly. As evening approached a slow, feverish paralysis seemed to encroach upon Eleanor's members. She was nearing the catastrophic moment of decision. She went into the drawing-room after the farce of dining, and took up a book as another act of the farce. An hour or two slipped away without a sound or movement from the lonely occupant of the room; not even the turning of a page deceived eye or ear as to her real employment—the deception had stopped with the picking up of the book.

At about half-past eight, in the deep quiet of the night, she heard a man's firm foot-fall mounting the outer steps. Immediately after the ringing of the bell pealed gently through the silent house. She felt herself turn icy.

She heard the sound of muffled voices, an altercation, an exclamation, a footstep; the heavy portière was pulled aside, and a keen, kindly face looked toward her from the threshold.

"Geoffrey!" she almost shrieked, the revulsion of anticipation throwing off all disguise. She swayed where she stood with outstretched hands.

He reached her side on the instant, and his firm, close hand-clasp, his silent greeting, the intensity of his gaze as it rested upon her changed face, brought her to herself at once.

"I saw your shadow upon the blind as I stood on the topmost step," he was saying, in quiet apology, "and I insisted upon the maid's letting me see you for

an instant. I thought you wouldn't mind me, even if
you have—'a headache.'"

"Oh, I am glad you have come—at last," she began,
in a high-strung key, as he seated himself near her.
"You always did deliberate till the clock struck the
hour, and then, pouff! it was done. How do you like
my drawing-room? Pretty, isn't it? That punch-bowl
you sent is exquisite—we'll drink your health every time
it is filled. I hope the wish won't conjure the contrary,
as some dyspeptic old pessimists want us to believe.
There's always a reverse side to every argument, and we
must listen to the testimony of those whose dinners
not only tasted good but agreed with them, mustn't we,
Geoffrey?"

"My dear Mrs. Kenyon, what *are* you trying to say?"
Geoffrey asked, sharply.

Eleanor drew in a swift breath at the sound of his
compassionate tone. Then she began to laugh hysterically. "My dear Mr. Brunton, what are *you* trying to
say?" she mimicked. "Have you lost your memory?
I am still Eleanor—crazy, madcap Eleanor!—who wanted
to sell her fortune for a mess of pottage on the day
she came into it. Don't you remember me now? And
can't you understand what I meant to say? I always
wrote gibberish on the lines and some invisible sense
between them—cap and bells on top, a polemic underneath. Make the bells tinkle, and— Poor old Punch-
inello! I mean—"

"That will do, Eleanor! Let us talk rationally.
Where is Kenyon?"

She rallied on the instant. "Is that all you have to
ask me, after a year and a half's absence?" she de-

manded, with a forced laugh, striving to drown his matter-of-fact question in another flood of words. "Have you grown so old that you can take stock only in the present? You can't be more than forty one or two at the utmost, Geoffrey! You have just reached the plateau; you can saunter now; before that one climbs. Only after fifty one begins to run down. Oh, I forgot," she broke off, catching the annoyed look upon his face, "you asked me where Kenyon is. Why, he—he—" She sat staring at him with eyes of helplessness. Her power of artifice had run its course. Not the glimmer of a parrying idea came to her relief.

She strove to say something, her lips moving spasmodically, but emitting no sound, her hands fluttering over her lap. Her agonized endeavor, the imprint of some unexplained torment in her whole aspect and bearing, filled Brunton with compassion.

"Don't, my dear, don't!" he implored, leaning forward and taking her feeble hands in his. "Wait!"

"Geoffrey," she moaned — "oh, Geoffrey, he — he has—" She began to sob in deep, painful gusts, like a storm long restrained that can only spend itself in heavy convulsions.

After a little she drew away from him, her wretched eyes regarding him wearily. "Forgive me," she entreated, in humble hopelessness, "but I did not want any one to know—not even the girls. But you were so kind, Geoffrey, and sometimes kindness is so painful, and—"

"You are not well; that is what upset you," he said, as if humoring a sick child. "But isn't there something your brother Geoffrey can do for you?"

"Nothing," she said, with sudden quiet. "I can trust you to let what has just passed go as though it had never been. You know, through accident, the truth—that I am wretched! But you are the only one who does know. Hush! I cannot have it discussed."

He studied her face sharply, and understood that his investigation was arrested. "Then there is only one thing to do," he said, cheerily. "I wonder you did not think of it before."

Her eyes mutely begged him to proceed.

"Why, Constance, to be sure, little girl. What else?"

She put up a passionate, repellent hand and cowered down in her chair. "No, no! not Constance now," she uttered. "It *can't* be Constance now."

"It must always be Constance," he asserted, with insistence. "There is no circumstance sad or miserable enough to call on Constance vainly. To stand aloof from your sister now would be to asperse your memory with the most profligate ingratitude. Have you forgotten everything, Eleanor?"

"Oh, Geoffrey," she sobbed, "I am so—so ashamed. I—"

"Ashamed? Before Constance? Eleanor!"

The whole volume of the man's secret, unswerving love and trust spoke in the exclamation. It sank like a plummet into Eleanor's memory. She understood. She arose and held out her hands. "Take me to her, Geoffrey," she said, simply.

.   .   .   .   .   .

Constance was sitting alone in the library. Her quiet hand shaded her eyes while she read. She heard the ringing of the bell with listless speculation.

A few moments later the door softly opened and the figure of a woman came silently in. Her white face, rising from the dark fur of her cloak, seemed to emerge from spirit-land. She advanced a step, and then stood quite still.

"Constance," she whispered, "I needed a mother, so I have come to you."

CHAPTER XVII

CONSTANCE'S motherly arms went quickly about Eleanor. "That is right, child," said the tender voice. "That is what mothers want."

She took the heavy cloak from her sister's shoulders and unpinned the hat. Her strong hand smoothed the pretty hair with loving touch while she did so. Presently she had drawn Eleanor down upon the divan into a nest of cushions, and, seating herself beside her, drew off her gloves, and began softly rubbing the chilled hands.

The house was still. For several minutes Constance's strong, reliable figure rose like a supporting oak beside the drooping form of the other; then, abruptly, Eleanor drew herself up, and the two women regarded each other silently. So different outwardly, an inward resemblance radiated from them, and proclaimed them for that one moment close almost as twins. The pale braids, olive skin, and noble proportions of the older next the glinting hair, white face, and slender figure of the younger were mere accidents of form and color, which faded into immateriality at this swift recognition of two souls. But reticence soon slipped unseen, like a shadow, upon Eleanor, and Constance looked into a pair of eyes too deep and sad for the young face.

"He has left me, Constance!" she said, breathlessly. "He left me on the day of our home-coming." Con-

stance did not answer; her firm, quiet hand pressed more
tenderly the one which lay beneath hers. "It was the
incident of the Louvre repeated," Eleanor continued, mo-
notonously. "Without warning, without a word, he was
gone. I have not seen or heard from him since."

"Was there any visible impulse?" asked Constance,
with frowning forehead but gentle voice.

"None but that of his ungovernable mood." The
hand upon Constance's rested lightly, as though waiting
for her to proceed. After a pause the answer came—
complete: "Yes, Constance. It was *you!* He heard
your voice—that afternoon in the house, you know."

A flood of color rushed over Constance's face and
neck. Her face contracted with pain. But her eyes
did not flinch in their gaze upon the cold, white face
before her.

"And that was all?" she asked.

"All."

"Are you quite sure?"

"Quite."

There was another pause. Then Constance spoke.
"Eleanor dear, he will return. It was not love; it was
memory. You must know this yourself. For *now* he
loves *you!—must* love you, Eleanor."

Her passionless voice spoke the words as an ultima-
tum; they bore no trace of self, no spirit of renuncia-
tion. She stated an incontrovertible, impersonal fact, as
one would say, "The sun shines."

"Remember," she went on, "your husband had not
seen me since the day when we parted in silence and bitterness. Linked with that parting were unspoken words
of violent emotions. It was the mere memory of these

old emotions; the sound of my voice recalled them.
Without premonition it threw him again into this state.
It was *not* love, dear, not despair. Don't fear it. He
is an honorable man. The moment he became your husband he buried me from sight. In all these long months
a living love, thus buried, must die. It *does* die, Eleanor. Inanition kills. Why, search your own conscience
and tell me truly. Don't you know, as only the woman
herself can know, by signs so delicate that only the one
who loves can interpret or even perceive — don't you
know that your husband loves you?"

The earnest voice ceased. For a long time the sisters
sat so still that the sound of the gas buzzing in the jets
was distinctly audible. And then Eleanor's hand moved
from under Constance's, and was laid as if in protection
upon it.

"Angel," she said, in a strange tone, "your words
recall a hope which for these two dark days has lain
dead. Now, since I am with you, I think—no, I *know*—
that he not only cared for me before we came home, but
was beginning to want my love! Oh, my dear, my dear,
which is the reality — which will prove the stronger—
the memory or the love?"

"You know what I have said. Now you must answer
for yourself."

"But it is sometimes hard to separate desire from
hope," she replied. "Sometimes, looking ahead, longing cries, 'It *is* so,' while reason corrects, in undertone,
'Would it were so.' I do not stop to listen to reason.
You do. Shall I tell you of the hope you have recalled
all at once?"

"Do, my darling."

"You remember I wrote you how he returned to me
in Paris? Before that we had seemingly grown into
congenial companions—a relationship for which he was
thankful, and which he had no desire to break. After
his—absence—he had been on a wild tramp through a
corner of Switzerland—he came back completely exhausted in mind and spirit. He came upon me in my
peaceful mood and—I did not upbraid him. That was
my salvation, Constance! I seemed to promise him
rest. He turned to me eagerly, as a tired head yearns
for a pillow. I let him woo me. I let him take my
hand—I did not put mine out to draw him. And yet,
Constance, I, who received it all with such calm, bore underneath the same old noontide passion. It was a seeming, a manner, a trick which Griff had taught me. I let
him woo me. He never left me but to return with some
token to show that only materially he had been separated
from me. He coaxed me with largesse to my better vani-
ties; he pursued the game with the eager delight of a dis-
coverer. I took it all with gentleness. He thought me—
indulgent. He never knew that the growing light within
him was with me an old, finished story. For I said to myself, 'A woman must hold her love so high that a man
must strain to reach it, or it may be held, like roses in
June, sweet, perhaps, but a cheap thing to be had for
the gathering.' He never knew I loved him, Constance."

The last words were long, with lingering hopelessness.

"Why, not at last, Eleanor?"

"I was waiting!"

"Waiting, child? For what?" She spoke in low, unexpected intensity. "It is never too early to speak words
of love. We are all too avaricious with tenderness. We

13

hoard and hoard it as a miser his treasure, and say to ourselves, 'Some day I will show it all; some day I will overwhelm him with my store.' But too often the day comes too late, when either the lips that wish to speak or the ears that long to hear have passed beyond human power. Love is the oil, Eleanor, that keeps the weary world turning without creaking. Why did you wait?"

She felt the hand upon hers suddenly raised. Eleanor had slipped to her knees before her with her old, impetuous abandon. She rested her arms upon Constance's knees and raised her face. The gaslight seemed to gain a softened lustre as it fell upon her uplifted countenance, and Constance caught her breath.

"I cannot tell you now," came the hushed words. "Some day, perhaps, you will know."

Constance's heart gave a curious leap, but she dared intrude no further into what was, perhaps, a shrine. They sat looking into the future without speaking.

After a little Constance put her arm around the kneeling figure and they both arose.

"You are going to stay with me now," she said, without question.

"To-night," replied Eleanor, quietly. "Geoffrey did not wait."

"Geoffrey?"

"He brought me here."

"That was like him. He always—he generally knows what is best. Let us go to bed, dear." She picked up her hat and wrap, but Eleanor drew them gently from her. "You have been doing for me long enough," she said. Constance turned off the gas. With their arms about each other they went up the broad stairs.

They stepped softly from the room where Grace and Marjorie lay sleeping, and came into Nan's shadowy room. Eleanor buried her face in the pillow beside the ethereal little face. When she raised her head the tears stood thick in her eyes.

"Hush! I know," whispered Constance. "She is slipping from me."

Eleanor buttoned the collar of the little night-robe which had become unfastened, and they went out.

They moved on to Eleanor's old room. Nothing had been altered here. Even the old-fashioned white rabbit pin-cushion, with the name "Eleanor" picked out in black pins by Nan's fingers, looked at her with pink eyes of recognition. Yet the room showed signs of occupancy.

"Grace sometimes sleeps in here," Constance explained, as she drew down the blinds; "but you will find everything as it was. You know Nan would be discomforted if she could not put her hands on things just where she expected to find them. Let me brush your hair for you, Eleanor, will you? It will rest you." Her hands ached to do something for the child who had returned to her in her need.

"No, no," protested Eleanor, shaking her head with a tremulous smile, as she looked into her sister's face. "I have grown so accustomed to taking care of myself. But just for a change, Constance, let me brush *your* hair for *you*, will you? It will rest you."

A glimmer of her girlish archness stole through her womanly tone as she drew Constance down into a low chair. "Just for a change," she whispered, drawing out the pins.

Constance's figure suddenly relaxed; she closed her eyes. She was unused to being cared for. "Eleanor, you seem so much older than— You make me feel childish," she laughed, through apologetic tears.

Eleanor did not reply. She was busily unplaiting the beautiful hair. Presently she drew back, as it fell in shimmering splendor about Constance's form, reaching, as she sat, almost to the floor.

"Oh," she cried, softly, "what a glory! How you are 'crowned,' Constance!"

"The crown is a great nuisance," returned Constance, lightly, moved by the lingering touch upon her hair. As the long braid fell from Eleanor's manipulation, Constance put up her hands, drew her sister's arms about her neck, and, leaning her head back upon Eleanor's breast, raised her eyes to the wistful face bending above her.

"You are going to be a great comfort to me," she said, softly. "You make me think of some one who used to love to smooth my hair. You have our mother's hands, Eleanor."

Eleanor did not answer. But before Constance left her, after tucking her in, Eleanor was startled to find her kneeling at her bedside.

"Eleanor," she said, in painful intensity, "I want your forgiveness. I have often feared that in my endeavor to save you and—and all the children—I have feared when *that* morning came to us three—to you, Hall, and me—I wrecked your life for you. It was done, dear, in a moral rigor which held no tenderness. I had grown despotic and self-sure. But I am beginning to doubt my every action. Did I provide nothing but unhappiness for you, child?"

Eleanor was sitting up in bed; her two hands closely framed the sad, beseeching face on a level with her own. Her eyes looked clearly, without restraint, into Constance's.

"Constance," she returned, steadily, "you must never torture yourself with such an accusation. When you gave me Hall for a husband, you unconsciously gave me the only happiness I craved! It was not a perfect happiness, because that lay out of your power, and, perhaps, out of your thought. But to one as selfish as I, possession is always the great nine points. When he became mine I ceased—to hate you! Was that nothing? You made me good again, because you gave me what I wanted. That appeals to what Eleanor Herriott always was, and what Eleanor Kenyon still is, perhaps. For I am a woman with more than my share of woman's weaknesses; there is nothing noble about me. If I have suffered, if I shall suffer, it will never be what I should have suffered if Hall, with all his faults, were nothing to me. Now you know me as I know myself. Now you know that no matter what may happen, no matter what I may do, out of my selfishness I bless you for what you have given me."

Yet for many hours Constance sat in her darkened room reviewing the past with doubting bitterness, as over and over in the past eighteen months she had arraigned herself.

"I did it for the best," was the repeated supplication her heart made, as if in justification to some invisible, condemning judge. And out of the shadows came fevered scenes: the night of Kenyon's avowal of love—to her, her heart giving no leap at the reminiscence, only an unresponsive stupor, like that which attends a strong lion lying strangled in death; the night of the Ferris dinner, when shame and fear had given her heart but one vision, had made her a monomaniac with one omnipotent necessity; the marriage of the two at Sausalito, as bizarre and seemingly unreal as an impressionist's frenzy. Why had such strange, unconventional things happened to them? They were quiet, ordinary, home-loving people. But the kaleidoscopic memories reintruded upon her questionings. Eleanor's first letter with its unutterable, unlooked-for confessions, and, after that, the months during which she, Constance, had hoped and doubted and hoped again for the welfare of her wandering child. Always she called up Kenyon's image, studying his features, gauging his possibilities, delving into her minutest reminiscences of him—the wilful, passionate, defiant face, true as steel, open as sunlight, with its curious contradictions of weakness and strength. "His faults are weaknesses, not vices," Eleanor had written, in love; but when weakness worked viciously, to one of Constance Herriott's controlled instincts, such weakness — moral weakness—was a vice.

"These flights of his must be stopped," she thought, with severe eyes and deliberate mouth. "They must end right here. She shall not submit to it. If it is physical, there are cures; if moral, there are other means of restitution. He is strong in effort; he can conquer what he desires, if it rests only with himself. He is stern in honor; there is not a trace of depravity in him. When he comes back your child shall have a life like other loved women."

In the dark she gave her promise to the ever invisible, ever attendant judge who ruled her life.

CHAPTER XVIII

WHEN Constance opened her door the next morning and was passing on to Eleanor's room, she was arrested by the chamber-maid, who told her that Mrs. Kenyon had asked her to tell Miss Herriott that it had been necessary for her to return to her house in order to arrange some affairs which needed her attention.

"Did she say nothing more?" questioned Constance, slightly startled.

"Nothing more," replied the girl; and Constance went on, explaining to herself that hope had probably flickered a little light before her, and led her, like a kindly demon, away from her passive inactivity.

"It is maddening for her to wait," she thought. "It is natural for her to want to stay where he left her. Perhaps she will not come back. If not, I will take Nan down and sit with her this afternoon. Although—" The rich color mounted to her face at the arresting thought of her possible undesirability.

The morning was almost spent when a messenger brought her a key and the following communication:

DEAR CONSTANCE,—I have gone to him. I have dismissed the servants and locked the house. Will you look in at it once in a while till our return? Am quite safe. Forgive me—and—again—again—pray for me.

ELEANOR.

That was all. No word as to her destination, no explanation of her knowledge of his whereabouts. She had slipped from Constance's hands as from a leash, and she could not turn to search for her. "It is the unexpected that always happens—with Eleanor," she thought, with a heavy sigh of resignation. "She will write to me when she gets to him. I shall have to let them go."

"Mr. and Mrs. Kenyon were unexpectedly called away the day after their home-coming," she informed the many inquirers. "But they will return immediately after the affair is arranged."

Her explanation bore two results: it stopped all outside speculation, and succeeded in giving her own conscience some assurance of their well-being.

"As long as she is with him," said Geoffrey, "there is no need to worry." Constance could not explain to him that his innocent view of the situation gave her small comfort.

A week slipped away with no further news, and had it not been for Nan's failing strength, the silence would have forced her to some definite action. As it was, the child's grave condition claimed her entire attention and thought.

She seldom left her, although Grace, with her calm womanliness, very much like Constance's own, was always ready to take her place. Nan, who was usually fretful when Constance left the room, made no complaint when these necessary substitutions were made.

"Grace isn't *you*, Constance," said her little lover, loyally; "but she is like you. And then it is always so lovely when you come home again."

And Constance, knowing that the child spoke from

her heart, left her thus in Grace's arms one day, slipped quietly out, and betook herself to Brunton's office. The knowledge that she herself was inadequate to advance a step toward Eleanor had given her the sudden impetus for this move. She could count the occasions on which she had entered her friend's business domain. Only an urgent case, which could not be satisfactorily arranged at home, had ever brought her here. There was a certain delicacy about this constraint which she could have scarcely explained. No outward sign from him, but a certain intuitiveness made clear to her that her coming into his unadorned law-office caused him more disturbance than she cared to inflict.

As she entered now he was standing in the centre of the large outer room, in earnest conversation with two men. He bowed courteously to her, and when the men had departed came over to her side.

"I don't wish to keep you many minutes, Geoffrey," she said, putting her hand into his extended one. "My business is of an entirely personal nature. I did not want to speak of it at home, and I thought you would pardon the intrusion."

"Come in here," he said, opening the door of his sanctum. "Now we can talk quite unreservedly and leisurely. How is our Nan?"

"The days are passing. But I—no, I won't sit down —I have come to speak about—Eleanor."

He nodded gravely, waiting for her to speak before committing himself.

"You know—at least, did she tell you that night— that she — that she did not know where Hall had gone?"

" No."

" Well, such was the case ; she had heard nothing from him. There had been no misunderstanding, you know, Geoffrey, but he left her the day of their return without premonition either to himself or to her. The cause, however, was perfectly clear to her and to me. You saw the note she sent me the day after you brought her to me. It is now almost two weeks since then, and I have heard nothing more. This silence alarms me. I don't know what to think. I don't know whether he sent for her, or whether she is searching for him, or has reached him, or—anything. It is entirely upon my own responsibility that I am confiding in you, Geoffrey. Do you understand ?"

" Entirely. And you have done nothing as yet to locate them ?"

" Nothing."

" You want me to lend a hand ?"

" Yes."

" Without Eleanor's ever knowing ?"

" Yes. She would never forgive me if she knew. But we— I dare not let her pass from me like this. It would be criminal."

" Yes. Let me manage it. The courts are beginning to close, and—"

" Geoffrey, I did not mean that you should go. I thought only that you would put it in efficient hands, with whom you could be in constant communication, and so could let me know whatever there is to know. I beg you, Geoffrey, not to think me quite so inconsiderate and tactless."

" A man may take a vacation once in a while, I trust.

But I'll see only to the laying of the wires. You will want them all underground, I suppose?"

"Yes, for many reasons. I will send you Griff's address—his friend, you know, who is with Severn. He may, perhaps, help you. You see, Geoffrey, I am as unhesitating in asking great things of you as in asking trivialities." His brow contracted—a word of thanks from her always displeased him—and she hurriedly continued: "Let no money or pains be spared. I shall be glad to spend my fortune in bringing them home again—together."

"Of course you will, and spend yourself, too, for that matter. Well, it is my affair now, and, everybody else aside, Constance, I should hate to hear that any harm had come to Kenyon. I like the fellow. We'll start in at once, but we don't want to do anything precipitate. Telephone me Griff's address when you get home."

"Ah, that is what I want—action. Good-bye, then." She liked action, and she went immediately, leaving in the cold office a memory which beautified the spot for many hours to Geoffrey Brunton.

But while she lightened one care, another moved on with swift, unswerving pace.

A day or two later Grace sat singing a tender ballad to Nan. The warm stillness of the May morning without had hushed the air within. All through the night she and Constance had watched, fearing that the frail cord would be snapped without their knowing. Now Constance sat near, in the heavy silence of impotent grief. A broad stream of sunlight bathed Grace and the child in a soft radiance, which swung in halos about their heads. The singing died into profound silence. They might have been transfixed by a spell, they were so still.

"And now, Grace," faltered the small voice, "if you don't mind, I should like to go to Constance."

During the moment in which the sisters changed places Nan lay with her eyes closed and a smile flickering over her pale little mouth. When the familiar arms closed about her she stretched out a wavering hand.

"Constance," she whispered, fearfully, "I cannot find you."

"I am here, my Nan, close beside you," said the voice of tenderness, broken with anguish and tears.

"You are—always here—Constance—aren't you—always here—you won't ever leave me—will you, Constance?"

"Oh, my bird!"

At the low cry of sorrow the small, cold hand sought her cheek, and, as out of a dream, came the indistinct murmur of consolation:

"Never—never—mind—Constance."

And with the beloved name upon her lips, little Nan passed on in safety.

CHAPTER XIX

Toward six o'clock in the evening of an unseasonably gloomy day in May, the sun, as if repenting for its erstwhile dulness, darted over San Francisco a rosy light, which, through the mist, gave to the atmosphere a mysterious charm. It was like that which lies in the unfathomable gaze of a child just awakened from a hazy dream. It lent a sudden spring-time vim to the departing day; and the shrill call of newsboys, the ringing of car-bells, the brisk step and alert eyes of pedestrians seemed to have caught the whiff like a cordial.

It was the hour when women, still busy with belated and vexatious shopping, hurry along the streets with an air of nervous purpose; when men stroll toward the car with a reminiscent smile for the appetizer just taken, and a genial looking forward to the gratification of the appetite thus aroused; when here and there a lighted street-lamp puts a premature seal on the day; it was the hour of finishing—the vanishing point of traffic.

Brunton emerged from his barber-shop, and turned down Kearney Street with a leisurely pleasure in the warm underglow of the vapory evening air. He went into his favorite shop and selected a fragrant sprig of jasmine with his usual near-sighted care. As he walked down the street the soft perfume caressed his nostrils with wonted delicacy, and he felt calm and benignant toward the world, himself included. He stopped for a moment to examine the photograph of the coming musical celebrity gravely regarding him from Sherman & Clay's window, sauntered on with an indulgent nod now and then to passing acquaintances, whom he seldom recognized in the evening light, and crossed over to his own particular little newsboy flitting before the *Chronicle* building with his armful of evening papers. He was at once besieged by an army of importunate venders with the shrill cry of "*Bulletin*, sir? Full account of the railroad accident!" "Want a *Report?* Returns of the Louisiana Lottery, and terrible murder by high-binders in Chinatown!" "*Post?* Lottery, great stage robbery, and—"

The eager little figures moved on and bestowed their attention elsewhere as he turned to the dirty-faced little urchin upon whom his favoring eye had, since a long time, fallen with material benefit.

As he took hold of the extended paper, his hand fumbling in his pocket for the customary dime, through the swaying, straggling crowd he noticed the figure of one man in particular passing up the street. The sight paralyzed all further movement. He stared after Kenyon's powerful form striding out of sight! He continued to look—utterly unconscious that the boy at his side was awaiting the reappearance of his hand.

"Change?" suggested the youngster, finally.

"Eh? Oh yes—yes," he vaguely answered, looking down at him, a line of perturbation showing at either side his thin nose. "Here, Pretzel," he exclaimed, seizing the boy by the shoulder and using his nickname with ludicrous gravity, "quick—you see that tall man going —there! He is out of sight—he has on a black cape-overcoat—soft hat—very tall—no mustache or beard. Run after him!—follow him!—see where he turns in, and come back to me—as fast as you can make it!"

The boy was off. Brunton watched the little figure darting off like an arrow with a dazed, uncomfortable sensation. Five minutes later Pretzel was on his way to him, his spindle-legs flying backward in alarming disregard to their striking him in the upward stroke. He reached Brunton, breathless and glowing.

" Jest caught de gent goin' in de rest'rant corner Bush and Grant Avenoo—he'd—"

"All right, Pretzel. Here you are." He handed him a half-dollar, the size of which made Pretzel's eyes emulous, and walked off in the direction indicated.

He entered the handsome, well-lighted restaurant with slow step and his usual air of indifference. He was before the footlights now, and his gait gave no evidence of what its nature had been in the wings. He nodded in courteous perfunctoriness in answer to one or two salutations as he passed down the long room, and paused with a preoccupied air at one of the side-tables near the end. Throwing his coat over a chair, his eye travelling leisurely down the vista of glittering glass and silver, he gave an apparent start as he met the gaze of the man at the table below his. He immediately picked up his coat and moved to his side.

"Kenyon," he said, in a low voice, holding out his hand. The other seized it, and for five or six seconds the two clasped hands were shaken in the honest demonstration which Americans are not ashamed to show, and which sends a glow of sympathy to the most callous spectator. During this time Brunton's eye noted, with-

out expression, the hair silvering at the temples, the
great gauntness of the hazel eyes, the stern leanness of
the steady jaw. The pallor of face and lip he passed
by—it might have been the result of the moment's sensation. They seated themselves, and after a moment
Brunton spoke. His voice was even lower and slower
than usual.

" Just get in ?" he asked, casually.

" An hour ago," replied Kenyon. He held the menu
card in a firm grip; the long, dark intaglio on his finger
seemed to stand up and out as though the flesh had
shrunken from it. The words escaped him like a missile—he could say no more; he was suffering, for the
moment, a lingual atrophy painful to witness. The
waiter came along with his bird and salad just then,
and Brunton carelessly ordered the same. Neither spoke
again until the latter's wine was placed before him.

" You are not eating," he said, extending the bottle
towards his companion's glass.

Kenyon put out a restraining hand. " I do not drink,"
he said, quietly.

A few minutes later, as Brunton was served, he asked,
with an assumption of ease and his entire attention directed to the duck, " How is your wife ?"

It was only after a few seconds that, conscious of his
companion's taciturnity, he looked up. Kenyon's eyes
covered him with bewildering intensity. " Why do *you*
ask me that ?" he returned, almost without expression.

" Why," replied Brunton, sharply, " whom else should
I ask ?"

" You can probably answer the question better than I."

" What !"

"I have not seen my wife for almost three weeks. She is not where I left her."

"I know that. Where is she?"

"Is she—is she not with her sisters?"

"No! Constance thinks she is with you!"

Kenyon's lips turned bloodless. He stared at Brunton as though he could not comprehend. Then, with a hasty movement, he started up.

"Your hat and coat," reminded Brunton's gentle voice, as he handed him the articles. The next minute Kenyon had passed rapidly out. Brunton paused at the desk, and then followed him closely.

He could discern the tall figure moving westward, but it was several minutes before he overtook him. Kenyon strode on like an automaton, his head raised, his eyes fixed before him; through the thin fog his face shone livid. On and on they walked, the athlete beside him seeming to Brunton to cover space without consciousness. Whither they were headed he did not know nor care. He had one thought, one object: not to let Kenyon pass again from his sight. A man in Kenyon's condition is like a drunkard—his muscles are as unfeeling as his brain is befogged. Brunton, however, began to feel winded and weary after an hour's steady pace. He resolved to appeal to his silent companion to halt.

"Hall, where are you going?" he gasped, brushing the fog from his mustache with his handkerchief.

Kenyon started and wheeled about. "Thank you," he said, after a moment, in an odd, restrained tone, as if recalled from some perilous verge. "I don't know where I was going—to the devil, probably."

"I protest," returned Brunton, with a forced laugh.

14

"I'm going with you, but not, knowingly, there, my friend. Nevertheless, we are on the road—another step will bring us into the cemetery. Turn around, Kenyon."

He grasped his arm firmly, and leaned breathlessly against the high stone coping surrounding the silent city of the dead. Kenyon stood still beside him.

"Take your hand off!" he commanded, finally. "It's none of your concern where I go! By what right do you interfere in my movements?"

"It is a self-imposed right, but a right, all the same," returned Brunton, with slow formality. "I restrain you in the quondam rôle of guardian of Eleanor Herriott, which office I reassumed upon my own account when Eleanor Kenyon was deserted by her natural protector. As her guardian, therefore, and in the interest of my ward, I must beg you now to tell me what you intend doing."

"Doing?" he repeated, violently. "What is there to do but to find her? For God's sake, Brunton, help me! I can't think."

"I don't think I care to do that," returned Brunton, almost lightly, in contrast to the other's distracted turbulence.

"You refuse?" demanded Kenyon, vaguely.

"Certainly. Why should I help restore the girl to a lifetime of misery?"

"Ah." He raised his hat as though to cool his brow. "Perhaps you are right," he said, dully. "You have no ground for believing it might turn out otherwise?"

"No," assented Geoffrey, stolidly, "I have none! I saw your wife two days after you had left her. I know nothing about the circumstance of your leaving. But if ever a miserable woman breathed on this earth, that woman was your wife the night before she disappeared, to go, as she wrote, to you. How do I know that she did not go to you? How do I know where you have left her now, or what you have done to her?"

"Great God, Brunton, what sort of a brute do you take me for?"

"Either a scoundrel or a maniac." He faced him with almost a smile which might have been insolent had not the stern earnestness of his eye challenged his dumfounded auditor menacingly.

"I am both," said Kenyon, finally, in a lifeless tone. "But," he broke forth, through clinched teeth, "that does not absolve me from my agony now."

"And quite right," retorted Brunton, suavely. "It is gratifying to find that it is not only in fiction that the criminal gets his deserts. But you must bear it. I suppose you can, since it is only the reflection of what she endured — she, the delicately - bred woman ; you, the strong, hardened man !"

"That is quite enough," enjoined Kenyon, hoarsely. The rays from the street - lamp glared down upon his ashen face like a confessor drawing out the secrets of a sick soul. "You don't know what you are saying." A singular light illumined his handsome, haggard features for a second. "My God !" Brunton heard him mutter, as though suddenly confronted with the horror of the situation.

"It strikes me," observed the lawyer, dryly, "that you are on easy calling terms with the Great Unknown tonight."

Kenyon bent his head. "You would not understand," he said, in a low voice. Then, "Come," he commanded, roughly, "I need your help. I can't stand still and explain myself here."

CHAPTER XX

"You have constituted yourself my judge," he began, as they veered around and retraced their steps. "You are evidently the *fidus Achates* of the family—you demand an explanation from me. I throw my confidence upon your honor, Geoffrey Brunton—it will find a solid resting-place.

"I don't know what you know of me," he continued, with simple directness. "To all intents my actions have pointed to those of a brute, or — maniac, as you have said. How much I am accountable for them you will judge according to your own standards. All that I know is that my life has always been the tool of uncontrollable impulses and emotions, over which reason and will held no restraint. Reason and will! It seems the veriest satire to claim such possessions in the face of the brainless miseries which I have perpetrated — and suffered. Whether the characteristic is the result of prenatal influences or an acquired habit I cannot determine.

"I remember an incident of childhood which might prove the latter supposition. I never knew my parents. My childhood was passed with a maiden cousin; I was brought up on theories—rules and isms and no favors were my pasturage. She bridled a young colt like a stately carriage-horse. I kicked at the traces—I had bumps and angles in unlooked-for places. But since, according to established authorities, they were accorded no place in the perfected form, the straps were buckled down over them as though they had no existence. One day, in a freak of childish indignation, I opened the door of a bird-cage and let her canary go. I was caught in the act, and the anger upon her face let loose in me a storm of accusation and invective. In the midst of it she grasped me by the shoulder. ' Run,' she said, in a horrified tone—' run from yourself ; you will hurt somebody. Run till you drop !' I took her at her literal word, and the lesson—it seemed a good one—has clung to me as a sort of preventive against active mischief. Once at college I made use of it with good results. Six or seven years ago I suffered a severe, thoroughly unexpected rebuff from a firm of publishers. It was my first experience in that line, and the disappointment disheartened me almost to morbidity. I simply rushed out of the city ! That was the first time I did it impulsively, almost without taking thought ; it was what I wanted, what I needed to do." He paused, drew breath, and plunged on with his narrative. " Again, something over two years ago, I asked a woman to marry me. My love was thrown back to me as lightly as a ball is tossed to a pitcher—or so it seemed to me then. I left her like a madman. It was a wild night, and I was in harmony with it. I spent myself walking in the storm, perfectly conscious, yet reckless—reason was having an orgy with despair, and despair, as usual with me, threw out reason. I hastened where my feet led, with no concern. I had but one thought, to end despair with myself. I was prevented—saved, you would probably call it.

" Well, you know I married Eleanor Herriott. In leav-

ing San Francisco I left behind me the woman who was all
—who was, at that time, at the root of all my bitterness.
One day, in the Louvre, I was suddenly confronted by a
strange image of her who, I thought, had become but
a bitter memory to me. The surroundings faded from
me—the statues, the crowd, the girl at my side. Only
the memory of our last meeting remained, and from it
I fled—blindly. Weeks after I returned—cured. It
would have been impossible to return to my wife otherwise. There is no need to tell you how she met me.
She understood, and— Some months later we left
Rome for New York; from there we came to this city.
We were both very happy over the thought of our home-
coming." He stopped an instant, and wearily pushed
back his hat. The confession was inevitable, but gall-
ing.

"When I think of what an ass I made of myself that
day," he continued, with bitter denunciation, "I could
willingly strangle myself. I came home in the afternoon,
feeling happier than I had ever expected to feel again—
happy as few men can feel. I entered the house door,
and the first thing I heard was— Did I tell you that
the speaking voice of the woman I had loved is to me
singularly beautiful? It had a note of tenderness which
struck the senses like a caress. At the first sound I was
undone—not through love, but memory of a frightful
delirium. It is hard to believe, Brunton, but harder to
endure the consequences, the helplessness of such a tyranny."

He stopped at the corner of a steep grade on California Street. They looked down over the city of hills and
valleys, lit here and there by lofty electric-lights poised

in mid-air like stars arrested in their fall. The sudden
flashing by of cable-cars at almost every alternate street,
the faint ringing of bells, broke the peace of night.
Brunton leaned against the lamp-post and said nothing,
looking with quiet interest into Kenyon's eyes, the flickering light playing in wilful shadows over the latter's
discomposed face. Two Chinamen passing by, tandem
fashion, looked curiously at the two men, and sang out
laughing comments to each other. A policeman, leisurely strolling past, regarded them suspiciously, but, after a
glance, moved on.

" I walked off—away ! It was the only thing for me to
do ! I could not have faced my wife or—the other, in
such a disturbed state. The demon of memory was pur-
suing me relentlessly, and—I could have cursed it for its
intrusion. I was endeavoring to rid myself of it for once
and for always. I found myself moving toward the
wharves. In the noise and hurly-burly I was suddenly
accosted by name. It was Joscelyn, the artist. I do
not know now what he said to me, nor did I care then.
I followed him indifferently, like a dog led by a string,
and we were soon on board the steamer A——, which
was bound that afternoon for Honolulu, and upon which
Joscelyn had taken passage. The sharp breeze made me
giddy, and he pressed me to come into his state-room,
where he had some whiskey. He knew there were only
a few minutes before sailing, but in his excitement at
seeing me he threw discretion to — the sea. He had
some project to suggest to me about a Honolulu romance, for which he would furnish the illustrations and
—what odds. ·

"The distraction and the idea interested me. He had

intended writing me, and now, in his enthusiasm over my unexpected appearance, he forgot the urgency of the moment, had forgotten entirely that I was no longer the ever-ready tourist he had known, and when the order was given for visitors to quit the steamer we heard nothing. The whistle had been tooting since our coming on board. Joscelyn, perceiving my interest, let the moment slip with all the recklessness of the adventure-lover that he is. He revelled in the consciousness of his bit of shanghaiing, until fifteen minutes later, when the whole miserable business presented itself to my consciousness. Brunton—"

"Better stop, Kenyon."

"No. I can't explain to you the remorse of my careless, insane oversight, the memory of my wife, the consciousness of the shock it would be to her, the horror of my helplessness there in mid-ocean! If I could describe the days which passed, you would probably scarcely believe me, knowing now that when I married Eleanor Herriott I did not love her. You cannot love two at once. I thought, then, that a man could never love twice. Come, let us be moving."

They crossed the street and continued eastward.

"However," he went on, his voice sounding dry and husky, "honor insisted that I should strive to forget the other after my marriage to Eleanor. After it I plunged into a sea of work totally at variance with thoughts of love. I imagined I had grown cold till that wretched affair in Paris. The knowledge, then, that I had duped myself was bitter indeed. But upon my return from Switzerland I was able to look upon *her* memory without a tremor. I regarded her as inaccessible to me as

is a star which may offer light but no warmth. In this
state I came back to my wife, and after the storm and
stress of my wandering Eleanor appeared to me like a
refuge of peace. Whether the change lay in her or myself, or both of us, I did not question, but I suddenly
saw her as I had never seen her before—I saw her individuality; she was no longer to me merely the pretty
girl with whom I happened to be travelling, whether I
would or no. She had been obscured before, as a star
is by the moon. I suddenly realized her womanliness,
which was deeper than I had ever cared to know,
and I wanted her forgiveness. I needed her tenderness
and kindness, and, to my surprise, she gave all. It
was pity, probably, but it was more than I had hoped
for. And, presently, I did not want her pity. My one
desire became to make her love me. I had her to myself and I did not despair. But it never became more
than the gracious sweetness of a woman who wishes to
make herself as true a wife as she was one inevitably.
God bless her for the endeavor, at any rate. Brunton?"

His hand fell like a weight upon the other's shoulder.

"Well?" returned Geoffrey, the old charm Kenyon's
personality had always wielded over him breaking down
the denunciation of his former attitude.

"Nothing." He strode on as if striving to outrun his
thoughts and footsteps. "Where was I? Oh," he added,
presently, "you can guess, perhaps, the torment I under-
went on board that steamer, going and returning and
during the four intervening days, with no means of communication to her who I now knew had become all in
all to me! If you can't guess, I have simply wasted
time in trying to gain your leniency, not for myself—

what do I care what you think of me? I must have your assistance! I have lost too much time already. Do you care to help me?" he demanded, shortly.

"I want to, yes. But—I confess I am a little doubtful. I will help you, upon one condition."

"Name it! What is your condition, Brunton?"

"I am sorry to appear so officious," said Geoffrey, in slow cautiousness, "but, in all conscientiousness, I could not honestly aid you in finding your wife with one doubt in my mind. I want you to go to this other woman; I want you to speak to her, to hold her hand. After that, if you find yourself as you now believe yourself to be, I shall move heaven and earth to aid you in your search. You have told me a peculiar history, and the case needs peculiar procedure, peculiar—certitude."

"Then," said Kenyon, moving away with a bitter laugh, "I shall go at once. The task is easy! I shall not be more than an hour at the utmost, after which— where can I meet you?"

"At my room at the ——— Club," he answered, giving him the address. "*Bon voyage!*" He turned away, and Kenyon walked southward down the hill.

Brunton took out a cigar and prepared to smoke. "It's a strange thing," he mused, as he strolled on, "to see a man, otherwise wanting in everything approaching formal religion, turn to the Power in moments of moral excitement as naturally as children turn to their mothers in time of need. Is it his faith at bottom, or only spiritual ecstasy? Is it an acknowledgment of a God beyond our knowledge, or only exclamations taking the name associated through habit with that into which one's reason may not enter? It is an impressive sign of human impotence, whatever its origin! Ah, a good cigar is more satisfying than the clearest elucidation of the most vexed problem!" His head was clouded in the fragrant fumes. He walked on in a disturbed mood. He drew out his watch presently and saw that it was half-past eight. "Poor wretch!" he apostrophized. "He's had his fling with sportive fate, I take it, if he does not overdo it to-night. Peculiar nature; this business of love-making to the exclusion of weightier interests is, I suppose, the province of all artists, as well as of women and—novelists. But where *can* that girl be? She is capable of any folly when in a fury. She always did give Constance more concern than all the others together. Too much like that charming, fiery husband of hers. I hope she has not — but no, I won't think of it. If we only find her it will be a pretty efficacious cure for both of them. I wonder who the woman was whom he imagined he loved. The genuine article does not give under so easily, no matter what considerations you bring to bear against it. Honor and circumstance! Twaddle! When you love, you love, and no change can kill it, though it may alter or perhaps die of starvation, non-fulfilment even of sight. But, after all, this ghost which he thinks so securely buried *may* rise again. I hope not. If it should, Kenyon won't meet me to-night."

He sauntered on for fifteen or twenty minutes, striving to imagine Eleanor Kenyon's possible whereabouts, the uncomfortable gravity of the question seeming to grow greater as he dwelt upon it. "By Heaven!" he thought, abruptly, "what a benighted fool I am! I have forgotten all about Constance! If any one can help us now, she can. Yet how can I approach her with this

bewildering intelligence? Another agony for her?"
His brows were knit hard, his lips pressed close.
"Well," he decided, finally, "I dare not keep it from
her. It seems decreed that she shall suffer all that is to
be suffered! We need her more intimate knowledge."
He looked at his watch. "I can make it," he considered.
"It won't take many minutes to prepare her—she is not
a fainting woman—and perhaps she can think of something yet to-night. If Kenyon gets to the club before me
he can wait." Geoffrey gave a shrill whistle to the passing car, ran toward it, sprang on as it slightly slackened,
and the next instant was gliding on to Constance.

Ten minutes later he walked up the steps of the Herriotts' home, in a somewhat slow manner. He was considering how best to break the news of Kenyon's return
without too severely shocking her belief in Eleanor's
having been with him throughout her silence. But two
days had elapsed since Nan's passing, and Constance's
quiet grief had impressed all who cared for her with the
pathetic knowledge that the going of the little blind
child had left a wide void which no tenderness could
fill. Constance had never possessed a confidant for her
inner life; but this frail child, like the blind fish of the
cave, had been furnished with an organism so sensitive
that she had perceived presences quite imperceptible to
any light-illumined eye. It was this unchildish, spiritual
insight to which, though wordless, Constance had grown
accustomed, and for the loss of which there could be no
compensation. Her going had left a coldness which
would some day add strongly to Constance Herriott's
stern reticence. Geoffrey rang the bell with evident reluc-
tance.

"Is Miss Herriott in, Kate?" he asked of the maid who admitted him.

"Yes, Mr. Brunton, but—". Her speech hesitated, and she moved away as Brunton, having laid down his hat, turned toward the drawing-room. He discerned Constance standing upon the threshold, and another form dimly visible in the brightly-lighted apartment beyond.

He came forward in some uncertainty. "Good-evening, Constance," he said, pressing her hand, keenly conscious of the unwonted silence of her greeting. "Did I—" The sentence broke upon his lips as he confronted Kenyon. His face turned red. He stood without speaking for several seconds, his stunned senses slowly rearranging themselves to meet this new, hitherto unexpected point of view. Kenyon met his glance with simple dignity.

Constance looked from one to the other in obvious surprise. "I thought you knew that Hall was here," she murmured, moving nearer. Brunton turned upon her quickly.

"Ye—yes," he stammered, "certainly." Then, observing her great pallor, he wheeled up a chair for her. "Sit down," he said, quietly. "I'm afraid Kenyon has unnerved you. I should have come—I came—to prepare you." As she seated herself he turned to Kenyon, who was still standing. "Were you going?" he asked, abruptly.

"I was going to meet you, as we had agreed," replied Kenyon, steadily.

"Yes, but having met here we can find no better place to discuss the trouble. Constance will aid us more than any one — that is, if the arrangement would be agreeable to you."

"Quite." He leaned against the piano in an attitude of one to whom the leisurely comfort of a chair would have been an impossibility.

Brunton seated himself at some distance from Constance. She sat between them, the woman to whose strength all had recourse in weakness or adversity, silent now and nerveless, her black gown deepening the pallor of her countenance. An unbroken stillness hung heavily over them.

"This is frightful, Geoffrey!" she exclaimed, at last, in the low tone which accompanies the moment immediately succeeding stupefaction. Her hands clasped the chair arms in a perceptible strain ; her eyes sought Brunton's in distress.

"It may look worse than it is," he assured her, as brightly as he could. "What we must do now is to try to recall every place where there is a possibility of her having flown. Can you think of any such place?"

"Of none where she would have gone alone. Griff will move entirely off the track."

"Griff?" questioned Kenyon.

She turned to him and explained that they had telegraphed to Griff, telling him of their departure, but supposing that they were together, and asking him, Griff, to endeavor to learn their whereabouts, as the silence had made them apprehensive. "He wrote that he would move westward at once," she continued, "and make inquiries at all corners which he thought might suggest themselves to you as good stepping-off places. Of course he has been looking for two."

"Yes," he answered, his slender hand, hanging over the piano, clinching itself unconsciously. "You said she wrote she was coming to me," he added. "Do you think she had any intimation of my whereabouts?"

"I do not know—I do not think so. But if she had had, do you think she would have started for you—to Honolulu?"

"No. I don't think she would have gone anywhere—for me."

"Why not?" asked Brunton, sharply.

"Why should she?" returned Kenyon.

"Hall means," explained Constance, carefully, "that she would not have been likely to go to him, even had she known where he was, without his having sent for her." Whatever shadow of the past may have rested upon this meeting between husband and sister, it was swallowed up—lost—in the calamity of the moment.

"Is that it?" demanded Brunton.

"Partly. But let the question drop. She had no intention of coming to me."

"Why did you ask, then, whether she had any knowledge of your location?"

"For—folly! What's the good of this cross-examination? Let us get to something definite. I don't think she has gone far."

"Why not?" questioned Brunton again.

"I don't know why, but that is my conviction."

"It certainly is definite. However, we must employ a detective. Her movements must be traced from the moment of her leaving this house."

"We must find the maids," suggested Constance. "We might advertise for them."

"Yes," acquiesced Brunton, jotting down a word or two in a little note-book. "Do you remember their names?"

"Marie —— and Gretchen ——."

"Good. They may furnish us with a clew. Were you thinking of any particular place, Kenyon, when you made that assertion of her nearness a moment ago?"

"No."

"What prompted the idea?"

"Eleanor."

The curt answer silenced them curiously. Kenyon suddenly began to walk the floor. Constance shuddered violently.

"What was that thought?" asked Brunton, conscious of her every movement.

"Geoffrey—suppose—she has—done away with herself!"

Kenyon wheeled around at the low, terror-laden words, his eyes blazing in his white face. "Hush!" he commanded, gruffly. "How dare you fancy such a thing?"

"From my knowledge of her."

"Knowledge? What knowledge?"

"Of her reckless, violent temper."

He gazed at her in astonishment. "She had no temper," he asserted, roughly. "She was quite passionless."

They returned his gaze with wonder. But the next moment Constance remembered the marked change she herself had noted in the girl's manner the day of her arrival, also Eleanor's confession of her constant straining and feigning to attain this effect.

"Your words are astounding," she heard Brunton saying. "Eleanor Herriott had a remarkably stormy

15

nature. The characteristic was so pronounced that any one interested in her was often fearful for her."

"You are mad," returned Kenyon, with a wretched laugh, as he turned away and continued his monotonous tread. He paused as he passed Constance. "Is that true ?" he asked, indistinctly.

"Yes," she murmured, burying her face from his tortured gaze.

"Well, she had utterly changed, then," he asserted, in a thick undertone. "And— Have you any old papers ?"

"Papers ?"

"Journals—of the past few weeks."

"I think so. I will look."

As she moved from the room Brunton came over to Kenyon. "I'm inexpressibly sorry for you," he said, in honest sincerity. "But don't despair ; I am convinced we'll find her. She has been gone only three weeks, you know."

Kenyon stared at him dumbly. Constance returned shortly with a number of old *Chronicles*, which Kenyon received from her with a word of thanks. He seated himself and began scanning them carefully, the only sound in the room being the crackling of the newspaper as he turned the pages. The other two watched him silently, wondering what his painful, unexplained search among the daily annals could portend. His colorless lips were compressed in a hard line, his eyes ran up and down the columns with startling rapidity and minute intelligence. Sometimes they saw him turn back to reread an article. Once a slight sound escaped him, and his face turned deathly as he read, but the next minute he had flung the paper from him, with the muttered explanation, "Thank God!"

Constance presently felt his dark eyes resting questioningly upon her. "Little Nan?" he asked, in sad gentleness.

She bent her head acquiescently.

"I did not know. Forgive me," he entreated, "for bringing my trouble to you."

"It is my trouble, too, Hall," she said, with the brave fortitude of custom.

And later, when they rose to go, he raised her hand to his lips. "It is good not to be alone in time of loss —or strife," he said, simply, in the expressionless tone which expressed so much to her.

She gathered together the papers he had read with such avidity. As she picked up the one he had thrown from him she moved with it under the chandelier. It was still folded where he had read to the page containing the important local news of the day. She remarked nothing at a glance that could have arrested his attention: there was a reported interview with a celebrated visiting explorer, an account of a murder trial, some theatrical notes, a— She had discovered the cause of his inexplicable disturbance. It was simply the sad, everyday story of the suicide of an unknown, beautiful young girl, who had taken into her own hands the only means of stilling despair and disgrace. As Constance reached the closing paragraph the suffocating weight upon her breath lifted. The "fair unfortunate" had been "flaxen-haired and blue-eyed."

"Thank God!" she, too, murmured, as though repeating Kenyon's unexplained train of thought. And with the explanation came the inexplicable but settled conviction that self-destruction would not prove the cause of Eleanor's disappearance. As long as Kenyon lived, life would hold jealous dominion of her battling soul.

CHAPTER XXI

HAD the earth suddenly opened in some obscure corner to ingulf her, Eleanor Kenyon could not have more
completely vanished from detection.

Every known medium and device at the command of
man was summoned to the assistance of the baffling task,
except that of open newspaper advertising. That her
disappearance had been deliberately planned by herself
there was no mistaking. They discovered that on the
morning of her going she had visited the bank and
drawn two thousand dollars in paper-money, a fact which
should have gone far toward assuring them that she
was materially protected. Yet the knowledge that she
had had so large a sum upon her person gave play to
grave fears to those whose love was following her in
every possible danger of life. Griff, slowly moving westward, was quietly conducting the search from the east
end of the continent; but Kenyon, still strongly imbued
with the belief of her proximity, gave all his attention
to California and, most indefatigably, the city environs.

This dominant idea, which held him in an absolute
tyranny, soon began to communicate itself to Constance,
Brunton, and Briggs, the detective. Griff's messages
were scarcely noted. There were days when they would
lose all sight and knowledge of Kenyon, only to see him
return from some wild dash into the interior, worn and
haggard, but never utterly discouraged, explaining that

he had remembered her mentioning such or such a place once in converse. Far from discountenancing these fruitless wanderings, Constance herself had several times . bidden Grace and Marjorie good-bye in the morning, and gone off to odd byways which they had passed and commented upon in the olden summers. There was no stone too heavy or inconvenient for their turning. But the weeks dragged into months, and no echo came to all their crying into the silent woods.

People were out of town. The Herriotts' movements were less constrained in consequence, and Kenyon's fitful appearances in the city without his wife remained unremarked—at least, to Constance. The atmosphere of the Herriott house was sadly changed. Only little Marjorie, singing in childish innocence and unconcern through the almost silent house, now and then recalled the ghost of its former sunshine and gayety. She had never lost her baby infatuation for Kenyon, and when he would come to them, weary, tormented, and dejected, the child's arms about his neck, her pretty caresses and crooning prattle soothed him as nothing else could. The sense of kinship is never more comforting or strongly felt than in time of trouble; Kenyon yielded to it insensibly. Between him and Constance rested the silent understanding of each other with which the memory of the past endowed them. It had been the forerunner of his quiet deference to her now in every circumstance. She liked to have him come to them so naturally when he was in town, and despite her own fears the sight of his changed face, which bore no trace of its former youth in its haggard leanness, filled her with a longing tenderness and pity for his torturing self-reproach, and she strove, as best she could, to make him forget his misery. Occasionally he would make a strenuous effort and talk to them in a quiet, interesting strain for a while; he would even smile when Grace repeated some merry anecdote or tale of the day's concerns which she had carefully fostered for his distraction. But more often he would sit for an hour, quite silent, with Marjorie on his knee, and then, suddenly, with a muttered word of apology, put her down, rise, and leave the house. And upon Constance's face the haunting corrosion of care began to leave deep traces.

As the months slipped away she would have caught at their fleeting skirts and implored them to pause, to go more slowly toward the catastrophe of utter hopelessness. But August was merging into September, people were returning to town, and the privacy of their strange trouble was no longer assured to them.

Kenyon had come in one afternoon, and Constance had just entered the drawing-room, when Mrs. Ferris was announced. She had been away since Nan's death, and had come to pay her visit of condolence. She entered clad in the stereotyped solemnity of consolation. She seated herself as though the very chairs must be approached softly. She gazed in deep-eyed solicitude upon the object of her sympathy when the latter assured her that she was quite well.

"But you do not look it," mourned Mrs. Ferris. "Have you been ill, Mr. Kenyon?" With impartial interest her head turned toward him.

"No," answered Kenyon, courteously, "though I believe I have lost flesh."

"And your sweet wife—is she with you?"

"She is still away."

"That must be loneliness."

"Yes, but it is inevitable."

"Circumstance is not always yielding, I suppose, even to a man of your pursuits. And yet, despite our crosses, we live and breathe." It was then time to sigh, and Mrs. Ferris led the charge valiantly. The *carte de visite* of her emotions had the condolence corner turned down; and her well-trained muscles responded, like good soldiers, to the call.

"Yes," she continued, with a slow shake of the head, "in moments of grief nature seems almost vulgar when it proceeds unconcernedly upon its wonted round of digestion and assimilation. But, as I have often said, it is by divine provision and intervention that we are being looked after at such a time when we might grow indifferent. Providence is never off on sick-leave, or drying its eyes, or on an excursion for amusement only. Providence is a hard worker. Well, well, as the Masonic service has it, 'So mote it be.' You have heard the funeral services, Miss Herriott?"

"Once."

"Impressive, are they not? Of course, it seems heartless to consider such things while a man is alive—just as it shocks one when one's husband mentions his life-insurance policy; but I have insisted upon Mr. Ferris's giving his consent to being buried by the order, with all the ceremonies. It must be a consolation to know that there will be no unseemly haste at one's final lowering. Don't you agree with me?"

"What will it matter after we are dead?"

"Nothing to the dead; but think how comforting the

idea of solemnity and prestige will appear to the one about to die. It gives him a proper estimate of his importance to the world, and is such an adequate expression of the mourners' voiceless grief."

"Do you not think we can mourn as deeply without the outward signs?" asked Constance, gently. "Grief is not expressed in ceremonies or the dye of the wool of one's gown."

"Black makes you look quite pale, or is it that white shawl, Miss Herriott? The house must seem very large to you now." A profound sigh punctuated this sentiment.

"Yes," replied Constance. She could not speak of her little folded-away flower to this woman, with her remarks fitted to the occasion like umbrellas unfurled in time of rain.

"Eleanor gone," proceeded the ferret-eyed one, "Edith away. By-the-bye, what do you hear from her? Excellent reports, I have understood. Is she quite well, and does she like it? I suppose Grace misses her, though I have heard that Grace, too, shows signs of flitting."

"Grace?" repeated Constance. "Oh no, I need Grace yet, you know."

"But, my dear woman, it is just when one needs a young girl most that she seems to be needed more peremptorily by some one else. And, seriously," with an inadvertent sigh, "you should not complain if she wants to leave you. We bring up a girl with the sole purpose of making her pleasing in the eyes of some possible bidder."

Constance smiled, when Mrs. Ferris had left, over the suggestion that Grace could be the subject of gossip.

She knew that young Glynn was a frequent visitor and attentive friend of the girl, and her smile abruptly changed to one of serious thought. She explained her visitor's innuendo to Kenyon in the confidential way into which they had fallen since a common adversity had thrown them together.

"Don't be disturbed about Grace," he said. "She will never marry any but a man with whom her happiness will be assured."

Constance was called away just then, and Kenyon, walking over to the window, was startled to see Caroll Glynn standing with Grace at the foot of the steps, taking an apparently lingering leave of her. His honest, intelligent face was alive with interest while she spoke, and Kenyon hastily drew back.

A moment later she came in softly humming. She had some spicy, dark red pinks in her hand, and a faint reflection of their color was in her cheeks. Kenyon's eyes rested upon her with quiet satisfaction.

"You here, Hall?" she exclaimed, coming up to him with the girlish, artistic delight she always felt at sight of his fine head and presence. "Let me put one of these pinks in your button-hole—they are so fragrant. Caroll Glynn gave them to me just now. I met him down-town and he rode home with me. Do you know him?"

"I met him on the street once with Brunton. He is studying law, is he not?"

Grace had laid down the flowers and was drawing off her gloves, as she seated herself on the broad window-sill. The late afternoon sun blazed upon the glass and shot flashes of gold from her fair hair. His quiet, sympathetic voice touched her with a swift desire to make a confidant of this grave, saddened man, who regarded her with such tender interest.

"He has gone into partnership with Steele & Grattan. Mr. Steele is losing his health and has gone to Europe, and, as he was the brains of the firm, Mr. Grattan has taken Caroll as a coming substitute. Geoffrey says he is recognized now as very clever. Geoffrey says a good deal of it is clap-trap, but that it is going to make itself felt. Geoffrey likes him immensely. He says he is so manly." She spoke in swift, low enthusiasm, wishing to make clear that even such a valued authority as Geoffrey Brunton approved of the man who had found favor in her eyes.

"I like his face," Kenyon admitted. "It is what one might call trustable."

"And that is a great deal, is it not?" She sat with downcast eyes, fingering the pinks upon the table, an eager, listening flush upon her cheek.

"It is the best recommendation a man can bring," he replied, forcibly. "I like Brunton's valuations of men and things. He goes straight to the core, and is never deceived by an attractive covering or frame. A great many worthless books come bound in morocco."

"Oh," laughed Grace, the color deepening upon her face, "Caroll is not very pretty to look at. But a man does not need that advantage."

"Then it is not by the long nail on his little finger that he has won your affectionate regard?" he observed, with a half-smile.

"No. I require something less brittle. I am not so silly! If I — if I had a — daughter," she went on, in earnest bravery, " I would rather give her to the plainest farmer living who had an honest, trustworthy heart than to the most polished courtier whose convictions might change with the season's fashions. I am woman enough to know that there are moments when it is good to feel that a strong-hearted, true man is always, always at hand to strengthen and uphold one." The young face looked toward him for approval.

"God help the woman who does not find such a prop," he returned, in bitter intensity. "You are right, Grace. Find your right sort of man ; You can let all the rest go."

He relapsed into silence after that and began pacing the floor. The bitterness of self-reproach obliterated the ardent, sweet-faced girl from his interest. Only the memory of the woman who had failed to gain this simple need filled mind and soul with exquisite remorse and longing, and made all else seem as shadows.

CHAPTER XXII

THE warm yellow haze of late October hung in the noon air as Kenyon made his way toward Brunton's office. He had been out of town for a week, and his jaded appearance testified to the uselessness of his excursion. Discouragement had at last overtaken him bodily. She was either dead or lost to him forever. Not the flicker of a smile came to his heavy eyes as Joscelyn accosted him with his usual gay exuberance just before the Mills Building.

"Be thou a spirit of health or goblin damned?" he exclaimed, grasping his hand. "Either the grave or gravity has got the better of you. Why so downcast? Why, man, you should be ablaze with stars and medals. I suppose you've just got back to sport your accumulated laurels. I congratulate you, old fellow. Never thought you'd let yourself out as you have in the book —it has caused a small flurry. You wear your honors too modestly. Come to luncheon with me, and we'll christen your latest in becoming fashion."

"Thanks—no. I don't understand your allusion in the least. What—"

"Fudge! Don't pretend indifference for glory to a man in the same boat with yourself. Ah, here comes Sire Coulter. He looks sentimentally this way—I'm off. See you later when less besieged."

As he moved along, a benignant-faced old club-man

came up close beside Kenyon, and intercepted his very
evident desire to get away.

"Hold on," he said. He stood leaning on his cane
held behind him, and shook his head at him sadly.
"You dog of a tourist," he slowly growled, with wag-
gish gravity and twinkling eyes, "you juggler of emotions, you time your entrance like a sensational Mephis-
topheles. You send your literary fireworks before you;
then, as they shoot up, appear on the scene to get the
full benefit of the 'Ah!' Your heroine has made the
men curious, and the women—indignant. They want to
know how you know, and I say to them, ' *Cherchez la
femme,*' or, better, *sa femme* in this instance—the tra-
ditional influence still bearing fruit. We can't growl at
your acquisition! No silent geniuses nowadays—every
man with a horn worth blowing blows it; and as to
your last perpetration, you're only showing what you
paid for—it took a wife, God help you, it took a wife!"
He had been laughingly edging away as he finished, and
before Kenyon could voice his annoyed confusion, the
garrulous veteran, with a jaunty salutation of mockery,
had turned the corner.

Kenyon moved on with an inward shrug of apathy
over the unintelligible purport of their words. He was
relieved to find Brunton in and disengaged for the hour.
The lawyer looked up as he entered, but made no inquiries, his eye interpreting the harassed countenance at
a glance.

"Sit down," he said, pulling up a chair.

"Any mail?" asked Kenyon, seating himself and laying his hat on the table. He pushed his hair from his
brow as though it molested him. Brunton leaned back

to a chest of small drawers, pulled out one, and, extracting several letters, handed them to him. He resumed his own correspondence, while his companion quickly disposed of his communications.

"What in thunder do they all mean?"

Brunton glanced up in gentle surprise at the exclamation of exasperation. Kenyon held a letter in his hand; his brows were knit in heavy anger.

"What's the trouble?" questioned Brunton, in his usual unhurried manner.

"No trouble. But here both Griff and Scott have been writing page after page of jargon about a book which I never wrote! Two men on the street surprised me just now with a similar peculiar tirade! Can you explain?"

"I suppose they refer to your newest book."

"Which book?"

"I don't remember the name; Constance can tell you. It was she who spoke to me of it. I have not seen it. She said it had been sent her from the publishers. She supposed you had directed them to send her a copy."

"Some error. I have not written a line since my return from New York! A new edition, perhaps!"

"Can't say. But Constance seemed unusually impressed with it."

"Strange! Well," he decided, rising wearily, "I'll go out to see her and investigate the piracy. Er—any news?"

"Nothing worth discussing. Briggs was in a day or two ago for a photograph. Constance had none of her taken later than six years ago, when she was seventeen. It is quite inadequate for his purpose, I am afraid, but the best we could give. I don't suppose you have anything more like her ?"

"Yes," said Kenyon; "Scott asked for a water-color of her before we left, and I had this done from it." He drew out his watch, opened the under lid, and passed it to Brunton. The latter took it, holding it closely to his eyes for inspection. It was Eleanor's pictured head burned into the gold of the watch-case ; but Brunton had never seen her with just that thoughtful look of womanhood in her eyes, nor the gentle musing upon her lips— the face seemed unfamiliar to him.

"Yes," he said, without further comment, in his customary undemonstrative fashion, returning it to its owner. But as Kenyon's hand touched it, he drew it back. "I suppose this is a good likeness?" he suggested.

"Perfect !"

"Well—um-m—had you not better leave it for Briggs ?"

Kenyon hesitated. "Perhaps," he acquiesced, finally. As Brunton separated the fob and handed it to him, he added, "I am going to resort to the newspapers to-morrow. It is my last throw. Some casual reader may help us."

"I wouldn't do that, Kenyon. When she returns, the knowledge of the publicity will hurt her mercilessly."

"When she returns ! Good heavens, Brunton, haven't you got over that insanity yet ? I have given in. Do you think *I* would court this notoriety for her if I were not pushed to the wall ? It's a wretched means, but a desperate hope."

"At least be discreet, Kenyon ; consult Constance about it."

"I intend to. Ask Briggs to be circumspect, and—careful with that picture, will you? Good-bye."

He met Constance on the door-step. "You are going out," he said, shaking her hand in the quiet greeting which characterized their meetings in those days. "Do not go back," he rejoined, hastily, as she moved to return with him, "I shall come again this evening."

"You are ill, Hall, or have heard something."

"Oh no; there is nothing to be heard. I have given it up, Constance."

"Don't do that," she implored.

They spoke so low their colloquy was almost whispered; no one passing and noting their unmoved exteriors would have guessed at the desperate nature of their converse.

"There is one more chance—but I will discuss it with you this evening. Don't let me detain you. Is Marjorie in?"

"No; she is at school."

"*N'importe!* I'll walk down the street with you. Oh, by-the-way, have you that new book of mine, of which one hears so much?"

"Yes; I have just finished it. It is— I cannot speak of it."

He looked at her speculatively as they descended the steps and stopped shortly. His curiosity was beginning to be piqued. "I should like to see it. No, don't turn back; I can find it if you will tell me where it is."

"Well"—she considered—"it is on the small table near the east window, in the library. Are you going in?" She never combated an unimportant point of etiquette, letting inclination decide the question at its case.

"Yes. Good-afternoon." She turned away as he lifted his hat and rang the bell.

The servants knew him now as one of the family, and he went into the library with a word of explanation. He found the book where she had indicated, and a line of amusement showed about his eyes as he recognized the usual dark binding of his previously published writings, and read his name under the unfamiliar title. He opened at the title-page, glanced through the list of his works, and turned to the next fly-leaf. "*A Message to H. K.*," he read on it. "I have been inditing to an unknown friend," he mused, with a faint smile. "Or— H. K.? Ah! my own initials." He turned to the opening chapter. The sentences had the evasive, familiar property of an echo. He seated himself in the deep chair near the window and began to read.

A singular stillness fell upon and about him. Marjorie returned from school, and, hearing he was within, rushed to him. He put his hand upon her curls, and in a low tone bade her leave him. The child went out, hushed by the indescribable tranquillity of his presence. Hour after hour passed, but no one disturbed the absorbed reader. Evening stole in softly, and Constance came to light the gas, her inherent delicacy hesitating even over this slight intrusion. She paused in her advance into the room as she perceived the tall figure standing by the window; his hand rested high up on the casing, his head was sunk in his arm.

"Hall!" she ventured, gently.

He turned at the sound. His face was deathly white in its stillness. He came toward her at once.

"That is not my book, Constance."

She started at the profound calm of his tone, which seemed to come from a distance, as though disembodied, and which she knew was his expression of powerful emotiveness.

"But it is your novel, Hall," she protested, in amazement.

"No, it is Eleanor's! I gave the manuscript to her—long ago. She has made the story her own. A word—a whole passage here and there—the cold framework filled out; she has given it what it wholly lacked—a soul! *Her* soul!"

Constance regarded him mutely. "Then," she breathed at last, "that woman is—Eleanor."

"In her entirety. Not the woman she appeared to us, but the woman she was! The woman she wished to be—the real, the ideal. We are all these three in one. She is *there!*"

"We did not know her, Hall."

"Whom do we know?" The color rushed over his face, and, receding, left him almost ghastly. "I have read her message," he murmured.

She mused a moment. "The message of her love?" she whispered, as though violating something sacred, the color staining her own pure face. "I have known it for a long time."

He took her hand almost blindly, and bent his brow upon it. Then he turned toward the door.

"Where are you going?" she asked.

"To get her address."

"Her address?"

"From the publishers. The clew is found."

She turned giddy at the unexpected turn to which his

words pointed, and caught at the door-lintel as she followed him into the hall.

" I shall wire to New York," he explained, the words dancing wildly upon one another's heels.

" Wear your hat, please," she laughed, tremulously, handing it to him. He laughed shortly as he took it from her, and was out of the door. " Address it from here," she called after him, " and—" But he was gone.

It was fully five hours after Kenyon's return to the house that the answer came to his despatch :

Have wired correspondent—must wait permission before giving address.

And Kenyon replied :

Do not delay—delay fatal.

Brunton had come in at about nine o'clock.

" Any news ?" he asked, struck by their curious aspect of restrained excitement. And after Constance had explained, he silently shook Kenyon's hand, and did not complain when the latter passed the following hours in pacing the floor.

" It was probably all premeditated," he decided. "Everything is dovetailed to a nicety."

But noon of the next day came before the feverishly-awaited telegram arrived. Kenyon opened the envelope with rigid fingers. The information was to the point :

Mrs. Hall Kenyon—care Mrs. Johnson—B—— Island—Alameda County—California.

He would have staggered had not Constance, who had been reading over his shoulder, laid her firm hand heavily against him.

"Where is that, Geoffrey?" she asked of Brunton, who, in his anxiety, had just come in. She took the paper from Kenyon's nerveless fingers and passed it to him.

"B—— Island?" read Brunton. "Never heard of it."

"Nor I, and I have lived here all my life."

They regarded each other with stern faces.

"Nonsense," said Kenyon, in indistinct impatience; "there must be such a place. How would they know? It will be easily located. I'll find out down at the wharf and telephone you the answer."

"I'll go with you," said Brunton.

A half-hour later the following dialogue vibrated over the wires:

"Is that you, Constance?"

"Yes. Is it all right?"

"All right. It is connected with the mainland by bridges. I am going on the half-past one boat. Good-bye."

She rang him up sharply.

"Hall!"

"Yes!"

"Listen to me. Be reasonable. Let me go. I will send for you at once if all is well."

"Are you mad? How can you demand such a thing?"

"You may make her ill. We know nothing of her condition. The shock of seeing you might kill her. Be patient and considerate, Hall."

"I cannot."

"You must."

"No."

She turned away with clouded eyes. The next minute the little bell summoned her peremptorily.

" Constance !"

" Yes !"

" You may go.   Take the 1.30 boat, and drive over from Alameda."

" Thank you.   All right."

CHAPTER XXIII

YET when she reached the deck she saw Kenyon's unmistakable form leaning against the railing. His hat was pulled down over his eyes, but he saw her approaching, and came forward at once to meet her.

"You are incorrigible, Hall," she murmured, reproachfully.

"No; but your demand was unreasonable. I tried, but could not stay away. I will not be impetuous, I promise—I will wait till you call me. You can't expect any more."

"Well," she sighed, as she seated herself.

Just as the boat moved away Brunton emerged from the cabin. He started at sight of Kenyon. "I thought you would be alone," he explained, apologetically. "Kenyon said you were going over first. I thought I might possibly be of some assistance in procuring a vehicle at Alameda."

She smiled her thanks, having learned that he preferred such quiet acceptance of anything he might wish to do for her. They spoke very little as they steamed over the sunlit bay. Kenyon's jaw seemed locked; he stood the entire distance, looking out upon the horizon. They boarded the Alameda train still in this strange speechlessness. Geoffrey secured a carriage for them at the station.

"Come with us," begged Constance, in an aside. "We don't know where or to what we are going."

So the three sat within when the horses headed eastward. Over the autumn-decked country they sped, the
horses making good time, the occupants quite insensible
to the glowing Indian-summer about them. The pace
slackened. They crossed the ramshackle bridges. Presently Constance looked out upon a green island, with its
long sandy beach, the name of which had never reached
her hearing. The least known of our possessions are
often those nearest home. Few of us know the sound
of our own voices. But the beauty of the waving feath-
ery asparagus-plant, rising knee-high, with its bright
scarlet berries, transforming the island into a sea of un-
dulating, tender green, was quite lost upon her. Great
shadows encircled her eyes, her face was weary, but she
gave no further sign of her excessive agitation. The
driver paused to make some inquiries, and soon struck
into the road leading northward. They passed, one after
another, the quaint farm-houses, many of them showing
traces of great age in their weather-beaten frames, and,
anon, they came to a stand-still.

The driver got down and opened the door. "This is
the Johnson farm-house," he announced.

She looked toward Kenyon in sudden dependence.
"I will walk up to the door with you," he assured her,
steadily, through pale lips. He alighted, and assisted
her with a firm hand.

"Courage!" called Brunton, softly, after them.

As they walked up the short mignonette-bordered
walk they perceived a white-haired, sweet-faced old lady
sunning herself on the porch, in a great, cane-bottomed
rocking-chair.

She arose as they drew near, and Constance watched

the chair swinging slowly back and forth till it grew quite still before she took a step in advance of Kenyon. The old lady looked with surprise at the evident discomposure of this stately young woman.

"Are you Mrs. Johnson?" finally came the question.

"That is my name," was the cheerful response.

"Have you—does Mrs. Hall Kenyon live with you?"

"Eh?"

"Does Mrs. Hall Kenyon live with you?"

"Not as I know of, my dear."

Constance turned a perturbed look upon Kenyon, and he came to her side.

"Perhaps," he said, in slow courtesy, which, added to the extreme pallor of his handsome face, impressed her singularly—"perhaps you do not know her by that name. She is a slight young woman, with brown hair and gray eyes."

The old lady's face flushed prettily. "Yes," she nodded; "she's in-doors."

"I am her sister," said Constance. "Is—is she well?"

"Yes, she's well—now."

"You mean—"

"Never mind, dearie. It was after all the writing; but Mother Johnson and Dr. Bronson pulled her through. Brain-trouble, he called it; heart-trouble, I called it."

"Will," she turned her back upon Kenyon—"will you tell her I have come? Say, 'Constance is here,' but do not mention any other. Tell her gently, please."

As she moved into the house Constance turned to Kenyon.

"Hush!" he commanded.

Neither spoke further. Mrs. Johnson came pattering out about five minutes later with a bright smile of welcome invitation. "She's been expecting you," she chirruped. "You can go. It's the third room to the right. But be quiet; she's not used to noise yet."

Constance walked in, and turned in the direction indicated. She stood for a moment before the door, then moved the knob and entered. She stepped into a flood of mellow sunlight.

"Constance!" she heard Eleanor cry softly.

Constance moved toward her with outheld arms. She sank upon her knees before her, and laid her arms about her.

"My child!" she said.

And presently the tender mother-arms of the older sister fell apart, and she looked deep into Eleanor's face as she knelt before her. A veil of strange peace seemed to enshroud and shimmer about her, her eyes looked out in pleading humility from the marble pallor of her face, her bright hair, slightly loosened, detracting from its fragile delicacy.

"It is the woman-look — the sorrow-look," thought Constance, as though answering the mystery of the beautiful young face. And then she met the sad eyes fixed beseechingly upon her.

"Oh, Constance," she cried, brokenly, as her sister rose and seated herself in a chair, "I had to do it! I had to do it!"

"All these long months?" chided the gentle voice.

"Yes," she returned, with intensity. "All these long months. I did it to save him."

"Ah, but you almost wrecked him."

" I know ; that was what I wanted—I wanted him to suffer. It was the only caustic that could cure." Constance gazed at her pale earnestness, scarcely comprehending.

" See," she went on ; " he was not the only victim of this thoughtless freak of his. I am not a patient woman, and in my first frenzy I decided to show him that he had taught me a game at which two could play. Then you stepped in with your tender reasoning, and I hesitated over the possible scandal it might create. But afterwards reason gave me another point of view. This recurrence had to be stopped, and I was the only one to save him —I, in my love for him. So I hurt him, willingly though painedly. To shock him almost to death was his only salvation from such a violent disorder. I wanted to live a normal, peaceful life, like other women. I knew it was possible, for I knew he loved me !

" To tell you would have been folly; you would have soon told him—too soon, in your compassion. I could not consider you. We — I never did. To me, ' Constance' means ' endurance.' I knew beforehand of your forgiveness, love." She rose, almost tottered over to Constance, and, sinking upon the low cassock before her, leaned her arms upon her knees. "And as for his," she murmured, with " starry eyes," " I did not fear; I had my day-dream : the book—our book." And Constance, looking at her, ceased to chide.

" How did you know of this unheard-of place ?" she asked, instead.

" I had read a description of it once. I remembered my surprise over its existence. I thought, even then, it would prove a good hiding-place for one seeking solitude. It recurred to me as in a flash that night. I came straight to it and found—Mrs. Johnson."

Her head drooped till it rested upon Constance's knees. "Constance," she whispered, "has he read it—the book?"

"Yes. Tell me about that, Eleanor. It is so wonderfully intimate, and yet — can that woman be Eleanor Kenyon?"

"I think so. You were surprised, perhaps; but why should you have been?" She paused, as though her thought had plunged into profound depths.

"Go on," urged Constance. "Tell me all about it."

"Do you mean what led me to do it? I had always intended to make use of it some time, but not as I have done. It was only the common story of a woman's picking up a thread and weaving a romance out of it. I thought to use it some day as a medium of confession. Day-dreaming is the occupation of only hungry souls, not of the truly satisfied. I used to pore over it as one does over a loved possession; it was so splendid, yet so *hard*. I wanted to make it less artistic, more human! I began to annotate; from annotating I came to strike out here, to add there; and finally—finally, Constance, in my extremity, I found the way—I wrote between the lines! I wrote my heart out. I have written there what few women would care to reveal; but it is written, not spoken. It was easy persuading his publishers to the secrecy, because they had read the first chapters before he ever came to San Francisco. They thought my request some little wifely surprise.

"Sometimes, after I knew he would read it, I have hidden my face at the memory of the revelation, but in stronger moments I was glad." There was a faint pause. Then, "Does he forgive me, Constance?" she whispered, almost inaudibly.

" He loves you," came the quiet rejoinder.

" Help me to keep him," she entreated, with sudden fear.

" You do not need me now," returned Constance, rising, and looking down at her. " You have him—and the future !"

Eleanor looked toward her, listening. In the shadowy room the stately figure rose like a dim column, distant and alone. Her voice, dim too, carried a sense of something lonely and apart.

She stooped abruptly and kissed her. " Good-bye," she said, lightly.

" You are not going !" cried Eleanor, catching at her gown in bewilderment.

" In another minute you will forget all about me— when some one else comes in. Now then, let me go, dear."

" Constance !"

" Yes, he is here — waiting. Why should you be afraid ? Sit there—so. Come, let me go."

Two minutes later Kenyon entered the room.

.   .   .   .

Brunton had gone, Mrs. Johnson told Constance ; he had hailed a wagon bound for Alameda, and left the carriage for the others. She stood for a while talking to the good woman, and then, with a message to those within, went out at the gate.

A sense of tranquil peace was upon her. She seemed scarcely to feel the motion of carriage or train as she was borne homeward. On the boat she sat in the sweet evening air as if soothed by gentle Ariels. The strain came from the harpist as from some distant sphere.

When she reached home Marjorie and Grace came bounding out to meet her, and she had much to tell them.

"Are you tired, Constance?" asked Grace, as she paused once.

"No," she answered, in surprise. "Why?"

"You speak so slowly—as though you were dreaming."

"Yes?" she returned.

Later old Mr. Glynn came in to borrow Grace. His wife wanted Constance to lend her to them for the night. Grace hesitated, divided between two loves. But Constance told her to go, and presently she was alone with the child Marjorie. She went up-stairs with her, lingering over the task of putting her to bed, the child prattling, prattling as usual, till she dropped off to sleep. And the house was quite still—and Constance was alone.

In the darkened room she went over and sat down by the window. A fair young moon hung upon the spire of the church, as though it loved it and belonged to it. It seemed to glow to-night with an unfamiliar glory, and to look in upon her with unrecognizing, alien eyes, as though in its darkened quarters lay a secret too deep and sacred even for Constance's reading. Yet she and the moon had long been friends. They had often kept vigil together. "It is the contrast," she thought, with a cold, icy feeling, and she could not stay the tears pattering slowly down upon the unresponsive window-sill.

The singular thought enveloped her that some one, velvet-shod, had softly closed a door upon her and left her alone in space; that at the other side were voices that she knew, voices that laughed and sang, and made merry, and moved ever farther away from her; and ever with the voices of youth and gladness came one like a wind sighing in accompaniment, "Never mind, oh, Constance, never mind!" but even that fainted in distance. And as the dream voices floated into silence, a slow, assured ring of the bell took up the sound like an echo.

"Geoffrey's ring," she thought, and she went down to meet him.

"As inquisitive as ever," he said, as she came in. "I want to know all about it."

"You mean of Eleanor, of course," she said, with a faint smile, as they seated themselves. "She has changed somewhat."

"Revised for the better, I hope."

"As he is," she returned, simply, and then, without further parley, she told him Eleanor's story. He made no comment when she finished.

"Well?" she said.

"You have been crying," he responded, with sharp irrelevance.

"Don't, please," she faltered, drawing in a deep-lying sob.

"Are you cold, that you shudder so? See, your fire is going out; there goes the last flame, Constance."

"Let it go," she said, looking into the white ashes. "There are many bright, warm things we must let go from us without a word or a staying hand. Only ashes, the memory of the fire, remain with us."

"You speak sadly," he said, with some pain. "Is there anything you—regret—to-night?"

"To-night, Geoffrey? Is not my Eleanor the happiest

woman in the world to-night?" She looked above and beyond him, a pale content resting upon her countenance. Brunton, his head sunk in his hand, watched her silently. "What should I regret?" she went on, quietly. "There is Eleanor, happy with her beloved husband; Grace is with the Glynns, absorbed in bright visions of the future; Edith is making us proud of her with her brilliant records; Marjorie is safe and warm and well just within call, and—yes, my bird is gone. But God knows I could not help that, Geoffrey!" She ended her accounting with a sharp cry.

"Hush, Constance; who could doubt it? Who would question you?"

She did not answer.

"You were lonesome," he said, bluntly.

"Perhaps. Mr. Glynn borrowed Grace, and Marjorie fell asleep, and there is no one else."

"No. And pretty soon you will give Grace 'for keeps,' as Marjorie says, to the Glynns, and there will be many evenings when Marjorie will be in bed, and there will be left but a lonely, companionless woman. Is it right, Constance?"

"Right? But how can it be otherwise?"

"How? You know how. Come, be reasonable. I—we will not speak of love. Let us be practical; that is the way you like to look at things, I know. Well, then, here are you and I, a quiet man and woman, who need each other. I need you, Constance; you need me—you have often needed me—and now, if only for the sake of having some one to talk to when the evenings are long, you need me doubly. Come, dear, why should you resist?"

" You forget my vow, Geoffrey."

" No. I remember it distinctly. You said you would never leave the children. Well, the children have absolved you by leaving you themselves, each in turn. Of course Edith will return to you, but she will be a woman; and there is Marjorie. But will you tell me, Greatheart, that you will not always find time and love enough for that one mite, no matter what the new life might ask of you? Be practical, Constance." A pale smile lit up his face while he spoke as to a child.

She brushed a hair from her forehead with a nervous gesture. " Will you tell me why you have never pleaded in court?" she asked, with a fleeting smile.

" Because I have never had a case in which I was so personally interested."

" Geoffrey, dear, why will you persist in making me hurt you so! You could not take from me or divide my responsibility. Ah, Geoffrey—my mother's eyes—they will not let me !"

" Do you mean that you think your mother loved you less than her other children ?"

" I did not say that," she answered, sharply, her face turning deadly pale.

" You imply it, then, by wishing to uphold a vow which is no longer tenable in the eyes of any one who loves you. Have you been harboring that cruel accusation against her all these years ?"

" Be still, Geoffrey," she commanded, imperiously.

" No," he returned, sternly, " I will not be still. I love you too dearly to allow you to make yourself miserable with such a false belief. Did she not trust you? Why, Constance, these others were as nothing to her

17

next the light in which she held you. Do you think if she could speak to you she would not plead with me? Do you think she would not say, 'Surely, Constance, *now* you can let Geoffrey take care of you?'" He arose as though to control himself. "Of course," he continued, with a short laugh, "if you could not tolerate me— I have been talking like an idiot. But I won't believe you don't care for me, or that I could not make you happy, and I suppose I'll talk that way to the end of the chapter whenever I get the chance. I'll worry you into it yet, if I can. But there! You are pale and tired, and I have talked enough."

He took her hand in both his, and looked long into her troubled eyes. "Good-night," he said, tenderly. "Don't rise. Think it over to-night—no, don't think. Sleep. You have thought too much already. Dream over it, love, and try to make a happy dream for both of us. Good-night, Constance."

"Good-night," she answered, lingeringly. "Good-night, Geoffrey."

THE END

By MARY E. WILKINS.

We have long admired Miss Wilkins as one of the most powerful, original, and profound writers of America; but we are bound to say that "Pembroke" is entitled to a higher distinction than the critics have awarded to Miss Wilkins's earlier productions. As a picture of New England life and character, as a story of such surpassing interest that he who begins is compelled to finish it, as a work of art without a fault or a deficiency, we cannot see how it could possibly be improved.—*N. Y. Sun.*

The simplicity, purity, and quaintness of these stories set them apart in a niche of distinction where they have no rivals. —*Literary World*, Boston.

Nowhere are there to be found such faithful, delicately drawn, sympathetic, tenderly humorous pictures.—*N. Y. Tribune.*

The charm of Miss Wilkins's stories is in her intimate acquaintance and comprehension of humble life, and the sweet human interest she feels and makes her readers partake of, in the simple, common, homely people she draws.—*Springfield Republican.*

By CONSTANCE F. WOOLSON.

HORACE CHASE. 16mo, Cloth, $1 25.

JUPITER LIGHTS. 16mo, Cloth, $1 25.

EAST ANGELS. 16mo, Cloth, $1 25.

ANNE. Illustrated. 16mo, Cloth, $1 25.

FOR THE MAJOR. 16mo, Cloth, $1 00.

CASTLE NOWHERE. 16mo, Cloth, $1 00.

RODMAN THE KEEPER. 16mo, Cloth, $1 00.

There is a certain bright cheerfulness in Miss Woolson's writing which invests all her characters with lovable qualities.—*Jewish Advocate*, N. Y.

Miss Woolson is among our few successful writers of interesting magazine stories, and her skill and power are perceptible in the delineation of her heroines no less than in the suggestive pictures of local life.—*Jewish Messenger*, N. Y.

Constance Fenimore Woolson may easily become the novelist laureate.—*Boston Globe*.

Miss Woolson has a graceful fancy, a ready wit, a polished style, and conspicuous dramatic power; while her skill in the development of a story is very remarkable.—*London Life*.

Miss Woolson never once follows the beaten track of the orthodox novelist, but strikes a new and richly-loaded vein which, so far, is all her own; and thus we feel, on reading one of her works, a fresh sensation, and we put down the book with a sigh to think our pleasant task of reading it is finished. The author's lines must have fallen to her in very pleasant places; or she has, perhaps, within herself the wealth of womanly love and tenderness she pours so freely into all she writes. Such books as hers do much to elevate the moral tone of the day—a quality sadly wanting in novels of the time.—*Whitehall Review*, London.

PUBLISHED BY HARPER & BROTHERS, NEW YORK.

☞ *The above works are for sale by all booksellers, or will be sent by the publishers, postage prepaid, to any part of the United States, Canada, or Mexico, on receipt of the price.*